THE NURSE WHO FOUND HERSELF IN 1916

Sally Lawton

Cover designed by Cover Creator

Printed in the United States of America

First Printing: February 2018
Independently published

ISBN-13 978-1-9770334-8-2

This book is dedicated to nurses of today, yesterday and tomorrow

CONTENTS

CHAPTER 1

The sound of the letterbox closing was like an alarm ringing for Charlotte. She walked through to the hall, saw the brown envelope lying on the doormat and sighed. She had been expecting this letter for a couple of days. She picked it up and opened the envelope slowly. And there it was in black and white. A request for her to attend a disciplinary hearing. It was the first time in her nursing career that she had been summoned to such a meeting and she was devastated. No amount of consolation seemed to help her overcome her sense of failure.

Her husband didn't offer much comfort.

'What's the worst that can happen?' he asked. 'They're not going to sack you for this, are they?'

No, she probably wouldn't be sacked. But it felt like such a blemish on her record to be in this situation. It was keeping her awake at night as she went over the incident again and again.

A simple mistake. That was the cause of all this distress. It had been a busy shift. Charlotte was the second checker as a controlled drug was being prepared. But as she was taking it to the bedside with her colleague, a distressed relative approached her. Charlotte had spent a lot of time with this family and the relative was so upset she felt she couldn't ignore her. So, instead of going to the patient, as the drug policy clearly stated, she had allowed herself to be distracted and her colleague had given the medication to the wrong patient. Although the patient had not been harmed, it could have been much more serious.

The event was noted as an error, and the disciplinary hearing was a consequence of the report that had been compiled. Charlotte knew the rules and understood she was culpable for the mistake. Her colleague, who was summoned to a separate hearing, seemed to be taking it in her stride.

Since the incident, Charlotte had lost her confidence and begun to question whether she should find another post or even leave nursing entirely. Her ward manager was very supportive and urged her not to throw her career away.

'I think you should take a few days' holiday,' she had said. 'Go away somewhere; get some breathing space to sort this out.' She put her hand on Charlotte's shoulder. 'You're a good nurse. I don't want to lose you from the unit. I can come with you when you have to attend the hearing.'

Charlotte had appreciated the offer of support and agreed that she could do with some time to think things over.

The letter informed her that the date of the disciplinary meeting was still two weeks away. She would go and visit her mother in Yorkshire for a few days.

'Are you sure it's alright for me to go by myself?' she had asked her husband that night, as they got ready for bed.

'Of course,' said Colin, setting the alarm on his clock. 'You've been working too hard, I kept telling you that. And now this thing with the controlled drug, it's affected you so much. I think you could really do with some time away from ...' He gestured vaguely. '... from all of this. From us.'

Even so, she felt guilty at the thought of going away, leaving him to look after the children, William, David and Anne. But he was right; she needed some time to herself. It would do her good.

'I can drop you off at the station before we head out of town if you like,' Colin said a couple of days later, as Charlotte got ready to leave.

She thought about it. 'No, it's fine. Thanks, but I think the walk will do me good.'

She could feel tears stinging her eyes as she kissed each of the children goodbye. Colin patted her on the back while he hugged her. 'You'll be fine and so will we,' he whispered. As she walked down the path, Charlotte turned and waved.

Aberdeen station was very busy. A group of teenagers was going on a camping expedition and had piled their rucksacks, tents and crates of food in the middle of the station concourse. Their squeals of excitement echoed as they welcomed each new member of their party.

Charlotte sighed. She walked towards the platform, hoping they would not be sitting in her carriage. She settled herself into the window seat, placing her weekend bag under the table. An older couple appeared, holding hands, and sat opposite her. Charlotte was intrigued; the woman's make-up gave her the look of a painted china doll. Her lipstick was bright red, matching a scarf draped around her neck. The old man smiled at Charlotte and said in a soft voice, 'My, I haven't seen you for a long time, dear. How are you?'

Charlotte was puzzled but smiled anyway. 'I'm fine, thank you.'

The woman tapped him on the arm. 'Now stop that, Andrew. She doesn't know you, just leave her in peace.'

To Charlotte, the woman said, 'I'm so sorry. He sometimes thinks he knows people when he doesn't. I apologise. It's his age. He's timeworn!'

'Please don't worry,' said Charlotte. 'It's not a problem.'

The old man continued to smile at her as he received his mild reprimand. There was a genteel look about him. He was dressed smartly in a shirt and tie. As he turned his head to look at his wife, Charlotte noticed a faded, vertical scar on his neck. She couldn't help it; her years of nursing meant that she continually assessed people, even when she wasn't at work. That will have to change if I leave, she thought. But what would she do instead?

The doors closed, a whistle blew a few long blasts and the train glided out of the station. It snaked over the River Dee and past the Duthie Park as it left the city. Charlotte yawned. The fields were bright next to the grey swell of the North Sea, which seemed to merge with the late September sky.

She realised the old lady was looking at her with an inquisitive expression.

'Are you going away on holiday, dear?'

Charlotte sat up straighter. 'Yes, to Yorkshire. For the weekend.'

'That's nice,' the woman said. 'We're going to see our daughter in London. Do you have any family yourself?'

'Yes, I have three children. But ... well, they decided I needed a bit of a break for a few days.'

'Why would that be?' the woman asked innocently.

Charlotte wondered what she could say. She thought about the drug error, the letter, the disciplinary hearing. Finally she said, 'They think I need a rest at the moment.'

The woman nodded. 'I take it you're a working mother, dear.'

'I am. Is it that obvious?'

'Perhaps. But it sounds like you have some wise children. How old are they?'

'William's the oldest, he's twelve. David is ten and Anne's seven.'

The woman's face was lit by a kind smile. 'And let me guess, you don't spend much time away from them on your own, do you?'

'No,' said Charlotte.

The woman glanced at her husband who appeared to be asleep. She turned back to Charlotte. 'You remind me of my granddaughter. She never stops – always working or looking after the house, organising her children. It was so much easier when I was young, you know. I was able to stay at home, even though it was hard physical work. My husband was a minister in the Borders for many years, but we moved north when he retired.' She leaned forward, as if sharing a secret. 'If you don't mind me saying, your generation all look exhausted. You're always running about, watching the clock. My advice is to enjoy your time off, dear. What are they going to be doing while you are away?'

Charlotte explained that Colin was taking the children to a friend's cottage in Braemar for the weekend.

'Well, it sounds as if they'll have a lovely time, too,' the woman said. 'I'm sure they'll be fine without you for a few days.'

'I'm sure they will,' Charlotte said, hoping she sounded convincing.

The drug error was one of several things at work that had been worrying her. Recently, she had often lain awake at night thinking about them all and feeling an unfamiliar sense of uncertainty about her career. She shivered as she remembered Mrs Ferguson whose husband had died a couple of weeks ago in her ward. For some reason, this death had scared Charlotte. Mr Ferguson had, apparently, been fit and healthy until three weeks before when he had suffered a heart attack and died, leaving a widow with three young children. Mrs. Ferguson was about the same age as Charlotte and although she had nursed many patients who had died, in this instance, she started to imagine that it was her who had lost her husband. I'm no good to anyone if I can't deal with death, she thought.

She had to stop thinking about work. The whole point of this trip was to leave all her responsibilities behind.

She reached into her bag and took out her copy of *Bleak House*. She loved Dickens but somehow had never found time for this one. Colin had bought it for her as a treat for her short break. Charlotte curled up in the seat and began to read. But within a few pages, fatigue began to grip her. She was so tired. Her limbs felt heavy and she struggled to keep her eyes open. The rhythm of the train rocked her gently in her seat and by the time they passed through Montrose, she was fast asleep, the book on her lap.

Distantly she heard a voice.

'Come on, now, wakey, wakey – we'll be arriving in a few minutes.'

Charlotte woke with a start. Someone was tapping her on her shoulder – an official in a dark blue uniform. She turned her head to glance out of the window, looking for the park and the small bridge which she knew sat just outside York station, but it was too dark to see.

'That's it, miss,' the guard said. 'Look lively. Glad you've woken up. You were dead to the world. You need to get off here.'

She looked at the guard as he walked away. Of course she was going to get off here, she thought, rubbing her eyes. She blinked a few times. The carriage's bright white strip-light now seemed weak and yellow in tone. The train was slowing down. There was a strange, loud hissing noise and a jolt.

She wondered where the old couple had gone. All the other people in her carriage were in uniform and were preparing to leave the train. She looked down. She was wearing different clothes. She'd got on the train wearing jeans, a shirt, a cardigan, and a new jacket. But now she wore a grey dress, a grey cloth coat, and flat shoes. She put a hand to her head. She was even wearing a hat. It seemed to be made of felt and was secured with pins.

She took a deep breath, then another and another, exhaling slowly in between. So, she thought, I'm in a uniform, on a train, in the dark. This is clearly a dream. In a moment, I will wake and everything will be as it was.

But she didn't wake. The dream continued. She didn't know what to do. She could feel her eyes darting to and fro as she searched for something familiar in the carriage, something to anchor her, to help her make sense of what was happening.

Her heart started to beat faster. She could feel it pounding in her chest. Her skin was flushing and her hands began to shake. Her mouth felt dry. What's happening to me? Oh God, where am I? Something's very wrong ...

She looked down, trying to find the tapestry weekend bag that was with her when she boarded the train. It wasn't there. Instead, she saw a brown leather suitcase under her feet, with her initials, 'CR', on its lid. And her handbag was gone, too. In its place was a small brown leather satchel. She looked under the seats, on the luggage racks, in the aisle. Where were her things? They were all gone. She snatched open the satchel. Inside was a letter, some papers and a small purse but she recognised nothing. None of it was hers. She struggled to open the purse because her hands were shaking so much. But she had to see if it had any money in. That would be a start. The clasp popped open. There were notes, including a few flimsy red ones which looked more like tissue paper, but she didn't recognise the currency.

She unfolded the papers to see if they held any clue as to her whereabouts. There was something with her name on. An 'embarkation permit', giving her permission to travel to ... she peered closer ... France. France? But she was going to York. This was madness. There was a pass card, too, the size of a postcard, allowing her to travel across northern France. It said the person whose name was on the card was permitted to pass within the area occupied by the British Army between 1 September and 31 October 1916. Her name, Charlotte Robertson, had been written in copperplate handwriting.

She leaned back in her seat. Impossible, she thought.

She looked through the papers again. There was a letter written on headed notepaper, signed by a Miss E Edmondson, Matron. The address was Woolmanhill in Aberdeen. Well, at least that was a familiar place. But Edmondson? She had never heard that name before and it had been many years since there had been a matron in post at the old hospital in the centre of the city.

The letter was written for the attention of a matron in the War Office, sent at the end of August, with a heading saying it was before a deployment to France.

'I can highly recommend Nurse Robertson as being a diligent, conscientious and attentive nurse on whom you will be able to rely.'

It appeared to be a reference but like everything else it just seemed impossible. At the top of the letter it said, '05 9/16'. What a curious way to write a date. It must mean September the fifth, 1916. Oh good God, if that's correct, thought Charlotte, it would mean I'm in the middle of the First World War. How could that be? I got on a train in Aberdeen this morning in 2001. She could feel her head spinning as she tried to make sense of what was happening to her. Her heart was pounding and she sensed a growing feeling of panic as her hands shook even more. A wave of nausea flooded over her.

Her hands started to shake even more.

She examined more closely the uniform she was wearing. It looked like the one in the poster she had bought many years ago in a museum showing the unqualified voluntary aid detachment nurses, the 'VADs'.

The train shuddered to a halt. A young man with a pipe and full moustache stood up across the carriage from her and smiled as he put on his peaked cap.

'You've had a good sleep I see, nurse,' he said, before moving to the door.

Charlotte stopped herself from asking him for help – her mouth was so dry it would have been hard to speak.

'Detrain now! Detrain now! You must get off the train now – in an orderly fashion,' said the guard. She stood up, stuffed the papers back into the satchel, grabbed the suitcase and made for the door. Her legs were like jelly and she felt sick. She had no idea what to do next.

Everyone else seemed to know their purpose but Charlotte felt invisible. She longed to see something or someone familiar. The train doors had been closed so she couldn't get back on. She felt trapped with no idea of how to escape. Her eyes were filling with tears.

The platform was very busy but what a contrast to the station at Aberdeen that she had left such a short time before. Here, the platform was full of soldiers waiting in small groups to board trains. Names were being called, and there was the sound of whistles blowing and steam engines. She noticed some soldiers lying on stretchers with bandages covering arms, faces, legs and heads. There were just so many of them.

An orderly called to her, 'Are you the nurse who is coming with us on the train to Étaples?'

'No, I don't think so. I've just got here.'

He looked at her for a moment, and then walked away.

She gazed around, not knowing where to go. But then she spotted two other women in uniforms similar to hers who were looking up and down the length of the platform. One of them saw Charlotte, tapped the other on the shoulder and waved. They beckoned her to go and join them. She took a deep breath to quell her nausea and made her way over. As she got near, one of them said, 'Hello there, are you Nurse Robertson?'

She felt a momentary sense of relief that someone knew her, but it was quickly replaced by incredulity. How could these people possibly know who she was? Nonetheless, she nodded. 'Yes, I'm Charlotte Robertson.'

'Good,' said one of the nurses. 'I'm Nurse Wishaw. We were returning from escort duty up to the coast and thought we would wait a few minutes to see if you would be on this train. It's lovely to meet you at last, Nurse Robertson. Am I right in thinking this is this your first time here?'

'Yes,' said Charlotte hesitantly. 'And to be truthful, I'm feeling very lost.'

'Oh, don't worry, we'll keep an eye on you, especially with Matron,' said the other girl with a laugh.

'Right, let's make our way back to the hospital. If we're lucky, there'll be some food left for us – I'm famished. By the way, I'm Nurse Ashville.' She began waving at someone behind Charlotte.

'I can see Tom over by the door.' She called, 'Tom, Tom, over here! We've found our other passenger for you.'

The three nurses picked their way through soldiers and equipment towards the man standing in the doorway of the station. Charlotte kept as close to the others as she could, now fearful of losing sight of them. When they reached him, she noticed what a welcoming, smiling face the man had. He was dressed differently from the majority of soldiers in the station, in a dark blue uniform.

'Good evening, ma'am,' he said, with an American lilt. He was looking at Charlotte. 'Can I assume you're Nurse Robertson? I was hoping you'd be on this train. Delighted to meet you. And welcome you to Albert – or what's left of it. I'm Tom Campbell and I'll be driving you back to the hospital.' His smile faded for a moment. 'Just a word of warning, though. Matron is on the warpath. She was expecting you to arrive this morning.'

Charlotte wondered how she could have been expected that morning but she said nothing.

Nurse Wishaw said, 'Tom, have you brought the ambulance or are we going on the cart?'

'I have the ambulance, but come along now. We should be going because I may need to go out again later this evening – if there's been a lot of activity at the front. James has had to take the other ambulance out already.'

They crossed a muddy forecourt towards a large, busy gathering yard at the side of the station. It was full of vehicles, horses, men and equipment. Charlotte could hear names being called out. Everyone else seemed to know what they were doing. They climbed into the back of the ambulance and sat sideways on an uncomfortable wooden bench that smelled strongly of carbolic.

One of the nurses turned to her. 'So, I'm Daisy Ashville. Do you mind if we call you by your first name?'

'Of course not,' said Charlotte.

'Where are you from, Charlotte?' asked the other nurse, adding, 'My name is Margaret by the way.'

'Aberdeen.'

'You've had a long journey to reach us from there,' said Daisy. 'It's long enough from London.'

Charlotte wanted to tell them so much more but instead said simply, 'Yes, it's been quite a journey.'

There was no opportunity to talk more as the noise from the ambulance's engine made it difficult to hear. In the gathering dark, Charlotte stole glances at her two companions as the journey went on. The tall, beautiful blond-haired girl – Daisy – looked as though she was in her late twenties. She had a cheerful expression and plump, rosy cheeks. The other girl, Margaret, was probably nearer Charlotte's age. She had an air of familiarity and composure about her that felt reassuring.

The drive was uncomfortable as they bounced around in the back of the ambulance. Charlotte held on tightly and tried to breathe deeply.

'It must be a nightmare to be transported in this vehicle if you're injured,' she shouted, above the noise of the engine.

'Yes, I suppose it must,' Daisy called back. 'But I'm jolly sure Tom does his best.'

The ambulance hit a pothole and they all heard a muffled apology coming from the front as Tom fought to keep the vehicle under control.

As they drove on, Charlotte tried to make sense of this bizarre situation. Tom had welcomed her to Albert. She had visited the town on holiday a few years before and knew it was not far from Lille in the north of France. The letter in her bag stated that the hospital she had been assigned to was situated there. So she now had the beginning of an understanding of where she was, but still it seemed impossible that she was experiencing all this. She remained convinced she was asleep but she had never had such a vivid dream where she could touch, smell and see things so clearly. And she didn't seem to be able to wake herself up, so she knew that she had little choice other than to go along with it.

She reminded herself again that in her world, the *real* world, she was travelling on a train in the year 2001. I know I'll return to that journey any minute, she told herself. But her pulse began racing again and she felt light-headed.

She was unable to see out of the back of the ambulance, which was closed by a tarpaulin, or the side facing her where there were two wooden shutters over the windows. When she looked through to the front, she could make out the vague outlines of the town's damaged buildings all around. There was no street lighting and little traffic, but Tom still had to drive carefully to avoid the piles of rubble in the road. He was not helped much by the poor quality of the ambulance's headlamps. She wondered about the danger they were in, but her two companions appeared to be calm.

They began to slow as they drove through a village, went up a small hill and round a corner. The engine groaned and Tom struggled with the gears. At the top of the hill, the ambulance turned right. Charlotte could see through the windscreen they had passed through a set of gates into an estate. She could see a large, well-lit building at the top of a sweeping driveway. They drove round the side and into a gravel courtyard at the back.

'This looks like a very grand building for a hospital,' she said, as the ambulance stopped.

Tom said, 'Yes, m'am. Welcome to the luxurious Bécourt Hospital.'

He opened the door and came round to the back of the ambulance, offering each of them a hand as they alighted in ungainly fashion.

'*Merci, monsieur*,' said Daisy with a giggle.

Tom grinned. '*De riens*.'

As the three nurses clambered out, Charlotte spotted a little girl peeking out from one of the outbuildings across the courtyard. She must have heard the ambulance arriving.

'*Bonjour*,' called Daisy, waving to her. The girl, who must have been about five years old, was wearing a dress with a cotton smock over the top. She waved back tentatively before disappearing into the darkness.

'Who's that?' asked Charlotte.

'Oh, it's little Monique,' said Margaret. 'She lives with her mother and grandmother on the estate, and they help us with the laundry and housekeeping.'

'I never knew that civilians lived so near to the fighting,' Charlotte said.

'No, I don't suppose that's commonly known,' said Daisy.

'That must be tough for them.'

Daisy nodded. 'I suppose it is. I've never really thought about it. I believe the locals are glad to have work, though.'

Daisy was heading towards a door. Charlotte was starting to follow her when Tom reminded her she had a suitcase.

'Oh, right. Thanks,' she said. Margaret picked the case up for her.

'Goodnight, Tom,' said Daisy 'And thank you for coming to collect us.'

'Any time.' He gave a mock salute and a wink. He wished them all goodnight, climbed into the front of the ambulance and drove off, the gears crashing as he got the vehicle moving again.

Charlotte followed the nurses through the solid wooden door and into the building. The red-tiled floor of the dark, narrow passageway was uneven. There was a powerful smell of cooked vegetables and a sound of pots and dishes being sorted as they passed an open door. People in the kitchen looked up as she passed. She nodded at them and they smiled back. Another new nurse was probably not exceptional to them.

The corridor opened out into a grand entrance hall. Margaret and Daisy headed for the staircase, taking Charlotte's suitcase with them.

Margaret called over her shoulder. 'I'll take your suitcase up as you're sharing a room with us. It's easy to find. Just come up to the next floor, look for the door at the other end of the balcony and come through there. Our room is the third door along on the left. But you'd better wait in the front hall for the moment until Matron comes to meet you.'

'Good luck!' added Daisy.

Charlotte took her coat off, folded it over her arm and gazed around the hallway. She cleared her dry throat and tried to take a couple of deep, calming breaths. The hallway had dark wood panelling and a high ceiling with an impressive staircase in the centre. A large, colourful, expensive-looking patterned rug covered the black-and-white tiled floor. There were fine, detailed tapestries hanging on the walls and two beautiful art-nouveau lamps at the end of the banisters. The lamps were lit and gave off a warm, golden glow.

Large French doors provided an entrance into the building. There were some brocade chairs and small settees arranged in groups with little occasional tables, as well as a large stone fireplace on the end wall and a grand piano, covered with a cloth. The place had an air of luxury. And here there was a smell of furniture polish – much more pleasant than the smell of the cooking that pervaded the corridor. The wooden banister was gleaming. Someone must spend hours polishing that, Charlotte thought.

A small curved reception desk stood at one side of the staircase, with little bells above, presumably connected to the bedrooms. An old-fashioned telephone sat on the desk and a bowl of pink roses. Charlotte wondered what would happen if she dialled her number. She bit her lip and tried hard not to cry. Keep looking around, she told herself. You'll soon wake up.

CHAPTER 2

The doors were suddenly slammed opened and two stretcher-bearers rushed in carrying an injured man.

'Evening, nurse. Where do you want him?'

Charlotte was confused. 'Sorry – where do I ... What do you mean?'

'I thought you were the reception committee,' the orderly said. 'Hold his leg for me while I will go and find out if they want him upstairs yet.'

Charlotte stepped forward, dropped her coat and grabbed the soldier's leg, which was heavy and bloodstained. The soldier, who was very pale and covered in mud, remained silent.

'Are you alright?' was the only thing Charlotte could think to say.

'It could have been worse,' he said quietly.

After a few minutes, the orderly returned. 'Righto, I'll take over now. Let's get him round to the assessment room.'

Charlotte eased the soldier's leg back down on to the stretcher, stepped back and looked at her bloodstained hands. She was reminded of how working in a casualty department had taught her to get used to the sight of blood. She was about to go and wash when she realised someone was speaking to her, but in a tone much less friendly than the orderly.

'Nurse! Nurse! What are you doing idling there?'

Charlotte looked up and saw a tall, overweight woman marching down the stairs towards her. She blinked twice, hoping it would be enough to wake her up. Nothing happened. She gazed up at the woman. It must be Matron McLean. Her instinct was telling her to run away, off down the corridor. But she stayed put.

Matron McLean had a fixed, direct, unsmiling expression. Charlotte's heart thumped even harder. Matron's long, thick grey hair was swept up into a bun which flopped in step with her as she stomped down the staircase. She was wearing a scarlet shoulder-length cloak over a long grey dress and a white bib. She loomed over Charlotte and carried with her a smell of violets.

'Good evening, Matron.' Charlotte held out her hand in greeting. Matron McLean looked directly at Charlotte, then down her outstretched hand, but made no move to take it. Charlotte lowered her hand to her side.

'You should have been here this morning,' she snapped. 'Most irregular, you know.' She gazed over her pince-nez. Charlotte could feel the steel-blue eyes boring into her and the hairs on the back of her neck stood to attention.

'The train took longer than it should have, Matron.'

'Such inefficiency!' retorted Matron. 'Where is your letter of recommendation? It had better be impressive.' She sniffed. 'Unlike your time-keeping.'

Charlotte fumbled with the clasp on the satchel and held out the crumpled set of papers. Matron McLean tutted, snatched them from Charlotte's hand and began leafing through them.

'I see you are from Aberdeen. Well, at least you did a three-year training. And you are from a recognised hospital.'

Charlotte said nothing. She wanted to say that actually she had done her nurse training in Edinburgh but at the moment keeping quiet felt like the safer option.

'When did you qualify?'

Charlotte hesitated. She could hardly say 1979 – the correct answer.

Matron growled. 'For goodness' sake nurse, you must know when you completed your training. Never mind, it will all be in the paperwork I received last week. I must say, based on this poor first impression I am surprised that your matron recommended you.'

This only added to Charlotte's bewilderment.

'And you are married?'

'Yes, Matron.'

'Are your belongings at the Front?'

'Are my ...' Charlotte was confused. 'Sorry, but I don't understand ...'

'I mean, nurse, is your husband serving in France as well? From my experience, your sort is unlikely to do well if that is the case.'

Charlotte stood a little straighter. 'No, Matron, my husband is at home.'

'Well, it seems rather strange that you are here, but I suppose the War Office is scraping the barrel now. I see you are part of the territorial nursing service, so have you worked in war conditions before?'

'No, Matron.'

Matron tutted again. 'Just what I need, another nurse who is green as grass. I hope you're better than the last one we had from Scotland. She only lasted two days. Couldn't cope with the work. At least you are trained, I suppose. And you have worked under the supervision of Miss Edmondson, who I believe I may have met. I do hope you are familiar with surgical patients.'

'Yes, Matron,' said Charlotte. 'Although it's some time since I worked in such an environment.'

'So what is it that you do now?'

'I work in a palliative care unit.'

Matron gave a little snort. 'Whatever that might be. It doesn't sound as though it will be very relevant here. Do you have any theatre experience?'

'Yes, I worked as a staff nurse in an operating theatre for a year after I qualified when I first moved to Aberdeen.'

'And what sort of surgery did that include, pray?'

Charlotte answered hesitantly. 'General surgery, plastics and orthopaedics.' She wondered whether such specialties even existed at the time.

'Well,' said Matron. 'At least that might be of some use to Sister Duke and me. But we can discuss your work schedule in more detail tomorrow. I do not have much time to explain the intricacies of our hospital now because you have arrived so late. You can attend my introductory lecture later this week. Suffice it to say that we are the most important part of the treatment of injured or ill soldiers. What you need to understand is that our purpose here is to return the men to the frontline again, in battle-ready condition and as soon as possible. Is that clear?'

'Yes, Matron.'

'Given your apparent lack of skill, I have decided that you will be working on the surgical ward under the supervision of Sister Craig but near me, too, so that I can keep a close eye on you. You will be starting tomorrow morning at eight o' clock sharp.'

Matron glanced down at her fob watch. 'Now, if you are lucky, there will be some food left over in the mess this evening. I suggest that you go and find your quarters. I have allocated you to share a room with Ashville and Wishaw, two of the qualified nurses.'

'Right,' said Charlotte a little hesitantly. 'Thanks.'

'Oh, and it is not regulation to wear your outside hat indoors, nurse or leave your coat on the floor.'

Matron turned abruptly and walked away. Meekly, Charlotte took off her hat and picked up the coat.

She walked up the staircase, hanging on to the polished banister to try and steady her shaking legs. At the top a series of rooms led off around the large, deep balcony. Now there was a different smell again; an old-fashioned disinfectant, possibly iodine. At the opposite end of the balcony, there was an open door leading into a corridor. She guessed it was the door she had been told to look for so headed towards it. The corridor beyond was narrow with whitewashed walls instead of wooden panelling. There were rooms with numbers on the doors and she assumed that one of these was where she was going to stay. Outside the third door, she stopped. She reminded herself of the nurses' names and called out softly.

'Daisy, Margaret, are you here?'

'Yes, yes,' came a jovial reply from behind the door. Charlotte entered and found a sparsely furnished room with three beds with wrought-iron frames. Her brown leather suitcase was lying on one. The bed had a lumpy-looking horsehair mattress and one of those long bolster pillows that were popular in France.

'So, how did you find Matron?' said Daisy, looking up from a letter she was writing. 'She's quite something, isn't she?'

'You can say that again,' Charlotte said. 'I seemed to be in trouble for being late, for not training at the right hospital and for not having the right experience. Matron then said something about my belongings which I didn't understand. Finally, I made the grave mistake of wearing my hat indoors.'

She hung the hat and her coat on a peg on the wall beside her bed. 'So overall, it could have gone better.'

Daisy laughed. 'Well at least she spoke to you. It took her three days before she even acknowledged my presence.' She pushed herself up off the bed and came closer. 'Whatever happened to your hands?'

'I had to hold a man's leg. It was bleeding. I've not yet had a chance to wash them.'

Margaret said, 'Don't worry, Charlotte. I'll show you where the bathroom is. We haven't got much time before all the food will be cleared away in the mess. We can talk as we go and you can unpack later.' She pointed at a battered chest of drawers. 'The bottom drawer can be for your things.'

That'll be interesting, thought Charlotte, who had no idea what was in the leather suitcase.

After she had washed her hands, the three nurses went back downstairs and sat at a table in the dining room on the ground floor – the room Margaret referred to as the mess. There were some large mahogany tables arranged in the centre of the room with smaller ones round the walls. A fire was glowing in the large fireplace at the far end. On each table was a tablecloth, glasses, cutlery, a bread-basket and a water jug. It reminded Charlotte of the dining room in a country-house hotel.

To distract herself, she decided to find out more about her colleagues.

'So where are you both from?'

'Oxford,' said Daisy, helping herself to some bread.

'Newcastle,' Margaret said.

'Have you been here long?'

'We both arrived during the same week three months ago. And luckily we're working in the surgical ward together,' said Daisy.

Margaret said, 'It's a beautiful building, isn't it?'

'Before it was a hospital, it was a country house, then a hotel,' said Daisy. 'Earlier on in the spring, Matron McLean was commissioned to adapt it to a hospital for officers. All that happened before the big push in July.'

'Big push?'

'Yes, you know – when we launched the summer campaign that's finally going to finish this war,' Margaret said wearily.

'So tell us a bit about you,' she went on. 'Do you work in a hospital or are you in private practice?'

'I work in a hospital. In a ward with twenty-one beds providing palliative care.'

Daisy and Margaret looked puzzled.

Daisy said, 'Is that a type of medical ward?'

Charlotte thought about it. 'Yes, I suppose it is. We look after patients who are nearing the end of life.'

'I've not heard of that,' Margaret said. 'But it sounds like it might not help you much in the surgical ward.'

Charlotte didn't know what to say so she changed the subject. 'How many beds are there in the hospital?'

'There are two wards on the first floor – our surgical ward has twenty-eight patients in the main room and the balcony has four beds, as well as all the other rooms you would expect,' Daisy said. 'The other ward is for medical cases and can hold fifty men at a push but I've never worked there. Earlier in the summer, we even had temporary wards in tents out in the front garden. One day, we had two hundred and fifty admissions.'

'The hospital has two floors,' Daisy continued. 'And you've now seen the reception area, but there's the kitchen, laundry room and store room on the ground floor, which you passed when we came in the back door. There's an assessment room that can be used for new arrivals and Matron's office as well. You'll soon find your way around. Oh, and I forgot to mention, there's also a room where up to six patients can go to release beds.'

'Release beds?' Charlotte said. 'I'm not sure what you mean.'

'Well, you know ...' Daisy lowered her voice. 'If a patient is clearly not going to make it – and if he'll not make it home – then we move him out of the main ward.'

A woman dressed in black approached and served each of them a steaming bowl of vegetable soup.

Charlotte wanted to know more about the room.

'So is someone allocated to look after the men if that happens?'

'Good gracious, of course not,' said Daisy, with a small, humourless laugh. 'Why on earth would you do that when there is so much work to do in the main ward? In fact, Matron refers to it as Darwin's room.'

'Darwin's room?' said Charlotte.

Margaret blew on a spoonful of soup. 'Well, according to Matron McLean, it's all to do with survival of the fittest. If a man's going to die, then he is obviously of no further use to the army.'

Charlotte sat back in her chair, shocked.

'Does it have to be used very often, this room?'

Margaret said, 'Well, it depends on how many injuries there are during spells of fighting. Sometimes, we're overrun with severely wounded soldiers and at other times, it's more of a steady pace. We're in a rotation with two other CCS units near here.'

'CCS? What does that stand for?'

Margaret laughed. 'Casualty clearing station, you silly goose. It sounds as though you have a lot to learn here.'

The soup bowls were cleared away and plates of mutton stew and potatoes placed before them.

'*Merci*,' said Daisy and Margaret in unison.

Nurses and soldiers who had already finished eating remained at their tables, drinking coffee and talking quietly.

A dark-haired man in uniform approached. 'Good evening,' he said, looking at Charlotte. 'And who are you?'

Both her companions jumped to their feet. Somewhat behind them, Charlotte did the same.

'Charlotte Robertson. I've just arrived this evening.'

'Pleased to meet you,' the man said. 'I'm Captain Clift, one of the surgeons. Please sit down and finish your dinner. I wanted to say welcome to our little unit. Have you done this sort of work before?'

'No. Actually, this is my first time in ...' She hesitated. '... in a setting like this.'

'Well, we'll have to look after you,' the captain said. He looked over to a nearby corner. 'Won't we, Nurse Brook?'

Charlotte followed his gaze and saw a serious-looking nurse glowering back at her. The nurse had been sitting so quietly, on her own, that Charlotte hadn't noticed her. The nurse muttered something, adjusted her round glasses and got up to leave.

Daisy said, 'Never mind Nurse Brook. She's always like that. Rather shy, I think.'

Captain Clift turned to leave. 'I'll let you finish your coffee in peace and no doubt see you tomorrow.'

The coffee that followed their meal was served in a bowl and tasted of chicory.

'Right, Charlotte' said Margaret briskly. 'Let's give you a chance to unpack and sort out your things.'

Back in their room, Margaret and Daisy lit the oil lamps beside their beds. Charlotte was relieved that hers was already glowing so she didn't have to demonstrate her ignorance about how to light it. She opened her suitcase, intrigued to know what was inside. There were a few sets of cotton underwear, four uniforms and a note from a uniform supply shop in Edinburgh detailing all the items of clothing she required for outside and inside wear. There was a pair of black low-heeled shoes with a label saying 'Dublup' – what a strange name for a brand of shoes. They were in her size, too.

There were a couple of books in the case – a Red Cross first aid manual and a nursing textbook.

'Oh, you lucky duck,' said Margaret. 'Is that the latest edition of Howard's book? Perhaps I can borrow it when you've finished reading it.'

'Yes, of course,' said Charlotte, putting the books on her small bedside table.

She changed into one of the long cotton nightdresses that had been in the suitcase and, with the help of the list, laid out the clothes she would need to wear in the morning when she would be starting work on the ward. As she climbed into bed, she immediately felt the lumps in the mattress. I wish I were in my own bed with Colin, she thought, suddenly feeling very alone again.

'So, tell me a bit about Matron McLean,' she blurted.

'Well, she's devoted to the army,' said Margaret, who was busy brushing her hair.

'She makes an ideal army nurse, too,' added Daisy from her bed. 'Being the scourge of the wrongdoer.'

Margaret said, 'She trained at one of the big London teaching hospitals, not exactly sure which one though, and joined the army in '95. She often says her skills were superior to other nurses. Then she served out in South Africa during the Boer War. I think it was in Bloemfontein ...'

Daisy interrupted. 'But that's not surprising because all her family had served in senior positions in the army.'

'Then after the war' Margaret went on, 'she spent time at Guy's. Her real interest is in how the operating theatre runs. And although she's very tough, she knows her stuff and seems to know everything that happens.'

She turned to Charlotte. 'All you need to remember is to show her that you're armed with all the facts about the patients and their treatments and you'll be fine.'

'I see,' Charlotte said. 'Thanks for the advice.' She thought for a moment. 'Matron also mentioned a sister.'

'Sister Craig is meant to be in charge of the surgical ward,' said Margaret. 'But Matron makes her life rather difficult for some reason.'

Daisy said, 'It's a shame because she's a real sweetie.'

'That's good to know,' said Charlotte.

There was a pause, then Daisy said, 'Charlotte, you've told us where you work, but who are you?'

Charlotte was uncertain how to reply. Normally she would have said, 'I'm married with three children and work as a nurse part-time in the National Health Service' – or something similar. But that would mean nothing to her new colleagues.

She took a deep breath. 'Well, I'm thirty-seven, from Aberdeen, married with three children. But to be honest, I'm not sure how I ended up here. It's all happened so ... unexpectedly.'

'Yes,' said Daisy. 'My papers came through very quickly as well. But you'll soon adapt, you know. And your family will be able to keep in touch by letter – the post is quite speedy.' She seemed to think for a minute. 'It's incredible they've let you come over. How old are your children?'

Charlotte said, 'I have two boys – William is twelve, David is ten – and then there's Anne, who's seven. I'm not sure they know where I am.'

Margaret laughed. 'Well, that's the military for you. Everything has to be rather secretive these days.'

'Do you have a photograph of them?' asked Daisy.

'No,' said Charlotte, a hint of sadness in her voice. 'I did have one in my bag but I lost it on the train.'

She felt her eyes filling with tears. Apart from the wedding and engagement rings she was wearing, she didn't have any reminders of her other life and she felt very vulnerable in this strange, new world. Her saw her roommates exchange glances.

'Homesickness is rather common, you know, Charlotte,' said Daisy. 'Margaret will tell you that I cried for about three weeks when I first arrived, didn't I, Peg?'

'Yes, I do believe you did,' said Margaret. She looked at Charlotte. 'We'll keep you right, you know. I'm on day duty in the surgical ward for a while along with you.' She lay on her back. 'Now, given that we're all working in the morning, I think it's time to put out our lamps and try to sleep.'

Charlotte tried to get comfortable. 'Thank you, both,' she said softly. 'And goodnight.'

'Sleep tight, Charlotte,' Margaret whispered. 'Sweet dreams.'

Daisy and Margaret quickly fell asleep, but lying there in the dark Charlotte began ruminating again. If this was a dream, it was lasting a long time. She wondered whether Colin or one of the children had tried to phone her or had heard that she had not got off the train when it arrived in York. She longed to know how things were in her world. She could feel butterflies in her stomach again at the thought of being here without anyone knowing where she was. If only she hadn't gone away on her own, then she wouldn't be lost like this.

Okay, Charlotte, she told herself, you just need to make the most of this experience and hope that you return to your normal life quickly – as quickly as you seemed to arrive here.

But it was no good. Despite her encouraging words, she couldn't understand why she had papers in her name, or a suitcase full of clothes that seemed to fit her perfectly, or that people had been expecting her. That was the strangest thing of all.

As she lay in the uncomfortable bed, she thought she could hear a distant booming sound, as though there were a firework display somewhere. Then the truth hit her. Oh my, she thought. That's the noise of the fighting. She suddenly felt even more vulnerable.

She tried to calm herself. If I can just get to sleep I can see where I am when I wake up. I hope I'm still on the train.

She began to focus on her breathing. Stay calm, Charlotte, everything will turn out right. She repeated the phrase over and over again until slowly the sound of the booming guns faded, her worries receded and, finally, she fell into a deep, black sleep.

CHAPTER 3

There was a knock on the door and a female voice called, 'It's six o' clock – time to get up.'

Charlotte opened her eyes, sighed and yawned. She looked around and immediately felt overwhelmed. She was still in this strange, foreign place. Her heart immediately began to thump again and her hands trembled. So many questions. Why has this happened to me? When will it end? What's going on at home? She wanted to say good morning to her children and give them a hug.

She stretched and noticed the rings on her left hand. How strange that all her other possessions had disappeared but not those. I must keep them safe, she thought. She knew she wouldn't be allowed to wear them on the ward. She would pin them in her pocket, just as she did when on duty at home. There was a packet of safety pins in her suitcase so she could use one to keep the rings safe.

She watched as Margaret and Daisy got out of bed. She would copy what they did by way of preparation.

'Did you sleep well, Charlotte?' asked Daisy as she got dressed.

'Yes, I did, thanks. I'm quite surprised. I didn't expect to but I must have been more tired than I thought.'

Daisy said, 'Yes, I find journeys tire me out as well. And I was so excited at the thought of starting work I hardly slept at all on my first night I was here.'

Daisy patted her stomach. 'Now, to more important things. Breakfast is served from half past six, Charlotte, so once you've had something to eat you have a few minutes to get some air if you like. I find that helps set me up for the day ahead, or at least until coffee time.'

'Yes, I'd appreciate a look around to try and get my bearings,' said Charlotte. 'Perhaps I'll do that first. I don't really feel like eating anything at the moment.'

Daisy looked at her. 'Well, my advice is to have some breakfast – it'll be a long day.'

Charlotte put on the underwear, stockings and grey dress she had laid out the night before. She had no idea if the uniform would fit her but it did. The dress had a texture like denim. She added the white apron, fumbling with the small buttons on each arm, followed by the starched white collar and cuffs. Margaret and Daisy had got ready much more quickly than she had. Charlotte noticed the exchange of glances between them as they put on their short capes.

'I'm sorry it's taking me so long. I'm not so used to this uniform.'

'No, you're fine,' Margaret said.

It was strange for Charlotte not to apply deodorant, moisturiser or a tiny bit of makeup to add a bit of colour to her pale complexion.

Like Margaret and Daisy, she too had a short cape, grey with a red border – another indication that they were all part of the territorial service. She noticed a small silver letter 'T' at the front corners of her cape but had no idea what they meant.

It was a strange feeling. Setting aside her trepidation, putting on the uniform was a treat for Charlotte. When she began her training she had worn an everyday shift dress but this – well, she felt she was dressed up as a proper nurse.

It occurred to her that she might need to write things down and found a piece of paper on the shared dressing table as well as a pen and pencil and she put them in her pocket.

There were some hairpins in the suitcase and she tried her best to pin up her chin-length hair inside the white cap that covered her head.

'You have such short hair, Charlotte – very modern,' said Daisy. 'My mother would not approve.'

When Charlotte was finally ready, Margaret said, 'Come on then, let's go and see what's on offer in the mess this morning.'

But downstairs, Charlotte said, 'Actually, if you don't mind, I think I'll just get some fresh air. I'll join you in a few minutes.'

She found her way to the back of the building. The smell of coffee and warm bread filled the air as she walked past the kitchen. She pushed open a heavy door and was back in the cobbled courtyard where the ambulance had dropped her off last night.

She took a couple of deep, steadying breaths and looked up at the blue sky. She noticed Tom and another man standing over by some outbuildings. Their sleeves were rolled up high and they were working on the engine of the ambulance. Tom turned as he heard the door closing behind Charlotte.

'Good morning, Nurse Robertson. I see you're getting some fresh air before you start your working day.' He gestured towards the other man. 'Let me introduce you to my colleague, James.'

'Good morning, Tom. Hello, James. Happy to meet you,' Charlotte said. She walked across the cobbles towards them. 'Yes, I felt I could do with seeing where I am. And I suppose I'm trying to steady my nerves a bit.'

She took a deep lungful of the morning air. 'I was quite surprised to see a little girl in the courtyard last night when we arrived.'

Tom said, 'Well, I guess it's just business as usual for the people who are trying to live their lives around here. But soldiers don't make superb neighbours.'

'Do you know how many people live here?'

'There must be about six or seven, I guess,' said James.

Tom said, 'Well, let me see.' He looked up as he thought about it and counted, waving the spanner he was holding as he mentioned each person. 'There's the old couple who work the gardens, the family in the cottage and the hospital. There are a couple of local girls who help in the kitchens ... Oh, and some older guys who help keep the place running ... Yep, that must be about right, James. I think they're glad to have some work.'

He turned back to Charlotte. 'So how are you settling in? Did you meet with Matron McLean last night?'

'Yes, I had a brief encounter with her last night in the hall. But I don't think she was very impressed with me.'

'She sure is a tough old cookie, isn't she?' said Tom with a wry smile. James looked up from the engine and nodded in agreement.

'Well, yes,' said Charlotte. 'You could say that.' She rubbed her hands together slowly then said, 'I have to confess to you, Tom, I'm very apprehensive about my first day.'

He smiled. 'That's not a surprise. It would be strange for anyone to be able to walk into a new unit and feel at home right away. But I'm sure you'll get on well. I can see you've got the makings of a good army nurse, you know. Stick with Daisy and Margaret, they'll look after you. Oh, and Sister Craig is delightful.'

Charlotte felt a little calmer. 'Thanks, Tom,' she said. 'That's reassuring. By the way, did you have to go out last night?'

'Yes, just after midnight. We were ordered to go up to one of the field ambulance stations to collect five injured men in both our ambulances – I guess you'll meet the men this morning.'

'Yes, I suppose I will. Tell me, where is your accent from?'

'Why, James and I are from the mid-west of the United States. Kansas City, Missouri. Have you heard of it?'

'Yes, I have.' Charlotte bit her lip. 'I once had friends who lived there for a while.'

Tom beamed. 'Well, what do you know! No one else has ever heard of it.'

Charlotte said, 'So how did you both end up here?'

It was James who answered. He straightened and wiped his hands on a rag. 'Well, Tom and I were set to graduate from law school last year when I read an article about the volunteer ambulance service. I thought, well, that would be a real good thing to do to support the people of France. The final straw for both of us was the sinking of the Lusitania. You know, the liner torpedoed off the coast of Ireland?'

Charlotte nodded.

'So when the opportunity to volunteer came up, we just grabbed it. We were with the Service Sanitaire Américaine for six months, but we've been here for over a year now. I started off further north, but was moved here to work with Tom about three months ago.'

Charlotte said, 'That's admirable. I'm afraid I haven't got a great sense of adventure.'

James laughed. 'I'm not sure that can be true, or else you wouldn't have volunteered for the Territorials.'

She wanted to let them know that she had not volunteered at all and had no idea why she was at the hospital. But she said nothing.

'I like gals with a sense of adventure, as you call it,' James said. 'By the way, how are my two favourite nurses this morning?'

'They're just having breakfast. And that's where I should be.'

As she turned and began walking back towards the door, she called over her shoulder, 'Nice to speak to you both. And see you later, no doubt.'

She was aware of a figure in an upstairs window looking down at her. She looked up. It was the nurse who had been in the corner of the mess last night. Charlotte smiled but got no response.

Back inside, she met Daisy in the hallway.

'There you are, Charlotte. I was just coming to find you so you have time for some breakfast. Are you all set for your first day on the ward?'

Charlotte said, 'I was just telling Tom and James I feel rather nervous. But in a strange way, I'm looking forward to seeing the work first-hand. I've always wondered what this kind of nursing would be like.'

Daisy reached out and straightened Charlotte's cap. 'Just as well as we'll have a long, busy day. It'll be late before you get to relax again.'

She hesitated then added, 'Yes, I saw you were talking to Tom and James. Aren't they wonderful?' Daisy blushed. 'They are very modest but all their colleagues say how brave they are. I worry about them when they set off to collect patients because they have to go near the front line to the first aid stations. And it's very dangerous, you know.'

Charlotte nodded. 'Yes, I think they're so brave to volunteer to do work like that.'

They went into the mess together where they each had a bowl of hot coffee and Daisy had another helping of bread which she slathered in butter and jam. Margaret was just finishing her breakfast. Charlotte looked over at her. 'Margaret, please will you take care of me today? I haven't been in this situation before and I don't feel very confident.'

Margaret smiled. 'Of course I will. Just ask me anything.'

As they headed upstairs to the ward, Charlotte wondered what the men would be like, how the staff would react to her and what sort of equipment she would be expected to use. Even with Margaret beside her, she felt an enormous sense of trepidation. Her heart was pounding, and her hands felt clammy and shaky. Had Margaret and Daisy felt the same on their first day? They seemed so full of confidence. She tried to focus on what Tom had said. How would anyone be able to walk into an entirely different environment and be totally familiar with everything? I'll try not to be too self-critical, she thought, although she knew it would be difficult. Colin found her lack of confidence an annoying trait – and regularly told her so. She wondered what he would make of her if he could see her right now. She could hear him saying, 'Enjoy the new experience and just ask if you don't know something. There's nothing wrong with that, you know.' She longed to speak to him.

At the top of the grand staircase, they turned to the right and walked along a corridor towards a big set of double doors. She let Margaret lead the way. The ward doors opened to reveal a long, wide room with panelled full-length windows on both sides. There was a large oak dining table at the far end and a small desk in the middle. It was a sight from Charlotte's past. I haven't been in a ward like this for the best part of twenty years, she thought. It reminded her of the surgical wards at the Eastern General Hospital in Edinburgh where she had spent some placements as a student nurse. The sight triggered a flood of memories of nursing patients with abdominal and amputation wounds following surgery.

She became aware of someone coughing, which brought her back to her senses. The coughing was followed by the unmistakable sound of sputum being spat out.

There was a hum of male voices from further up the ward and was she was shocked to see some of the men were smoking in their beds. There was not much space between the beds and no curtains to divide them, although wooden screens surrounded one bed and she wondered who was behind them.

She knew she was being looked at, not only by many of the patients but by the other nurses, too. Three of them, wearing uniforms similar to hers, were standing around the desk along with Daisy and Margaret. Two orderlies were already working in the ward, bustling to and fro, and didn't seem to be coming over to join the group.

'It's Nurse Robertson, isn't it?' asked one of the nurses whose uniform was slightly different from that of the others. There were two scarlet stripes on the forearms of her dress. She offered her hand in welcome and Charlotte took it.

'Hello, I'm Sister Craig. You'll be working for me. I understand from Matron that this is your first time in an army hospital – is that correct?'

'Yes, Sister Craig. I'm very glad to meet you.'

'Well, we will try our best to settle you in gently but you need to understand it will be dependent on the workload. You may have to work things out yourself to some extent.'

Sister Craig had a soft, gentle expression and her large red-rimmed eyes were framed by swept-up chestnut hair that seemed to be escaping from all the pins she had in it, battling in vain to keep it under control.

'Thank you, Sister. I'll try to pick up things as quick as I can.'

Sister Craig turned to the nurse who it seemed had been on night duty and was looking exhausted. 'Right, Nurse Collinson. Let's get on with the morning orders, then you can finish for the night and go to your bed.'

Charlotte fished in her pocket for her paper and the pencil and over the next few minutes scribbled notes as the nurse made her report. No one else wrote anything down. Matron McLean, who joined halfway through, glared at Charlotte over her glasses as she came and sat down at the desk. Charlotte could see that everyone, including Sister Craig, stood a little more upright the moment Matron appeared.

Nurse Collinson began her report.

'Let me say in the first instance that we had five admissions overnight, but Lieutenant Francis died shortly after being admitted. We have no empty beds at the moment.'

She reported on each of the thirty-two patients in turn, bed by bed. But she spoke quickly and although Charlotte tried her best to write down as much as she could, there were so many names ... Burns, Cameron, Bremner, Fulman, Manson, Gibson ...

The equipment mentioned meant nothing to her either and she had abandoned her notes by the time Nurse Collinson had got to bed number eight, the patient behind the screens. This was the soldier mentioned at the start who had died shortly after admission.

Nurse Collinson finished her report with Godman in bed five and Douglas in bed three, two patients newly added to the dangerously ill list.

Before Sister Craig had a chance to speak and organise the staff's duties, Matron McLean said, in a matter-of-fact way, 'Well, we shall see what the CO says, but we will probably move them nearer the door before they lower morale in the ward. Has the paperwork been completed for the new admissions?'

Nurse Collinson hesitated. 'Not quite, Matron. Unfortunately, we were diverted by Francis.'

Matron said, 'That is "unfortunate", as you call it. Or more probably, a lack of efficiency. So, tell me how they have been categorised, then?'

She didn't wait for a response. 'We will be forced to finish off your work, Nurse Collinson.'

Nurse Collinson went bright red and bit her lip.

Matron turned to Sister Craig. 'Please make sure in future that your staff complete the paperwork. You know it is most important.'

'Yes, of course, Matron,' said Sister Craig 'I'm sure we will be able to attend to that.'

Nurse Collinson was trying hard keep herself together. 'Higgins, Ellis and Wilson are Bs, Deans and Fellows are As,' she said, in response to Matron's question.

Charlotte didn't understand what this meant – it was something else to ask about when there was time.

Matron was silent for a moment, then she said, 'Sister Craig, I am not happy with how the ward is laid out at the moment. I cannot understand why we have new admissions in the balcony. Rectify this as soon as possible today.'

'Yes, Matron. It was the first thing I planned to do this morning.' Sister Craig remained expressionless in the face of Matron's criticism. Charlotte wondered how she managed it.

'Besides,' Matron went on, 'I fail to understand why we keep getting these non-abdominal wounds admitted. We are an abdominal unit. I will speak to the CO again about it. Also, we need to move some of these men on. They have been here far too long and we are not a stationary hospital.'

She stood. 'Now then, enough of this sitting around. It is time to start with the day's work. Sister, report to me at eleven this morning. I need to speak to you about a complaint.' She turned to leave the ward but then stopped to look at a document on the desk.

'Of course, Matron,' answered Sister Craig, whose expression gave no clue as to her inner thoughts. She turned to Nurse Collinson. 'Thank you so much for your hard work. You deserve a good, long sleep and we'll see you again tonight.'

Nurse Collinson looked grateful. With a smile she said quietly, 'Sorry to drop you in it, so to speak, Sister. I just couldn't manage to move all the men around last night.'

Sister Craig told her not to worry and the weary night nurse left the ward, having wished everyone a good day.

'So, we will have another busy day today,' said Sister, glancing round the small team of nurses. We have at least five going to theatre so Nurse Wishaw, I want you to be on theatre duty and to complete the observations, with particular attention to the head injury in bed eleven. Please let me know directly if there is any change in his condition.' Matron didn't look up, but Charlotte could hear her tutting as Sister Craig spoke.

Undeterred, Sister Craig turned to Charlotte. 'Nurse Robertson, as this is your first day with us, I want you to work with Nurse Brook on the admissions and dressings. I would prefer it, though, if you could avoid taking notes. It is standard practice here to be able to remember the details contained in morning orders. After today, I want Nurse Wishaw to supervise you for the rest of the week until I decide when you are ready to work independently.'

She called over two staff in different uniforms so she could speak to them. Charlotte recognised them as belonging to the VAD. Both looked very young and very nervous. They were wearing bright blue dresses with white collars and cuffs and a white apron over the top. One of them had a red cross on the bib of her apron.

Sister Craig said, 'Please do the cleaning and the feeds, just as we discussed yesterday, Miss Giles.' Miss Giles nodded.

'You need to attend to our stores today, Miss Hill, as I notice we're low on our dressing supply and Dakin solution. You can also check the state of the rubber gloves as I think a few pairs require some repairs. We need to catch up and replenish our stores after the busy time we've had. Is that clear?'

'Yes, Sister,' said the two volunteer nurses in unison.

Charlotte thought it very old-fashioned to call someone 'Miss' but she noticed that Sister Craig's tone was kindly and she had given them clear and direct instructions about their tasks for the day.

After Sister had left them, she noticed Daisy whispering to one of the girls as they started the day's work. The girl giggled and nodded. Charlotte wondered what was going on.

She had a feeling her work would be scrutinised by the nurse she was assigned to work with and that it would not be done with such kindness. She had not made a good start with Nurse Brook last night.

The VADs scuttled off quickly to work with the orderlies as they prepared the breakfast. A tray was laid for those soldiers who were on bed rest. Of the remainder, those who were able were encouraged to eat at the dining table and help with the table setting and serving of food.

Out of the corner of her eye, Charlotte saw Tom coming into the ward. He nodded and smiled at Charlotte but he paused when he saw Matron McLean who was still looking at documents on the desk.

Matron looked up. 'Yes, what is it?' she said sharply.

'Good morning, Matron. I was just passing and wanted to inquire after Captain Francis and Lieutenant Wilson. I brought them in last night.'

'Well, Francis died. And it is too early to say much about Wilson, but I'm sure the jostling of your ambulance won't have done his injured back any good. Furthermore, I am not clear why you brought him here. We are not orthopaedic specialists and he will probably block a bed for an abdominal wound.'

'The other hospitals in the area were full, Matron. I had no choice,' Tom replied in a matter-of-fact way.

Again, Matron tutted. As she turned to leave the ward, she announced to the assembled staff, 'Now, as I have already said, enough of this idle chat, there's work to be done. Someone open the windows and let some fresh air into this ward.'

Charlotte wondered whether Matron was choosing to be mean deliberately or whether she was just thoughtlessly blunt. She didn't know her well enough to decide yet. But from her experience of riding in the back of the ambulance last night, she knew the suspension and the road conditions would not be good for anyone with a serious injury, let alone someone with a damaged back.

She thought briefly of the differences between a modern nursing handover and the 'morning orders' she had just observed. There was no mention of anyone's first names, just their rank and surname along with a list of tasks that had to be done for each patient. And it was a strange thing to hear problems with bed occupancy being discussed in a similar way to the 21st century.

She knew she would spend a lot of the time today asking how to do things and was relieved to be working with another nurse, even if it was Nurse Brook. She was unsure what to do first but it didn't take long to learn the general rhythm of the ward even though it was such an alien environment to her.

As Matron McLean left, Charlotte heard her say, 'Keep an eye on her for me, Sister Craig. I must go and ensure theatre is prepared for the day.'

Nurse Brook also heard. She sighed and said to Charlotte, 'I always get lumbered with the new staff. Come along then, quickly. I suppose I'll have to tell you about the ward routine as I show you round. Surely you won't need to take notes for that.'

Charlotte merely raised her eyebrows in response. But the hair on the back of her neck bristled. Stay quiet, Charlotte, she told herself. This is your first day and she might be able to help you become familiar with the ward and its routine.

There were fourteen iron-framed beds on each side of the large ward and four on the balcony which had glass doors at either side. As Matron had observed, these four beds were not meant to be used by new admissions who were more likely to need closer observation. There was a small bathroom by each of the balcony doors. Every bed had a small table beside it where the soldiers could put their limited possessions. There were wicker-backed wheelchairs next to some of the beds.

'We have a clear daily routine,' said Nurse Brook briskly. 'Morning orders happen at eight, followed by the observation round when we record temperatures, pulses and the occasional blood pressure. Each patient has a chart to record these above their bed and both Matron and the previous sister like it if you note down in the temperature book on the desk any patients who have a fever. Can you take a blood pressure?'

'Yes, of course I can,' said Charlotte. Nurse Brook looked disappointed. She resumed her monologue.

'We have two MOs on the ward and they'll make their rounds at ten before they begin surgery – unless there's an emergency – and the CO will often make an inspection during the morning. If the men are able, they should be encouraged to stand at the end of their beds in preparation.'

Charlotte had to stop her. 'I'm sorry but I don't know what those abbreviations mean.'

Nurse Brook sighed and folded her arms. 'MO stands for medical officer and CO stands for commanding officer. Did they tell you nothing before you arrived here?'

Charlotte said, 'No, actually. You're right – I've had no preparation for this assignment at all.'

Nurse Brook ignored her and carried on as she walked Charlotte around the ward.

'The dressing round starts at nine and will probably take about three or four hours. A few will be done by the MOs as well so be aware of that. Work from clean wounds to dirty ones. Observations happen at least four times a day. The soldiers are encouraged to do as much as they can and they need to be discouraged from lying around. Lunch is at noon when a bugle will sound and tea is at four o'clock.'

'A bugle sounds at meal times?'

'Army regulations,' said Nurse Brook. 'Orderlies assist patients with washes and make the beds. Every soldier must have a wash and shave daily. Someone will tell you later when you can go for a short morning break. You have some time free for lunch if we're not too busy, but sometimes we work a split shift, depending on the day's events. Neatness, observation, procedure and record-keeping are the keys to our success.'

Nurse Brook pointed at the beds by the door and continued talking without giving Charlotte any time to ask questions.

'The soldiers on the danger list are nearest the door and we move patients as needed. Our biggest enemies, apart from the Hun, are sepsis, bleeding and tetanus. You must ensure that the soldiers have or have had their anti-tetanus serum.'

She paused for a moment. 'I do hope you have a strong stomach. You're going to see some sights you're probably not prepared for, and you must be able to react swiftly to a change in condition and alert a more senior nurse first. This person is then responsible for conveying that information to the MOs.'

Charlotte was beginning to feel overwhelmed with information but Nurse Brook had more to say.

'When a bed is vacated, you must ensure it's prepared for the next admission as quickly as possible. Clean each bed frame with carbolic lotion and, if possible, fumigate the mattresses and bedding. However, you need to check the orders book to ensure there will be time to do this.'

She pointed over at the desk, saying that was where the book was kept.

'Some forms require completion and I'll show you them in due course. On admission, soldiers are undressed, bathed, re-clothed in hospital shirts, have their temperature and pulse taken and recorded, and are then tucked up in blankets and hot water bottles. The only exception to this is if there's no point and we'll try to transfer them to the side room directly or put them behind screens.'

Here again was mention of the room the others had last night called 'Darwin's room'.

As well as feeling she was facing a deluge of detail, Charlotte was finding some of Nurse Brook's information was annoying her and she could not keep quiet.

'What do you mean, "if there's no point"?'

Nurse Brook looked directly at her. 'There's no point in wasting resources when someone is clearly done for. The goal of the Royal Army Medical Corps is to return men to fight.' Her voice held no trace of emotion.

Charlotte shook her head. What an awful attitude to the welfare of injured men. But Nurse Brook had begun again.

'When a patient is taken through to the operating suite, their bed is readied here in the ward. Unlike other units, Matron prefers the men to come back to this ward rather than move to another. You are, I assume, familiar with a theatre bed.'

'Yes, I can do that.'

'At last! You know something!' Nurse Brook said acerbically. 'At the end of the daily care rounds, there will always be preparatory tasks to do regarding equipment and dressings. You will see the preparation room when we start on the dressings. You must ensure that the volunteer staff do their bit. I find them rather lazy.'

Charlotte said tartly, 'Well, I'll work that out for myself, if it's all the same to you.'

Nurse Brook ignored her and carried on. 'So, we have six admissions to finish and then nineteen dressings to complete. We'll have to take the bandages off the wounds the MOs will change and prepare the dressing trolleys when they arrive. Let's start with the admissions and see where the night nurse got to. Pretty poor stuff that she didn't finish all the documentation. The previous sister would not have allowed that to happen. Of course, she was a proper army nurse – like me.'

This was the second time Nurse Brook had referred to a 'previous sister', but Charlotte chose not to comment. Nurse Brook was clearly not a fan of Sister Craig, but Charlotte's first impression of her was of someone trying her best to run a ward in the face of some opposition. That must be a difficult task. Finally, it seemed, her introduction to the ward was complete. It was time to start work.

CHAPTER 4

Charlotte and Nurse Brook turned their attention to the new admissions. A brown leather patient record book sat on the desk in the ward and all the new names had been entered into it. The other columns remained empty, although Charlotte could see the essential details of each patient were on their medical cards.

'Well, I suppose that's something,' said Nurse Brook.

She turned to Charlotte.

'You use black ink for a new admission and red ink if we have a soldier transferred in from another hospital or casualty clearing station. You'll find the pen and red ink in the desk drawer. And you'll see there's a space for the reason for admission. If a soldier has multiple injuries, then the most severe one is entered.' She paused. 'I wonder if you're senior enough to do that.' She seemed to think for a moment. 'Oh well, you'll have to do. It's imperative to include all the details as each book returns to the army for compilation. The date of discharge and the patient's status are added later. Make sure you're accurate.'

Charlotte smiled as she picked up the fountain pen. She recalled being made to write with one at school and managing to cover herself in ink. Nurse Brook watched over Charlotte's shoulder as she made her first entry, noting down that Francis had died on the same day as admission.

'What strange writing you have,' said Nurse Brook. It was true. Charlotte's handwriting was very different from the copperplate script of previous entries.

'Would you prefer to write, then?' Charlotte said.

'No, you need to learn how to do this properly.'

A field medical card had been partially completed for each soldier at the time of injury at an advance dressing station and transferred with the patient to hospital. Nurse Brook added more information to one of the cards.

Charlotte was surprised to see such bureaucracy. There were several different forms to fill in and no obvious way to avoid duplication. Observation charts were completed for each soldier and were similar to those she used at work.

When the paperwork was complete, Nurse Brook said, 'Right, come with me and we'll make a start on the admission washes.'

They got up from the desk and passed Margaret who was completing the observation round.

'Is everything alright?' she asked Charlotte quietly.

Charlotte smiled. 'Yes, I think so. But I have information overload.'

The three preparation rooms were by the main entrance to the ward. One was used to store linen, another was a 'clean' room for dressing material, medicines and equipment for procedures, and the last was the sluice where all the personal care equipment was kept and items disposed of – the place for the 'dirty' things that came from the ward. A couple of large wicker baskets were already filling up with soiled linen that would be taken away for boil-washing. In each of the rooms, everything was tidy and ordered. Beyond the open door of the laundry cupboard, Charlotte could see wooden slatted shelves full of neat piles of starched sheets, blankets, pillowcases, draw-sheets, hot water bottles, night shirts, pyjamas, undershirts, bed-socks, knitted hats ... A little table and chair in the room had a sewing box and oil lamp on it. Someone was kept busy darning and repairing the linen. Perhaps the VADs preferred to be in here, away from Matron's glare.

They went into the sluice, which had all the necessary equipment to attend to the personal needs of the patients – glass urinals, lidded enamel bed-pans, a couple of commodes and a sink about two feet off the ground. It had taps and a cistern with a chain, and a moveable grate on the top – a bedpan washer, 1916-style.

What struck Charlotte was the absence of plastic. Even the pots and the different number and type of bowls used to collect various bodily fluids or for washing patients were made of enamel. Everything was designed to be re-used. She was gazing round the room when she realised Nurse Brook was speaking,

'You might need some turpentine as well as soap and water to get the dirt off them. Oh, and you'll need this.' Her hand stretched up and took a bottle of carbolic off the shelf.

'What's that for?'

'Their heads, of course – dilute it one to twenty and rub it in their hair to get rid of the blighters.'

Nurse Brook attached a laundry bag to the side of the admission trolley. It would be used to put the soldier's uniform in before it was taken away to be fumigated.

'I'm surprised you don't know this,' she said. 'Obviously I'll need to supervise you more thoroughly than I thought when you do a blanket bath so I can see if you know what you're doing.' She sighed exaggeratedly. 'Honestly, sometimes I wonder what they teach in the minor civilian hospitals outside the capital.'

Charlotte gently bit the inside of her lip. She filled one of the enamel bowls with warm water and placed it on the trolley. She felt piqued that her core nursing skills were being challenged and her training questioned. She could understand the criticism about not knowing the equipment but this was different. It made her wonder where Nurse Brook had trained. Her accent sounded as though she was from the north of England but perhaps, like Matron, she had moved to London.

They started with Lieutenant Deans in bed nineteen and Captain Fellows in bed twenty-six as they had been graded 'A', which Charlotte now understood meant they were dangerously wounded and may need to go to the operating theatre that day if it was deemed that surgery could make a difference. Presumably, a 'B' meant a wound of lesser gravity. She would learn later that that the soldiers referred to a 'B' category as a 'Blighty wound' – severe enough for them to have a spell at a hospital back home but not bad enough to kill them.

However, both the 'A' men clearly had very severe abdominal wounds. Fellows's abdomen, which had blood-stained padding over its left side, looked enlarged and tense, reminding Charlotte of women who were at the full term of pregnancy. The two nurses turned down the top layers of the bedclothes and placed a towel over his chest. They managed to remove his uniform and they put it in the bag for fumigation. Charlotte observed as Nurse Brook rinsed his hair with the carbolic solution. She seemed more interested in doing that than in Fellows himself, whose colour was that of a ghost. Was this really more important than ensuring he was warm and comfortable before theatre?

He groaned quietly each time they moved him. Nurse Brook instructed him to stop making such a fuss and 'get on with it'.

'Do you think this could wait until he's been to theatre?' asked Charlotte.

Nurse Brook stopped in her tracks. 'The admission procedure should be completed in full. Were you not listening to me earlier?'

Charlotte nodded. 'I appreciate that but he seems to be in such pain. Would it be possible to give him some analgesia?'

'No, he'll have to wait,' said Nurse Brook. 'He had some morphia administered when he came in last night, and I've already told you that the medicine round is at ten.'

Charlotte turned to look at the soldier. She rinsed a cloth in the warm water and gently wiped his face and then dried it with the towel.

'I'm sorry to be making such a fuss,' he whispered.

'My goodness,' said Charlotte. 'You're badly injured and you look like you're in a lot of pain. I don't think that's making a fuss at all. We should be apologising to you for all the moving you're having to endure.'

She wiped some dried mud off his dirty hands, wondering what the conditions must be like at the front line. She remembered what she had learned at school about the terrible mud in the trenches.

They managed to put a clean nightshirt on him without making him move too much.

'I hope we can sort something out for you as soon as possible,' Charlotte said, gently touching him on his hand. It felt clammy. She looked up. Nurse Brook was glaring at her but said nothing.

'Will I wash his feet as well?' asked Charlotte, seeing that Nurse Brook was tidying away the washing trolley.

'No time. The night staff should have completed these admissions and I fail to see why I should have to do all their work for them.'

Charlotte was about to say something about helping others who were working hard as well but she was distracted by a voice calling out.

'Nurse, will you come and hold my hand as well?'

She turned to see a smiling face looking over at her from bed nine. McLeod had relatively minor leg injuries so was well enough to watch what was going on in the ward. When so much of the care was given without screens being placed round the beds, it was easy to watch procedures as well as the comings and goings of the ward.

'That will not be necessary,' said Nurse Brook severely, but with a smirk on her face. 'Come on with you, Nurse Robertson. You're taking too long with this and we have lots to do. When you're finished there, you can get him a couple of hot water bottles to keep him warm. That will do him for now.'

Charlotte patted Fellows on the hand as she left, much to the amusement of McLeod.

'You have to be careful not to pander to them,' Nurse Brook snapped.

'We obviously disagree on the meaning of the word "pander",' Charlotte said. 'I think it's important to provide the appropriate care to a patient, even if that does interfere slightly with a routine. That's not pandering. In my ward, we would administer analgesia not just at set times but as it's required to ensure someone was not in such awful pain.'

'Well, you are not in your ward now,' Nurse Brook said. 'And you have to make sure they don't get too used to morphia.'

'That's unlikely to happen when someone has such a severe injury and is clearly in such pain, Nurse Brook. I'm surprised you don't know that.'

Nurse Brook was clearly not used to someone answering back to her. She opened her mouth as if to speak but then turned away.

The remaining three patients were all admitted in the same perfunctory way. Charlotte noticed that Nurse Brook worked in silence as she checked that the injured soldiers had received their anti-tetanus serum.

After the third patient had been washed, they pushed the blanket-bath trolley back to the sluice. 'I take it you have a copy of the current anti-tetanus policy,' Nurse Brook said.

'No, I don't.'

'Well, you should have been issued with the new policy that came out in August. You should make yourself familiar with it, you know. You could have been doing that last night, rather than fraternising with the staff in the mess.'

Charlotte laughed and shook her head in disbelief. 'Thank you for letting me know. I'll ensure I read it just as soon as I can.'

She watched Nurse Brook marching away.

Daisy was in the sluice.

'How's your first morning going, Charlotte?' she asked.

Charlotte leaned against the wall and sighed. 'A bit of a blur, if I'm honest. I'm being told lots of things and I can see I have lots to learn. What about you? Did you see Tom when he came into the ward?'

'No, I missed him,' replied Daisy, as she rinsed out a bowl.

'I felt rather sorry for him. He came to ask how the new admissions were and looked very upset at the news of Captain Francis.'

'He tries to be as unobtrusive as possible to keep out of the way of Matron and Nurse Brook. They're so awful about him and James. I heard Matron saying they interfere in ward work when they should be fighting – but I think that's jolly unfair when they're clearly volunteers.'

Charlotte closed the lid of a full laundry basket. 'Yes, I agree. Tom seems to care about the soldiers he transports.' She paused. 'So what happens to Captain Francis now?'

'What do you mean?'

'Well, do we wash him as well?'

'Charlotte, what would be the point of that?' Daisy said. 'A wash won't do him any good now and we don't have time for such luxuries.'

His body would be wrapped in a cloth, covered with a flag, removed by the orderlies and buried in a nearby cemetery, she explained. 'Matron thinks it lowers morale if they're here too long after they've gone. It's a pity they didn't move him into the side room to get him out of the way during the night – it would have saved a lot of trouble this morning. Unfortunately, there have been plenty like that around here over the last couple of months.'

Charlotte felt uncomfortable that she would not be able to wash and tidy the body. It was something she always did with great reverence; the final thing you could do for your patient.

Back on the ward, with the paperwork and tasks associated with the new admissions complete, Nurse Brook and Charlotte turned their attention to the dressing round, which would take many hours. They began in the clinical preparation room.

'I'll go and get the dressings book – you make a start on the preparations, Nurse Robertson.'

The shelves were stocked with bottles, jars with labels that were a mystery to Charlotte and lots of different pieces of equipment. Dressing material was put in silver-coloured boxes and then sterilised in the small steel machine in the corner. She gazed around the shelves, at the many different sorts and shapes of bandage material – muslin, calico, flannel and gauze.

One of the VADs, whose job it was to make and roll the bandages, was cutting gauze, putting it into wire baskets and then sterilising it, ready for use.

Charlotte introduced herself. 'Hello, we haven't met properly. I'm Charlotte Robertson.'

The VAD looked up. 'Good morning. I'm Miss Hill. But I'm just a volunteer.'

'Good to meet you,' Charlotte said. 'But I'm sure you're more than that. What's your first name?'

The girl looked surprised. 'Isobel,' she said.

'Is it alright if I call you that?'

'Only if no one else hears. Or else I'll be in trouble.'

Charlotte said, 'I'll be careful. What are you doing? It looks like a tricky job you've got there.'

Isobel nodded. 'I'm a bit apprehensive about it. Nurse Brook may check that my measurements are exact and I don't want to be reported to Sister Craig again and give her more work to do.'

The small dressing trolleys were covered with white linen and had an array of kidney-shaped dishes on them. Daisy was busy making up a solution.

'What are you up to?' asked Charlotte.

'This is one of my favourite jobs – making up the Dakin solution. I managed to get Miss Hill to agree to let me do it instead of her.' At this, Isobel looked up and smiled.

'So that's what you two were whispering about at the report,' said Charlotte.

Nurse Brook re-appeared. 'I'm not sure why you're doing that,' she said to Daisy. 'It's typical that the VAD has managed to extract herself from her duty.'

Daisy said, 'Nurse Brook, that's unfair of you. I asked her if I could do it.'

Nurse Brook simply shook her head and gave Isobel an unpleasant look before leaving the room.

'Isobel, my dear, never mind her,' Daisy whispered.

Charlotte watched as Daisy continued with her work. She measured out chloride of lime and added it to a large flask of water, then mixed sodium carbonate and sodium bicarbonate with more water before adding it to the large container. She then shook the flask energetically before looking at her watch.

'I'll come back in half an hour and siphon off the liquid and then it will be ready to use. By then it'll be clear, just like magic! Isobel, please will you remind me when it's ready?'

'Of course,' said Isobel. She checked her watch and looked pleased to have been given a little responsibility.

Captain Clift, one of the two surgeons who worked on the ward, arrived just after ten o'clock to begin the ward round. Nurse Brook reappeared, following him into the clinical room.

'Perfect timing,' he said. 'I can see you've not yet started on the dressings.' He turned to Nurse Brook. 'Let me borrow Nurse Robertson for the next few minutes. She can assist me with the dressings. Please go ahead with your work, Nurse Brook. I'm sure we'll catch you up in due course.'

Nurse Brook began preparing her dressing trolley, clattering the metal trays and dishes louder than seemed necessary and then muttering something under her breath.

'Did you want to say something, nurse?' Captain Clift asked.

'No, sir,' came the reply.

Charlotte felt uncomfortable watching their exchange, so she changed the subject.

'Who do you want to see first this morning, Captain Clift?'

He thought for a moment. 'Stills, Stevenson and Jones, but perhaps I should have a look at Fellows, the new chap. I was a bit concerned he might still have some internal bleeding.'

'Yes,' said Charlotte. 'I helped to admit him this morning and I noticed how distended his abdomen was. I also think he's in a lot of pain. He's trying to be very stoical but as we were moving him, he seemed to be finding it hard to cope with it all.'

Charlotte was unsure whether Captain Clift was listening to her. He stared intently at the floor with his arms folded while she was talking. She wondered if she was speaking out of turn so was surprised when he said, 'I agree, we need to give him some morphia. Let's say a quarter grain, and I may have to reconsider when we take him through to surgery. In fact, let's go and see him first.'

To Nurse Brook he said, 'Please will you administer a quarter grain of morphia? I'll write the instruction on his card.'

'Yes, Captain,' said Nurse Brook. 'I wanted to raise this issue with you as I think he's in a lot of pain.'

Charlotte said nothing.

Following Captain Clift, she pushed the dressing trolley to Fellows's bedside, wondering what the modern equivalent of the morphine dose might be. The poor man had closed his eyes and was lying extremely still.

She touched him gently on his arm. 'Here's the doctor to have a look at you. I'm just going to open your nightshirt so he can see what's going on.'

The young officer was doing his best to move and it looked to Charlotte as though he was attempting to stand.

'Please don't worry,' Captain Clift told him. 'I'd prefer it if you stayed where you are.'

'Sorry, sir,' Captain Fellows mumbled.

Charlotte undid his hospital shirt to expose the dressing. There were fresh bloodstains on it.

'I think his abdomen is more distended than it was earlier,' she said.

Captain Clift gently palpated the taut belly. Fellows groaned.

'Is that very tender, old chap?'

'Yes,' said Fellows weakly.

'Tell me, when did you sustain this injury?'

'Last night.' Fellows's voice was little more than a whisper.

'I see.' Captain Clift straightened and said to Charlotte, 'I think there's some internal bleeding. I want to take him to theatre now but we need to give him some fluid rectally first. One pint of saline solution with an ounce of brandy should do. But in the first instance, Nurse Robertson, please go and prepare Sister Duke in theatre. I don't need to see under the dressing.'

He turned to speak to the soldier. 'Now then, old chap. I'm going to operate on you shortly to try and stop this bleeding. We'll have you on your feet again in no time.'

The nearby theatre room had been converted from a series of pantries, making it pleasantly cool and Charlotte found the theatre sister preparing all her equipment for the day ahead. She was wearing a thick white cotton gown, full-length, a white cap that contained all her hair and a mask. Charlotte was impressed with the way all the instruments were organised.

'Yes, nurse, what is it?'

'Excuse me, Sister Duke, but Captain Clift has just reviewed Captain Fellows and feels he needs to come through to theatre immediately because he has started bleeding again.'

'Well, that will put my schedule out a bit,' said Sister Duke, not looking at Charlotte. 'But please let the captain know he can come through directly as Captain Goodman is here already. What sort of injury does he have?'

'An abdominal wound. A dressing is covering his spleen.'

'I have a laparotomy set ready now. Thank you, nurse.'

'I'll go and let Captain Clift know,' Charlotte said. 'Is there anything else I can do to help with the preparation?'

Sister Duke glanced up at her. 'Yes. Remember your place on the ward and be careful not to become too familiar with the patients and medical staff.' She turned her attention back to her preparations.

Charlotte thought about this as she returned to the ward. She was used to speaking very informally to her medical colleagues. How different it must have been for most nurses in the early part of the twentieth century. It was true that Nurse Brook had told her the ward sister was the liaison between nursing and medical staff – but when an opportunity came to update a colleague or request a particular form of treatment for a patient she knew about, she would not expect someone else to do that for her.

Captain Clift was writing notes at the ward desk.

'Sister Duke is all prepared for Captain Fellows,' Charlotte said. 'And she wanted me to tell you that Captain Goodman is there, too.'

'Fine,' he said. He put down his pen. 'She is a wonder, you know. She can even turn her hand to the administration of an anaesthetic if needed, using a Skinner mask and chloroform. But I'm glad to hear Captain Goodman's there. He's like his name - a good anaesthetist. In fact, they're quite a team.'

'Should I accompany Captain Fellows through to theatre?'

He smiled. 'In an ideal world that would be delightful, but I don't think you'll have time to do that, Nurse Robertson. We're not in private practice now. It'll be more important for you to monitor him once he returns to the ward.'

At Fellows's bedside, she could see Nurse Brook had already started the infusion and was clearing away a syringe. Charlotte had hoped to see the procedure so she would know what to do. She had of course given injections many times but not with a glass syringe and reusable needle.

She walked over. Even though she could not accompany Fellows, Charlotte could not let him leave the ward without telling him what was about to happen.

'I'll see you later when I hope your pain will have eased. And by the way, I do think you're in good hands.'

He made no reply. When the orderlies came to take him through to theatre, he groaned as he was lifted onto the trolley.

Charlotte made a theatre bed, which meant putting a piece of mackintosh across the bed, covered by a smaller sheet. This made it easier to change a patient, without having to replace the whole lower bed sheet. In the modern world, such sheets had been replaced by disposable pads. While she was doing this, she thought again about the differences between this world and home. The pre-operative preparation had only consisted of a two-minute talk, and Captain Fellows probably had no clue about what was going to happen to him or the possible risks associated with anaesthesia and surgery.

She looked at her watch. Late morning. Daisy came over and asked if she would like some coffee.

'That sounds fantastic.'

'Well, let's go down to the mess and have a seat for five minutes or so.'

There was a pot of fresh coffee waiting for them in the front hall.

'Oh, lovely,' said Daisy. 'And there's time for a freshly baked croissant.'

Through the mess doors, Charlotte saw Sister Craig walking along the corridor, presumably on her way to her appointment with Matron. Poor thing, thought Charlotte. What bad news will she be receiving? Perhaps I'm not the only one who's uncertain about things round here.

CHAPTER 5

Daisy wanted to pop up to their room for something and disappeared with her coffee so Charlotte decided to take hers outside for another chance to have a breath of fresh air. This pleasant weather was surprising. She had always associated the First World War and the Western Front with rain and mud. As she sat on the low courtyard wall, she watched the orderlies putting a wrapped body on the back of a cart. What an unpleasant task, she thought.

She mulled over Daisy's comments about Francis, the soldier whose body was behind the screens and the wish to move him out of the way quickly to make it easier for the other patients. Charlotte was puzzled by this attitude, given that the soldiers must be surrounded by death when they were on the front lines. She wondered whether it might provide comfort to see that their dead comrades were well looked after, rather than bundled up and rapidly disposed of.

How difficult it must be for people like Tom and the girls who were civilians, finding themselves in such a regimented world. The strict order of the military command was very different from her experience. She was already finding it confining.

Tom had shown genuine concern earlier that morning and clearly felt the loss of any soldier he had brought to the hospital for treatment. The constant pressure must affect you. Had people developed compassion fatigue in the war? They must have, surely, being surrounded by suffering and death all the time. She compared it to the feelings of uncertainty she was encountering at home. Were there any similarities?

She laid her empty cup on the wall and turned to walk out of the yard in the direction of some outbuildings and cottages. There was a wisp of smoke coming from of one of the chimneys and it was hard to believe that life looked so normal when such devastating fighting was happening in the vicinity. A few yards past the cottages, there were chickens scratching about in front of a gate that led into a large walled garden where there were vegetables growing and a large orchard with full fruit trees. She went through the gate and saw, at the far end of the garden, an older couple working but they did not look up. The vegetable beds were well ordered, laid out in neatly tended rows. This is lovely, thought Charlotte, just the sort of place I would enjoy spending a few days on holiday.

She walked a little further up the lane and stood at a fence by fields and watched some cows grazing lazily. Perhaps my real world is just over the horizon, she thought. She hesitated for a minute then retraced her steps back towards the hospital.

Tom appeared in the courtyard, armed with a large spanner.

Charlotte went over. 'Hello, Tom. I was just thinking about your visit to the ward this morning and your concern for Captain Francis.'

'Well, my pal James tells me just to get hardened to it and not think of them as human.' He smiled. 'But I don't seem to be able to do that.'

He shifted the spanner to his other hand. 'I know Matron thinks I get in the way, but I think showing some concern for your fellow human beings is a good quality. And to be frank, it's what keeps me going.'

He paused for a moment, then said, 'You know, I was taught that unintentional movement could make things worse for an injured man, and I do try to ensure they're well strapped in before I move them. So I'm real concerned that Wilson seems to have been made worse by me.'

Charlotte said, 'I'm sure you do your best, but from my journey in the ambulance last night the suspension is no help.'

He looked downcast.

Charlotte went on, 'But I think the problem lies with Matron's attitude towards volunteers.'

'You may be right,' he said. 'We're not under her control and perhaps that annoys her as well.'

'Is that why your uniforms are different?'

He nodded. 'We report to a French medical officer.'

He stood aside and gestured towards the dusty vehicle behind him, smiling again. 'Seeing as how you've mentioned one of my favourite gals, let me introduce you formally to Camille, my ambulance.'

She laughed.

'James calls his Paulette,' Tom said. 'These cars are made with a Ford chassis and the bodies from old packing crates. We say that they can be bent but not broken, but with the state of the roads around here, they need a daily work-over. There's always something to do, even when we're not collecting soldiers.'

'Well, I'm delighted to meet Camille,' said Charlotte. 'And I have to say I admire your concern for the soldiers.'

Daisy appeared at the back door.

'There you are, Charlotte. I wondered if you'd still be outside.' She spotted Tom. 'Oh, good morning again.'

'Good morning, Daisy. And can I say you're looking mighty pretty today?'

Daisy blushed. 'Thank you,' she said. She turned to Charlotte. 'Come on Nurse Robertson, we need to return to the ward.'

She grabbed Charlotte by the arm and guided her towards the back door.

'See you later, Tom,' said Charlotte, over her shoulder.

'You need to be careful, Charlotte,' Daisy said. 'A staff nurse who came to work here last month was redeployed for spending too much time with one of the orderlies. Do you know you've already been reported for talking to Tom earlier this morning?'

Charlotte was indignant. 'Do you think exchanging pleasantries with a colleague in the yard would fall into that category?'

'Probably,' Daisy said. Charlotte shook her head in disbelief.

Back on the ward, she found Nurse Brook in the preparation room.

Nurse Brook sighed. 'Now you're finally back, we need to make a move with the dressings. Fellows has knocked our schedule out.'

'Have you had your coffee break yet?' asked Charlotte.

'No, I'm too busy to take breaks for coffee,' Nurse Brook said. 'And by the way, remember that when you make a theatre bed up, the pillowcase opening must face away from the door and the hot water bottle should be further up the bed.'

Charlotte laughed inwardly. She had encountered people in her nursing career who followed similar little rules and rituals that had no bearing on the care a patient received. Her amusement must have shown on her face because Nurse Brook said, 'I'm not sure why you find that amusing. It's important that things are ordered. By the way, you need to write to Francis's family today to let them know he died.'

'Is that a nursing task?' said Charlotte.

'Yes, and you had better get used to doing it – even with your fancy writing.'

Before Charlotte had a chance to say anything, Nurse Brook turned her attention back to the dressing trolley. Her brisk efficiency meant she had got through several dressings while Charlotte had been organising Fellows's trip to the operating theatre and having her coffee break.

'Right,' said Nurse Brooks, pushing a dressing trolley towards her. 'Go and set up the Carrel tube on Peters in bed twenty-two. I assume you know how to do this.'

'No,' said Charlotte. 'Sorry. I've never seen this piece of equipment before.'

She could see Nurse Brook was just about to launch into another tirade about other people's poor training and experience, but Charlotte just looked at her and said as calmly as she could, 'Please understand this is my first day on this ward. This is a new experience for me and I'd be grateful if you would show me how things are done with a bit of kindness. Believe me, I can appreciate how annoying it is to have a new person joining the ward and the extra work it gives you, but everyone has to have a bit of time to become orientated. So, rather than being unpleasant about my apparent lack of knowledge, please can you tell me what the Carrel tube is?'

Nurse Brook stared at her for a moment then sighed and said, 'It's a way of irrigating a wound to prevent it becoming infected.' She began moving the dressing trolley into the ward. 'I suppose I'll have to show you how to set it up, then. Honestly, I'd be as well doing the dressing round on my own.'

Charlotte chose not to react to this remark and was amazed she had spoken to Nurse Brook in such a direct way. In other work settings, she had never managed to be so assertive and as a result had been on the receiving end of some dismissive or rude comments about her knowledge, appearance or experience. She felt pleased that she had stated her case and was holding her own. If only she could be more like that at home, she would feel more confident.

The dressing trolley was set with all the equipment they were likely to need and they arrived at the bedside as Lieutenant Peters was finishing his morning coffee. His left arm was in a sling and Nurse Brook silently set about organising the equipment while Charlotte prepared their patient.

'Good morning, Lieutenant Peters. We're about to set up this special cleansing equipment on your arm. Is it alright if we do it now?'

The soldier seemed amused. 'Of course. I'm not golfing until after luncheon today, nurse.'

He was obviously not used to being spoken to like this. His response drew a smirk from Nurse Brook.

They began setting up the Carrel tube. It was fascinating to watch as a glass flask was hung upside down from a stand with a set of rubber tubes inserted into the bottom of it.

Nurse Brook explained. 'This fills the wound with the Dakin solution and it's packed lightly. We need to replace the gauze every two hours. Over the next couple of days, the wound will gradually become sterilised.'

She cleaned the surrounding skin with iodine, placed the tubing across the extensive and deep wound, tucked some gauze around it, and then put wadding over the top and secured it with a bandage.

'The renewal of the gauze will be one of your tasks for the rest of the day, Nurse Robertson. Do you think you will actually manage to do this?'

'Of course. Thank you for showing me how to do it.'

Nurse Brook looked at her with surprise when she realised Charlotte had thanked her.

As they cleared up, Charlotte asked if the same approach was used for all wounds.

'No, we wouldn't use it if it could get directly into a blood vessel or the peritoneum. Not every doctor uses them, but Captain Graves does. And the procedure works very well in my experience. I don't know why they have to keep trying new-fangled things when we have perfectly good dressing material on our shelves.'

The procedure complete, Charlotte noticed another doctor was reviewing the wounds of Still and Lawson, with assistance from Daisy who was looking rather pale. The doctor called to Nurse Brook.

'I need a hand with Beattie, please, as I think Nurse Ashville has other duties to perform.'

'Certainly, Captain Graves. Nurse Robertson will assist you,' said Nurse Brook. She turned to Charlotte. 'This will test you. You won't have seen anything like this before. It's a "have a go, Harry" special!'

Charlotte walked over to join Captain Graves who was standing near the ward door.

'Hello, Captain. I'm ...' She was about to say 'Charlotte'. 'I'm Nurse Robertson.'

'Right,' he said. 'I want to do Beattie's dressing – and you can assist me.'

Daisy looked relieved to see her. 'Thanks Charlotte,' she whispered. 'I just can't bear this sort of wound.' The colour was already returning to her cheeks as she walked away.

Charlotte tried to remember what the night nurse had said about Beattie, who was in a bed near the door. He was an army chaplain and had been in the ward for three days, having sustained a large shrapnel wound in his neck. But his unstable condition meant he was not yet ready for onward transfer. He had been operated on the day before in an attempt to excise the damaged tissue. But an infection was now developing and the wound was leaking pus copiously. That meant he might start bleeding from one of the main arteries in his neck and there would be ghastly consequences if he did. In the 21st century he would have been on intravenous antibiotics – although she had noticed how scrupulous all the staff were about washing their hands in between patients.

The dressing had been changed under light anaesthetic on the first evening after the surgery so that the wound could be inspected thoroughly, but yesterday Captain Graves had re-dressed it in the ward.

'Let's have plenty of hydrogen peroxide and gauze on the trolley, nurse,' he told her. 'And I think we should have some screens around the bed. Just in case.'

Charlotte fetched the screens from the linen cupboard. She then put together all the items needed for a dressing on a trolley and wheeled it to the bed where Captain Graves was waiting. He had put on a gown and was wearing a pair of surgical gloves.

'Thanks. Just put the trolley beside me here and pour some of the hydrogen peroxide into the kidney dish.'

Beattie was staring out of the window opposite as they made their final preparations.

'Right then, Padre,' said Captain Graves. 'Please let me look at that wound on your neck.'

‘Good morning, Captain. Apologies for not getting up.’ Beattie had a soft, lilting lowland Scottish accent. He seemed distracted. ‘I was just thinking what a beautiful day it is. It’s hard to believe we’re so close to all that fighting.’

‘I was thinking the same when I popped outside earlier,’ Charlotte said.

What a lovely accent he has, she thought. It reminds me of someone.

Captain Graves removed the dressing and when Charlotte saw Beattie’s wound, she was shocked. There was a gaping hole in his neck.

His eye caught hers, looking for a reaction. Charlotte tried her best not to show her surprise at his disfigurement but she could appreciate why Daisy found it so horrific.

She could also understand why the doctor who had operated on him wanted to change the dressing. It was a perilous procedure. Captain Graves cleansed the area with some hydrogen peroxide, which frothed on contact with the wound, which was then re-packed with sterile gauze.

Captain Graves said, ‘As I’ve been interfering with the wound, please keep an eye on Beattie’s pulse and temperature for the next few hours, nurse. If there’s new soakage on his dressing, make sure I am informed immediately. Is that clear? Tell me directly if there is any change rather than report it to Sister.’

‘Yes, of course, Captain Graves,’ Charlotte said.

Every hour for the rest of the morning and early afternoon, she returned to Beattie’s bedside to check on his wound. In between she carried out her other tasks, including the two-hourly re-packing of the Carrel tube.

‘ Tell me, Padre, where are you from?’ she asked when she made one of her checks.

‘Berwick upon Tweed,’ he replied, without moving his head to look at her. ‘Would you like me to show you a picture of my family?’

Charlotte nodded and he pointed to a small photo frame on the table beside his bed. It was sepia-tinted and showed a family, formally posed, with a little boy in a sailor suit and a woman holding a baby.

‘What a lovely photo. What are your children called?’ She could see the pride on Beattie's face.

‘Alexander – he’s three years old, named after my father – and the baby is William, but I’ve not seen him yet. My wife is called Flora.’

He sighed. 'Now that I'm in this ... predicament, I seem to be thinking about them a lot and missing them even more than usual. I'm rather looking forward to seeing them – if I'm lucky enough to be transferred to a hospital back home.'

'That would be good for you if it happened. But I suppose it is rather uncertain.'

'Yes,' he said. His voice had dropped to a whisper. 'It is.'

Mention of the name William caused Charlotte to think about her children. What would they be doing now? She missed them so much. She forced away the tears that she could feel were stinging her eyes and made herself think about Beattie.

She hoped she would be able to spend more time speaking to him about his situation and finding out about the work he had been doing nearer the front line. She was far from being the only one uncertain about their present situation and what might happen next. It was all a matter of degree. Speaking to the padre had been both revealing and thought-provoking.

Later, about three in the afternoon, Charlotte was doing another of her wound checks when a man in a long frock-coat and wide-brimmed hat arrived at the ward.

'Excuse me, nurse,' he called in very clear English. She went over to him and he introduced himself as Monsieur Gosset, the curé at Notre Dame de Brébières, the church in the centre of Albert. 'Please could I see Padre Beattie? I heard that he was with you and I have met him on a couple of occasions.'

'Please let me see if he wishes you to visit him, Father,' said Charlotte.

She walked over to Beattie's bed. He had dozed off. She touched him gently on the arm. 'Padre, there's a French clergyman here to see you. Would you like me to bring him to you for a few minutes?'

Beattie opened his eyes. 'Yes. Thank you. That would be very pleasant.'

She noticed how little he moved his head. She would be the same in his situation.

She took the priest over to the bedside. 'I would be grateful if you only stayed for a few minutes, Father. He's exhausted, although I'm sure he will benefit from seeing you.'

The curé kept to his word, stayed for about fifteen minutes and when Charlotte did the next wound check, Beattie seemed more settled.

'How kind of him to come and see me,' he said. 'We prayed together. It's especially considerate of him with all the damage in the town and at the church. He tells me that the statue of the Golden Virgin has been secured at the top of the steeple by chains, even though it's still hanging on at right angles. He thinks the fact it's still there is a sign we will all come through this war. I do hope he's right.'

'Yes, Padre. I do, too,' said Charlotte.

Beattie closed his eyes. 'We prayed together even though we come from different religious backgrounds. Nurse, I prayed for strength to endure this uncertainty.'

'I do hope that was comforting for you.' Charlotte thought she might benefit from a similar prayer, even though she had lost her faith many years before.

The flow of the work continued throughout that first day. Margaret looked after the patients before and after they went to theatre, so Charlotte spent little time with her. The patients who were further along the road to recovery helped serve the drinks, even though some had serious injuries. It was remarkable, given the extent of their wounds, but was in keeping with the goal of getting patients back on their feet as soon as possible. All the staff worked efficiently and there was little time to speak. Charlotte kept an eye out for Captain Fellows and was relieved to see that he returned from theatre and seemed to be more settled. Over the rest of the day, his swollen abdomen reduced and his pain seemed to lessen slightly. He was kept flat, and hourly checks were made on his pulse, temperature and wound.

After the patients had eaten supper, Matron McLean appeared for her evening ward round. Charlotte admired her hands-on approach. Nurse Brook was quick to assist, without letting Sister Craig know that Matron was in the balcony.

'No, I'm not sure where she is,' said Nurse Brook when Matron asked. But she quickly retreated when Sister Craig noticed that Matron had arrived and the two of them discussed who was improving and who was worsening, which would influence their decisions about which beds the men should occupy and who was ready for discharge, whether back to their units, on to a stationary hospital nearer the coast, or back to Britain.

There were two empty beds in the ward. Cosworth had left earlier in the day to start his journey back to England. Charlotte had been so busy she hadn't even noticed he had gone. The other empty bed had been occupied by Francis, the patient who had died the night before.

The general rule was that men who were improving were moved towards the balcony while those whose conditions were deteriorating or who needed closer observation moved nearer the door. As mentioned at morning orders, Matron did not like new admissions to be in the balcony, where no-one could see any change in their condition as had happened during the previous night. That was one of the advantages of having everyone in the same large room – at least you could see them, Charlotte thought, although it didn't make for any privacy. She could see how difficult this situation would be to manage as it could involve moving patients to free up beds during the hours of darkness.

The orderlies were called to the ward and instructed by Matron McLean and Sister Craig which men to move. Luckily the beds were on wheels which made the task relatively easy. Charlotte was relieved that no one was moved into 'Darwin's room', but she wondered if this was the likely outcome for Godman and Douglas, the two soldiers who had been moved nearer the door as their conditions deteriorated and their chances of survival lessened. Here was another, more profound example of uncertainty – not knowing whether they would survive their injuries.

She had not yet opened the door to the side room which was a few feet away from the main entrance to the ward, so didn't know what it looked like and whether there were any men in there at the moment.

Once the ward round was completed, Sister Craig let the staff know that they would all be working the day shift again tomorrow.

Charlotte couldn't believe how quickly time had passed. She had been so absorbed in what she was doing that she had not had any time to think about her real world since the incident with Beattie. It was as she was clearing away some equipment that her mind jumped back to her family. The questions that caused her distress last night resurfaced and her hands started to shake again. I wonder if the same amount of time has passed there, she thought. What would Mum have done when I didn't get off the train when it arrived in York? Colin and the kids will be worried I haven't been in touch. Where are my things? What if I can't get home and I'm trapped here?

An unfriendly voice interrupted.

'Have you written that letter yet?'

Nurse Brook was standing beside her, glaring.

'I was just about to make a start on it.'

'It doesn't have to be a novel you know. The facts will do. And it should have gone in the evening postal collection.'

'I didn't know that there was a collection tonight,' Charlotte said. 'But I'll make sure it's written before I leave the ward. When's the next post?'

'In the morning.'

Charlotte found some writing paper and copied the hospital's address from another letter that was sitting on the desk, awaiting a signature.

She contemplated what to write. Nurse Brook had told her to stick to the facts, but that would make it a short letter. *Lieutenant Francis died of his wounds on arrival at the hospital.* There, that said it all. But Charlotte thought about the impact on the person who opened the letter. How cold and unfeeling. It was an important task that she was about to undertake. This will be the ultimate in bad news; a letter out of the blue, written by someone the reader had never met. Everything about it felt wrong. In this wartime situation, the families at home must have lived with the dread of receiving such awful news and people must have been aware of the losses from reading their newspapers or watching what was happening in their neighbourhoods. How would she be able to do this with compassion?

Her first challenge was uncertainty about the recipient of the letter. She didn't know if Lieutenant Francis was single or married. She was mulling this over when Nurse Collinson, the friendly night nurse, approached her.

'You're working hard for your first day. What are you up to?'

Charlotte smiled. 'Oh, I'm writing a letter to Francis's family.'

'Why are you doing that when you've not been in charge today?' Nurse Collinson tutted. 'Let me guess – Nurse Brook asked you to do it, didn't she?'

'Yes,' Charlotte said. 'But I don't mind.'

'That's not the point. She always manages to avoid things like that. Did she tell you we have a template?'

'No, she was more annoyed that I'd missed the evening post.'

'She's talking nonsense, as usual. We usually manage to write these letters within a week of the soldier dying, so to even begin it today is good going. Do you want me to write it for you?'

Charlotte shook her head. 'No, thanks. My hesitation was more about the form of words that would show some compassion for strangers.'

'Well, we often don't know much about them, so we tend to leave the beginning rather general in these situations.'

'That's helpful – thank you.'

Charlotte started writing. But then Daisy and Margaret appeared and Daisy called over to her.

'Charlotte, we'll meet you in the mess in a few minutes, once you've finished there.'

'That's fine,' Charlotte called back. She turned her attention back to the letter.

I am very sorry to have to write to inform you that Captain James Francis died earlier today. He sustained serious chest injuries yesterday and despite his immediate transfer to the hospital and treatment, he died shortly after his arrival. I can assure you that he was in no pain when he died, and I am very sorry for your loss. I am sure you must have been so proud of him.

Yours with regret

C. Robertson

'Will you have a look at this and tell me if it is suitable?'

Nurse Collinson was standing by the desk, checking through the admission book. She picked up the letter and read it. 'Yes, that sounds about right, but it's more than we would usually write. How do you know he wasn't in any pain?'

'I don't, but I wondered if that would be of some consolation to them.'

Nurse Collinson read the letter again. 'Yes, possibly. Right, you head off now and I'll put it in an envelope for you. See you in the morning if you're working.'

'Thanks. Yes, I am. I hope you have a better night.'

Nurse Collinson laughed. 'I don't normally have to look around for work.'

The daily report book was lying open on the desk. Each day, Sister Craig wrote a summary and Charlotte glanced to see what had been written for today.

Saturday 23/09 at 10pm. Number of admissions: 6. Number of discharges: 1. Number of deaths: 1. Patients to operating theatre: 6.

Patients remaining in surgical division: 30.

Staffing changes: Nurse C. Robertson arrived at the hospital last night and commenced day duty on the surgical ward today.

J. Craig

How funny to see a busy day reduced to just a few words. Sister Craig's short entry confirmed that nurses have never been good at describing all the things they do for patients, Charlotte thought, as she walked out of the ward and down the stairs to the dining room. A pleasant smell of cooking pervaded the air and she realised she was hungry.

Another bugle call heralded the arrival of the staff supper and she found all the day staff ready to sit down and have their meal. Those from the medical ward were sitting at another table, sharing news about their day. As she sat down beside Daisy and Margaret, Charlotte could feel the muscles in her legs and back aching from the constant activity. She wondered how far she had walked over the last few hours.

The food arrived, interrupting her thoughts. The first course was rabbit terrine with toast, followed by some cold meat with salad. It wasn't the sort of food that Charlotte would usually eat, and the salad leaves were a bit chewy, but she enjoyed it and the fact that it was being served to her. At home, she was thinking about cooking every day after work and had lost any sort of inspiration.

At the end of the meal Charlotte leant back in her seat with a cup of coffee in her hand.

'What a day,' she said.

Nurse Brook, who was sitting at the far end of the table, at a slight distance from everyone else, said, 'You should try it when it's been busy. This was very quiet.'

'I'm sure it must be utterly exhausting then,' said Charlotte, to Nurse Brook's apparent surprise.

'Did you finish that letter?'

Charlotte sipped her coffee and nodded. 'Yes, I did actually.'

Nurse Brook's lips pursed but she said nothing.

Later, as they made their way upstairs, Margaret asked Charlotte how her day had been.

'Not too bad,' Charlotte said. 'I did find I had to keep asking what things were for and I could see it was annoying Nurse Brook.'

'That's not surprising. It was very difficult for us, too, you know, when we first arrived. How did you find the medical staff?'

'They were very kind to me, all things considered. What are they like to work with?'

Margaret said, 'Captain Clift finds it difficult to adapt to the military way of things, I think, but he's rather more conservative in his approach. Captain Graves is a more experienced surgeon and comes from the school of thought that surgery shouldn't be halfhearted.'

'Is that why Nurse Brook referred to him as "have-a-go Harry"?' Charlotte asked.

'Yes, although that's rather mean of her. His theory is that one larger surgical intervention should prevent further operations. But as you'll have seen with Beattie, the consequence of that is rather large wound excisions.'

Letters were waiting for Margaret and Daisy when they got to their room.

'What a lovely way to end a long day,' said Daisy, 'This one's from my mother.'

She lay down on her bed and began to read. At one point she laughed and said, 'Listen to this. "Please take care of yourself, darling girl, we don't want another situation like Edith Cavell on our hands." Goodness me, what does she think I'm doing here?'

'Have you no post today, Charlotte?' asked Margaret.

Charlotte hesitated. 'No ... I ... I'm not expecting to receive any letters.'

Margaret was shocked. 'Why on earth not?'

'Well, I've only just arrived and ...' Charlotte thought quickly. 'I don't think they'll know where I am.'

'Well, hopefully you'll hear something tomorrow. If you want, I can give you some writing paper.'

'That would be lovely. I'd love to speak to them and tell them about my first day here.' Charlotte knew it was impossible.

To distract herself from the distressing thoughts she knew would follow, she contemplated having a relaxing soak in a bath. But at that moment there was a knock at the door and Sarah, one of the volunteer nurses, came in.

'Excuse me, Nurse Robertson, but Matron McLean wants to see you in her office directly.'

Margaret said, 'Gosh, I wonder what you've done.'

'Who knows?' said Charlotte. 'Thank you, Sarah. I'll come to her office straight away. My bath can wait a few minutes.'

She followed Sarah back down the stairs to the ground floor and went to find Matron in her office. She knocked and a voice said, 'Enter.'

Charlotte felt she was entering a museum exhibit of an Edwardian drawing room. The room was full of dark wooden furniture, carved and ornate, with many exotic-looking ornaments and plants on side-tables. It was all immaculate and ordered but with no photographs anywhere, Charlotte noticed. There were two small chairs arranged in front of the fireplace and beside one of them there was another little table with a tray and an empty plate on. Matron McLean had eaten her supper alone in here. Her desk sat in one alcove and her bed in the other. There was a pair of heavily brocaded curtains and the oil lamps gave the room an amber glow. What struck Charlotte most was an unusual smell that she couldn't immediately identify.

Matron was sitting at her desk with her back to Charlotte. She stood, turned round and walked over to one of the small chairs.

'Please sit down,' she said, pouring herself a sherry from a decanter. 'I wanted to find out how you had got on during your first day.'

Charlotte was not expecting this. She sat. 'Fairly well, thank you, Matron,' she said. 'Considering it's all very new and very different from what I'm used to.'

Matron McLean settled herself on the chair opposite, fixing Charlotte with a steely gaze. There was a pause but Charlotte held her nerve and looked back without blinking.

'Sister Craig tells me that you are rather unfamiliar with the admission procedure and paperwork that we use. Is that correct?'

'Yes, it's true. I've not seen this sort of paperwork before.'

'I have to say, Nurse Robertson, that I cannot work you out at all,' continued Matron. 'You seem so uncertain about many routine tasks that I believe you should know, but seem so confident in the manner in which you talk to the medical staff and patients. I am going to assume that this is because you have not worked in war conditions before and because you trained in a hospital outside a leading medical community.' She took a small sip of sherry. 'But I also wanted to tell you that I am keeping my eye on you and will be writing to the matron in chief and the matron in Aberdeen if I have to.'

Charlotte was unsure how to respond so kept quiet but held Matron's gaze.

Matron stood up abruptly and brushed past Charlotte on the way to open the door.

'That will be all. Good evening, Nurse Robertson.'

Charlotte rose. 'Good night, Matron McLean,' she said as she left the room. The unusual smell she had noticed earlier was strong as she passed Matron.

This dream is getting more ridiculous, she thought, walking along the corridor. That felt as though I was at school again and had been sent to the headmistress's study for being naughty. I wonder what would happen if I told her the truth. What could she do to me? Perhaps I should have said go ahead, write to Matron Edmondson if you feel you want to.

Walking back through the grand front hall, she noticed Sister Craig sitting in the corner. She was sipping a cup of coffee and appeared lost in thought.

'Good evening, Sister,' Charlotte said.

'Hello, nurse.' Sister Craig answered slowly, apparently having forgotten Charlotte's surname.

'It's Robertson, Sister.'

'Yes, of course, please forgive me. Good evening, Nurse Robertson. How did you find the work today?'

Charlotte walked over. 'Well, to be honest, it was hard but I enjoyed it much more than I thought I would – although Matron doesn't seem to share my opinion.'

'Oh? And what has Matron had to say about your day?'

'Well, I've just been called to her study because she wanted to speak to me.'

'I can assure you that I made a favourable report about you, nurse.'

Charlotte smiled. 'That is kind. You know, somehow I didn't think you would have reported me.'

'Thank you for that.' Sister Craig stifled a yawn. 'Now, I'm so tired. If I don't go to my room soon, I'll fall asleep in this chair. And that would never do.'

'It must be difficult to be in charge when everything is so unpredictable.'

Sister Craig looked at her for a moment. 'Yes, it is. But I'm fortunate that most of the staff are so supportive of me.'

'Most?'

Sister Craig seemed to hesitate. 'Yes,' she said. 'Most of the staff.'

Charlotte was not sure what to say. 'Oh, I ...'

Sister Craig cut her off. 'We just have to grin and bear it. When I compare my situation to that of the soldiers, it's of less importance. I just have to tolerate it until it ceases. It will, you know.'

'Yes, Sister Craig. I hope it does so soon. As long as I'm here, you have my full support.'

'Thank you. I appreciate that.' Sister Craig looked as though she might start crying but instead she suddenly stood and said, 'Goodnight, Nurse Robertson. I shall see you in the morning.'

Back in the bedroom Daisy and Margaret were waiting.

'We were so worried about you. What happened?' Daisy said.

'Why did she want to see you?' asked Margaret.

Charlotte sat down on the bed, sighing. 'She's puzzled why I don't know about all the paperwork and some of the procedures that are used on the ward. Someone had said something to her.'

'That seems very strange,' said Margaret. 'The paperwork is different from what we used at home as well, but she didn't speak to me about it.'

'Well, she said she can't work me out and is going to keep an eye on me.'

Daisy smiled. 'I think she should include Nurse Brook and make those four eyes. One thing's for sure, though. It won't have been Sister Craig. She's too kind to do anything like that.'

'I spoke to her in the front hall as I was making my way back from Matron's office. She was as shocked as you are that I was summoned to her room.'

'Well, what a strange thing,' said Daisy.

Charlotte thought she would have her long soak in the bath now. She deserved it. She went along the corridor to the main landing. The bathroom was the most fantastic she had ever seen. So stylish. It must have been cutting-edge Edwardian design. There was a four-piece white porcelain suite that included an oval shower hanging over the middle of the huge bath. But she decided to leave the shower for another time and filled the bath instead. She climbed in and lay back in the warm water.

She thought about her first day on the ward. She recognised the need for good nursing skills, just like at home, but remained confused about the names of the all soldiers, never mind the equipment she had seen for the first time.

She looked around to see if there was any shampoo. There wasn't, so she soaked her hair in the water. But something in that mundane action triggered a sudden, overwhelming feeling of separation from her home and family. It flooded over her and as she lay there she allowed herself to sob. All she wanted was to be back with Colin and the children. She had such a longing for familiar faces, familiar routine. Her tears flowed unchecked.

But after a few minutes, she pushed herself up and wiped her eyes. Come on, pull yourself together, for goodness' sake, she said to herself.

She stood and reached for her towel. She had stopped crying now but was feeling completely exhausted. She looked at herself in the mirror and said out loud, 'Just believe that it will turn out alright. Think about the Padre's prayer.'

The back of her neck was red and sore from the starch on her collar. The striped towel was rough and made it sting even more. When she was dry, she put on the long cotton nightdress and returned to her bedroom.

'Are you two working in the morning?' she asked hopefully, as she climbed into the uncomfortable bed again.

'Yes, we are,' said Daisy, yawning.

The lights were put out. As she closed her eyes, Charlotte thought, when I wake up, I'll be back on that train. She lay there in the dark for a while, the day's strange events tumbling through her mind, and finally she fell into a dreamless sleep.

CHAPTER 6

The daylight streamed in through the curtains. Her wish had not been granted. She was still here – in 1916.

She stretched her arms above her head and rubbed her eyes. 'Good morning, you two.'

There was a groan from Margaret who was peering out of the window. 'What a racket,' she said. 'I hope you weren't disturbed too much by the sound of shelling during the night. I found it so unnerving when I first arrived.'

'Shelling?' Charlotte said. 'No, I heard nothing at all. My husband says I could sleep through anything. I didn't even hear the alarm going off in the house the other week. I only woke up because he was leaping out of bed.'

'Good grief,' said Daisy. 'What do you mean? An alarm in a house? I've never heard of that.'

Charlotte had been caught off-guard and had to think quickly.

'Oh, I mean the noise of the neighbour's dog barking. We refer to him as the alarm when we look after him if they're away,' she said, unconvincingly. She noticed Margaret's doubtful expression.

Charlotte changed the subject quickly. 'Does shelling like that happen very often? Now that you've said it, I did think I heard sounds like fireworks in the night.'

'Now and again it happens,' Daisy said. 'But what a funny way you have with words, Charlotte. Fancy calling artillery fire "fireworks".' She stretched and yawned. 'The front line does seem to come and go a bit but it would be unusual for a shell to get to us here. It has happened elsewhere, though.'

'Gosh, I didn't know that,' said Charlotte.

As she dressed, it dawned on her that she was possibly in danger, although she didn't have any sense of the level of risk. Questions began to flow again. How long this will go on? What would happen if I got injured here? Or if I was killed? What if I never see Colin and the children again?

Like last night, she could feel her pulse rate rising again as the feeling of being lost resurfaced. She distracted herself by preparing for the day ahead. She applied some cold cream to the raw skin on her neck before putting on her starched collar. And she managed to get dressed more quickly this time. Soon they were ready and the three nurses went downstairs for breakfast.

'By the way,' Margaret said, 'a laundry basket is put outside the room each evening if you wish any washing done.'

'Who does that?'

'The mother of the little girl we saw the night you arrived. It gives her some income.'

'Thanks, Margaret' said Charlotte. 'That's useful to know. I wouldn't know what to do without my washing machine at home.'

She had said it without thinking. It probably made no sense to Margaret, but she said nothing as they walked along the corridor.

Charlotte had more of an appetite today so treated herself to a little bowl of apple compote along with her bread and coffee.

After breakfast they went up the main stairs to the ward.

'Back again are you, Nurse Robertson?' said one of the orderlies who was brushing the hallway outside the ward. 'Glad we didn't scare you away after your first day.'

Charlotte smiled. 'Yes, I'm back for another go today. I'm sorry but I don't think we met properly yesterday.'

'No, we didn't,' said the orderly. 'But I've heard all about you. I'm Alexander Brown – known as Sandy for short.'

'Well, it's nice to meet you, Sandy.'

'And where are you from?'

'Just like you, nurse, I'm from Aberdeen. I live in the Hardgate. Do you know it?'

'Yes, of course. It's just behind Holburn Street, isn't it?'

'That's right. And where do you stay?'

'I live in Rosemount, near Victoria Park. It's nice to know that someone else is here from home.'

'That's a lovely part of the city,' Sandy said.

'Yes, it is. Tell me, have you been here long?'

'I wasn't fit for the army, what with this bad leg of mine. But I signed up to be an orderly so I could do my bit. I've been here in France since the beginning of the war and I've seen a lot of folks come and go.'

He carried on with his work. 'You'll get on better today, you know.'

'Thanks,' said Charlotte. 'Was it that obvious I was out of my depth yesterday?'

'No, no,' he said quickly. 'But I overheard someone speaking about you while I was sweeping the floor out here and I thought it was uncalled for.'

'Well, thanks for letting me know. I had a feeling I was being closely observed. See you later, no doubt.'

He stopped sweeping for a moment. 'Perhaps you'd like my copy of *The Press and Journal* when I've finished with it. My brother sends it to me every week.'

'Thanks, Sandy,' she said. 'That would be lovely. I'd enjoy looking at it.'

She walked into the ward and saw Nurse Collinson.

'Good morning. Have you had another busy night?'

'Yes,' she said. 'But better than our previous night, that's for certain. And I should manage to avoid a reprimand this morning with any luck.'

Charlotte stood at the desk with her colleagues and took out her piece of paper, ready for morning orders. Sister Craig looked even more tired this morning and Charlotte wondered if she had slept at all.

'Good morning, everyone.'

The nurses replied in unison. 'Good morning, Sister.'

'I hope you all managed to have some sleep last night in spite of that nearby shelling.'

The nurses confirmed that yes, they had, although Nurse Brook said nothing.

Nurse Collinson gave a summary of the soldiers' conditions and made a point of describing how the ward had been reorganised. Sister Craig smiled and nodded in approval.

Matron, who arrived just as the handover was starting, made no comment. Charlotte had never been impressed by leaders who stayed quiet when good things happened but seemed to delight in highlighting errors.

She tried hard to remember all the patients' names before Nurse Collinson mentioned them. She managed about half: Burns, Cameron, Bremner, Stills, Lawson ... And so it went on, right around to Beattie and Wilson. Now at least she understood how the beds were numbered so she could match the name to the bed.

The conditions of Douglas, Fellows and Godman had deteriorated overnight. Some men had moved places in the ward. The admissions from yesterday had been accommodated in the main ward and a couple who were nearing discharge had been transferred into the balcony. One patient, Murray, had gone to theatre after Charlotte left the ward last night to have his chest wound cleaned out. Three men were leaving today. She had spoken only briefly to McLeod yesterday when he seemed full of bonhomie, but not at all to either Fulman or Manson. Such things happened on busy units. She wondered what it would be like for Fulman to travel with a fractured pelvis in the rickety ambulance. Very painful, probably, even with the positive prospect of him being transferred home.

The discharge of patients meant there would be more empty beds by lunchtime and no doubt more new faces later in the day. The ward would probably not stay quiet for long.

At the end of the short report, Sister Craig issued the notices for the day. One of her evident strengths was her ability to plan work priorities and allocate tasks precisely so everyone knew their duties.

'Right,' she said. 'Let's prepare as best as we can for both the certainties and uncertainties in our ward today. There will be four discharges to free up some beds. If we only have a few admissions, I would like us to catch up on the ordering of supplies and ward cleaning. We can see to that this afternoon, please.'

The nurses, who were gathered around her, nodded.

'Once the men have gone, I will decide who can be moved and I want the moves to be completed this morning before lunch. That will give us space if we do have any admissions this afternoon. I will decide what to do with Godman and Douglas when I've consulted with Captain Clift after the ward round.'

Matron interrupted.

'I do not want empty beds in the balcony and I do not want to have to tell you all this again, Sister. The CO, who will be inspecting us today, will be annoyed if this occurs.'

If Sister Craig was irritated by the interruption she showed no sign of it. 'Thank you, Matron,' she said. 'With the planning that we can do today, I'm sure it will not happen.'

She turned to the night nurse. 'Nurse Collinson, you look exhausted. Thank you for all your hard work. Please go off duty now.'

'Thank you, Sister. Yes, it's a bath and bed for me.'

Nurse Collinson nodded to Charlotte as she headed for the door. 'I hope your second day goes well.'

Charlotte said, 'Thanks. And I hope you have a good sleep. You look as if you need it. Watch that you don't fall asleep in the bath.'

Sister Craig was still allocating work.

'Nurse Brook, I would like you to be on discharge and admission duty today and ensure they are completed by ten so they can be ready for the hospital train that leaves Albert at noon. Please make sure you complete all the relevant paperwork and that everything goes with them today – unlike last week.'

'I'd like to see McLeod's face when he's told he's not a B,' Nurse Brook said.

'That is unnecessary and rather unkind,' said Sister Craig. Nurse Brook skulked away.

'Nurses Robertson and Wishaw, you can do the observations, dressings and anti-tetanus checks. Nurse Wishaw, please offer guidance to Nurse Robertson who may not be ready to be left to administer this medication yet. Nurse Ashville can be on medication and theatre duty. And you can help with the laundry duties today, Miss Giles. That will keep you busy as there's a lot of sorting out to do – but I know you will manage it well.'

Sarah Giles blushed at being singled out for praise and seemed relieved to be given a task that would take her out of Matron's direct vision for a while. Charlotte was also relieved to know that she would be with one of her 'girls' today and felt a sense of relief that she was not going to be working closely with Nurse Brook.

'Let's divide up the observation round and dressings between us,' Margaret said as they headed for the clinical room to prepare.

'That sounds a good idea. But you will make sure I'm on the right lines, won't you?' Charlotte had not taken offence at Sister's comments, which were, after all, accurate. She wouldn't have any idea how to prepare the anti-tetanus injections.

The language she had heard the previous day about medication doses was incomprehensible to her.

Back in the ward, Nurse Brook immediately began to prepare the soldiers for discharge and Charlotte noticed McLeod's change of expression when it was confirmed he would be returning to the front line. Nurse Brook had been smiling when she approached his bed and Charlotte wondered how he had been told. She guessed it would have been done in a brusque manner. Perhaps he had been hoping to be going back to 'Blighty' for a while. But he had no choice. He would be returning to duty. That was the main aim of this medical service, as Matron had so forcefully told Charlotte when she arrived.

After the observation round, Charlotte turned her attention to Lieutenant Inglis in bed ten who had a collapsed lung and a chest drain in place. He was in pain when he breathed and became breathless on the slightest movement which he admitted was incredibly frightening. A severe cough caused the pain and breathlessness to become a lot worse. What a horrible situation for him, she thought.

He had been to surgery two days earlier to have the chest drain inserted and a section of rib removed to help the process. He had started to cough up blood, which was not a good sign and was often a precursor to a life-threatening infection. Charlotte had already taken his temperature and pulse and so far his temperature had not risen. His nursing care involved keeping him warm but they also had to keep an eye on the leakage from the chest drain and encourage him to lie as still as he could – although as he was in pain, lying still was not difficult for him.

The chest drain, which was sitting on the floor, was connected by a long piece of rubber tubing to a glass bottle that had about two inches of clear fluid in it and the tube sat in the water. Charlotte had always been rather frightened of these drains when she was a student nurse. They had the potential to harm a patient if they were lifted up as the water could run into the lung. However, they helped to keep the lung expanded and she remembered one of the things she should do was examine the fluid to check it was clear.

'Right, Lieutenant Inglis, I'll be back later to check your temperature again,' she said. 'Is there anything else I can get you at the moment?'

'A new lung perhaps,' he replied wearily.

'Yes, that'd be nice if we could do that for you,' Charlotte agreed. 'Let me go and see if there are any in the cupboard.'

He laughed, which caused him further pain.

She apologised. 'I didn't mean to make things more uncomfortable for you.'

'I appreciate that but laughing does make the pain a lot worse, you know.' He smiled but was then consumed by a fit of coughing.

One of the other nurses brought a Nelson's inhaler over to him and Charlotte smelt the sweet, woody odour of Friar's Balsam. I haven't smelt that in years, she thought. They would never use such a thing now – a stoneware jar with a glass mouthpiece and full of boiling water. Such a dangerous piece of equipment, although she recalled that these inhalations were always popular with patients who often described them as very soothing. Charlotte helped Lieutenant Inglis sit up so he could use the device. She was then ready to help Margaret make a start on the lengthy dressing round.

One of the ten patients who required a dressing change was Captain Burns in bed one. He had a large abdominal wound and a drain that needed to be shortened. Charlotte remembered learning how to do this and had spent many hours during quiet spells on night duty practising with a section of plastic tubing, a safety pin and two pairs of forceps. She had now learned the routine of preparing her dressing trolley with all the things she would need, including some kidney-shaped dishes, forceps, one-in-twenty carbolic solution to clean the wound, some antiseptic powder, gauze, lint, a many-tailed bandage, which she had never used, before and a heap of safety pins.

As she did with all her patients, she introduced herself to Captain Burns and asked if she could change his dressing.

'Yes,' he said. 'Please go ahead.'

'How are you feeling today?'

He grimaced a little. 'I don't feel too bad if I lie still but it's pretty sore when I move.'

'Have you had any pain relief this morning?' Charlotte asked.

'I don't like to make a fuss. I'm trying not to take anything unless it gets unbearable.'

'Could I give you a wee bit of advice?'

Captain Burns looked up at her. 'Well, yes, of course, nurse.'

'Well, I've found that pain tends to settle more readily if you take a pain killer regularly,' she said.

He didn't respond for a moment, then said, 'Perhaps that's true, and I thank you for your advice. But I'll carry on with my approach.'

'As you wish then,' Charlotte said. 'But I hope I don't make it worse for you as I change your dressing.'

She carried out the task as confidently as she could, realising that the principles of doing a wound dressing had not changed over the years. She undid the safety pin securing the drain, asked Burns to take a deep breath and as he did so, she tugged at the drain to remove it about half an inch from the wound.

He yelped.

'Sorry to hurt you.'

She put in a newly sterilised safety pin that would stop the drain disappearing into the wound. The final task was to sprinkle the antiseptic powder over the wound and she had never done this before. The wound was large and ran down the middle of his abdomen. It was stitched neatly but a little red at the top.

'Does it feel more tender here?' she asked.

'Yes, it stings a bit.'

She glanced up at his observation chart. He had a mild fever but that was to be expected so soon after surgery. As with all the tasks in the ward, there was a book to record temperatures that was regularly checked by Sister and the medical staff. When she looked, Margaret had already added Burns's name to it.

She then replaced the many-tailed bandage that was keeping the dressing in place. She had paid particular attention to its removal so she could replace it accurately. She was about to begin putting the flannel bandage back on when Margaret appeared at her side.

'Captain Clift has asked that you apply a fomentation to Burns's abdomen once you've put this dressing on. I can help wring it out if you like.'

'Thanks, I'd appreciate that,' Charlotte said. 'You've turned up at just the right moment to make sure I put this on correctly. Tell me, do you start at the top or the bottom?'

Margaret said, 'I was taught to fix the tails at the lower end first and then work your way up, crossing each tail over, but keep the tension even, and the safety pins in a line – or Matron will make a comment.'

Charlotte attended to the bandage. It stretched from hip level up to the captain's armpits. It was a bit like plaiting hair, she thought. It seemed to her to be the right tension. It was staying in place but not too tight, and he said it was comfortable. Charlotte thought he was trying to be kind but she had a sense of satisfaction at seeing it neatly in place.

Once the dressing was completed, she and Margaret went to the preparation room to get the fomentation ready.

'Is this like a poultice?'

'Have you not used a fomentation before, Charlotte?' Margaret sounded surprised.

'No, we ... Well, we don't use them at all where I work.'

'I'm surprised because they're common. But to answer your question, yes, fomentations are similar to a poultice, used for pain relief rather than to draw out an infection.'

Charlotte watched as Margaret put a flannel in a bucket which she then filled with hot water from a kettle.

'Right, Charlotte, you lay out a towel on the table and I'll get the flannel out.'

Margaret used some wooden tongs to lift the hot cloth out of the bucket. She then dropped it onto the centre of the towel.

'Oops-a-daisy,' she said with a laugh, as the flannel flopped onto the towel causing a splash.

'Quick, let's get wringing. You turn your end to the left and I'll turn mine to the right, and that will get the excess water out of the way.'

They did it over the sink and a surprising amount of water dripped out of the towel. It was folded up, put in a dish and covered with a lid, and they then returned to Captain Burns's bedside.

'This will help relieve your pain,' said Margaret, as she unwrapped the towel. She placed the hot flannel over the centre of his dressing, covering all of it. Dry dressings were put over the top to help keep the heat in and secured with pins. Charlotte felt pleased she had learned two more procedures but the fomentation seemed to be another very time-consuming technique.

'We'll come and change this every hour for you,' Margaret said. 'And just before we leave you in peace, the final thing we have to do to you is ensure you're in the right position.'

They moved Captain Burns into an upright position and put a couple of sandbags under his thighs to ensure he didn't slip down the bed.

'Thank you,' he said, looking relieved to be left alone for a while. He was quite pale.

Back in the treatment room, Sarah Giles was clearing up the dressing trolley and was already preparing another many-tailed bandage.

'Thank you so much for doing that for us, Sarah. That's quick, efficient work,' said Margaret. Sarah blushed but seemed pleased.

In bed twenty-four, Charlotte found Second Lieutenant Thomson, pale-skinned with sandy hair and lots of freckles, whose family, it turned out, had emigrated from Glasgow to Calgary at the beginning of the century when he was a small child.

Charlotte was not surprised to learn he had Scottish blood given his Celtic appearance. He had been injured by a mortar and had sustained compound fractures of the bones in both lower legs. He had two open wounds on his legs and the priority was to ensure they did not become infected. He lay on a fracture bed, which meant he had wooden planks to lie on instead of a soft mattress. He had not been to surgery until a week after the injury to allow the surrounding tissue time to recover from the initial trauma. It was three days since the surgery, which explained why he was still in the ward rather than having been transferred back to Britain for convalescence. In spite of his discomfort, he was in remarkably good spirits.

'I'm beginning to feel I'll up and about soon, nurse. But I might be a bit shorter when I get up on my feet again.'

'How tall should you be?' Charlotte asked.

'About five feet and six inches – the tallest in my family,' he said proudly. 'Still, it won't make any difference when I'm wearing my kilt.'

'Well, that's true. Do you have family in Glasgow now?'

'Yes – all living on the south side of the Clyde, in Newlands. I guess I'm quite near them here in comparison to Calgary. Perhaps I could be sent to a hospital up there to recover. I'd love to see Scotland again. I was just a wee lad when we left for Canada.'

Charlotte remembered nursing patients with compound fractures when she worked in an orthopaedic unit, but the cause was usually road traffic accidents, not explosions. What those young patients shared with these soldiers was a similar age and finding themselves on bed-rest for a long time. In this ward, everyone on bed-rest was treated as being at risk of developing pressure sores. Twice a day, all of them had their lower back, sacrum and buttocks washed with soap and water – by the orderly, a VAD or one of the qualified nurses. To ensure it was recorded, there was a 'pressure sore book' to note when it had been done, and Sister Craig and Matron checked the book every day.

When the patient's skin was dry, it was rubbed with spirit and sprinkled with powder. Immobility and pain meant shifting position was difficult for soldiers such as Lieutenant Thomson and Charlotte told him to lift his bottom off the mattress on a regular basis to help keep his circulation moving.

'I'll try my best,' he said. 'It might help relieve the boredom.'

As ever, Nurse Brook was on hand to make sure Charlotte was doing her job properly, even though she was meant to be focusing on the discharges.

'Did you rub the spirit in?' she demanded.

'I applied it gently so as not to damage the underlying tissue.'

'You should rub it, you know.'

'No, you shouldn't,' Charlotte said firmly. 'It damages the skin if you rub too hard.'

'Well, Matron says it's a sign of bad nursing if a pressure sore appears and we've had our fair share recently.'

'Oh, why's that?'

'Poor leadership,' said Nurse Brook emphatically. 'The last Sister made sure such things were attended to properly.'

'Really?' Charlotte said. 'I have to say that Sister Craig doesn't strike me as someone who would neglect such an important element of nursing care.'

Nurse Brook said nothing.

By the time lunches were being served, the bustle associated with the departing patients had settled and the ward had four empty beds. Charlotte noticed two envelopes on a table with 'Manson' and 'Fulman' written on them. Nurse Brook had forgotten to attach the notes to the patients before they left. Was that deliberate, she wondered.

Earlier, at the ward round, the decision had been made by Captain Clift to move Godman and Douglas into the side room if their conditions had not improved by mid-afternoon. But everyone on duty knew that any such improvement was a forlorn hope. An older man had joined Matron, Captain Clift and Sister Craig and the ward round. He'd had a lot of decorations on his uniform and Charlotte assumed he was the commanding officer.

So now there would be six empty beds. If they were filled at once, that would make for a very busy period. But if there were any quieter times, then ward stocks could be replenished and tidied, as Sister Craig had hoped, ready for the next onslaught of injured men.

Captain Clift returned to the ward to review the patients later in the afternoon. His approach to wound care was different from that of Captain Graves and he didn't use equipment such as Carrel tubes very often. Margaret had told Charlotte that he felt wounds should be left undisturbed for a few days after being excised and he favoured the use of salt soaks. The wound would then be re-dressed under anaesthetic for the first time. Once an injury showed an indication that it was healing the salt soaks would stop.

But there was another, more pragmatic reason for this approach. The use of complex equipment was very time-consuming and if the ward was busy it was hard to ensure that the treatments could be performed correctly. How sensible, Charlotte thought. Margaret also told her that Captain Clift had said a doctor could not simply come over from civilian life thinking he could work in the same leisurely manner as he did in private practice. She wondered if this was a reference to Captain Graves. She would need to understand more about how each of them approached their work. In every other place she had worked, she had found that each senior doctor had a preferred way of doing things – and it could make life more complicated for the nursing staff.

Captain Clift turned his attention to Second Lieutenant Macdonald who had a gunshot wound to the head. He had a small dressing on the upper left side of his skull, from which clear fluid was leaking. The dressing had already been changed today but it was thoroughly soaked again.

But Macdonald's biggest problem now was a headache that seemed to be getting worse and over the day he had felt increasingly sick. He was now complaining of double vision.

'I think he needs to go to theatre so we can remove the bullet,' said Captain Clift. 'Otherwise the pressure will just increase and that will be an end to him.' He paused, then added, 'I would rather not lose three patients today if that's possible.'

Charlotte said, 'I heard Sister Craig mention that Sister Duke isn't here this afternoon, Captain.'

Nurse Brook had appeared beside them, eager to see what was going on. But she hesitated, apparently unsure what to do in Sister Craig's absence – the second day in a row she had not been in the ward after lunch.

But then she said, with some glee, 'You told us you'd worked in an operating theatre, Nurse Robertson, so why don't you assist Captain Clift?'

Charlotte looked first at Nurse Brooke, then at Captain Clift. ‘Well, I could. As long as you appreciate it’s a long time since I did any theatre work.’

Captain Clift was blunt. ‘There’s no time to prevaricate. This patient needs to be treated now. You’ll have to do.’

CHAPTER 7

Macdonald was taken through to the operating theatre by Sandy, the orderly, and Charlotte began trying to get the appropriate instruments ready. Captain Clift was less gruff now.

'I'll talk you through it,' he said, putting on his theatre gown. 'The first thing we'll need to do is shave his head and then wash it with peroxide of hydrogen. We need to try and prevent infection getting into the brain which would be fatal. Why don't you get on and do that and I'll look out the rest of the instruments. Then you can get your gown and gloves on.'

'Yes, of course, Captain.' Charlotte thought how kind he seemed.

Shaving someone's head was something Charlotte had never done – except for the clippers she had used when her sons were small and 'buzz cuts' made their hair care more manageable. But she had used electric clippers then. This time it was scissors and a razor.

'I'm just going to cut your hair, Lieutenant Macdonald.'

He said nothing in reply. Poor bugger, this is not exactly an expert haircut, she thought, as she chopped through his blond hair, which was matted with blood and mud. A few lice were crawling through it.

'At least you won't have any of these creepy crawlies in your hair for a while,' she added brightly.

He didn't move as she hacked away, lying with his eyes closed. She tried to put the hair into a basin but some of it spilt onto the floor. Then she poured hydrogen peroxide over his scalp.

Sandy was suddenly there with his brush and quickly swept up the locks of hair. 'Thanks,' she said. 'Sorry, I've made a bit of a mess.'

'Nae worries. We'll soon have it tidied up.' He stopped sweeping for a moment. 'I'll tell you one thing, nurse. You'll no get a job as a barber anytime soon.'

She laughed. 'That's true, Sandy.'

She took a deep breath and began scrubbing her hands. Isobel, one of the VADs, had come to act as the 'runner' so Charlotte had someone to help tie her into her gown and fetch any instruments or equipment after she'd pulled on her sterilised rubber gloves. They were too big and it was awkward to hold anything but she managed to set out a trolley covered with a sterilised cloth and place the instruments in order.

To anaesthetise Macdonald, Captain Clift put a cloth mask over his mouth and dropped some chloroform on to it. Once Macdonald had lost consciousness, the anaesthetic was maintained with ether spray. Captain Clift gave a commentary as he worked, which was interesting for Charlotte but, she thought, perhaps also acted as a way of reassuring himself.

'I can see the bullet entry hole here on the upper aspect of his skull,' he was saying. 'But there doesn't appear to be an exit wound. That means the bullet is probably still inside, which might explain why he's beginning to deteriorate. Let me feel around his head to see if there are any indications of a fracture. That would give us a clue where the bullet might be.'

Carefully, he felt around Macdonald's skull, starting on the opposite side where the bullet was likely to have lodged. After a few moments he said, 'Yes, there's something here, a few inches above his right ear. I can feel a break in the skull.'

He turned to Charlotte. 'Right, as this hole is likely to be cleaner, let's start here. Let me have a scalpel and then the trephine.' Charlotte handed the scalpel to him and he made an incision on the side of Macdonald's head. Charlotte made a guess that the trephine was the hollow metal tube lying on the trolley and she picked it up and passed it over. He used it to open up a small hole in the skull. Charlotte peered closely and could just see the tip of the bullet lodged in Macdonald's brain. 'He's lucky,' said Captain Clift. 'The brain's not a place to start fumbling one's way around.'

He asked for forceps. Charlotte passed them to him. He tried to grasp the bullet but seemed to push it further into the brain tissue. 'Bigger forceps,' he growled, stretching out his hand, which was shaking. Charlotte looked at the instruments on her trolley and saw another, heavier pair. 'Here you are,' she said calmly. She held her breath as he made another attempt to get hold of the bullet. After a few seconds, he gently eased it out. It dropped with a clunk into one of the metal pots she was now holding.

Once Captain Clift had completed the work on the exit wound, he turned his attention to the other side of Macdonald's head where the bullet had entered.

'I need to clean out any debris that entered his head along with the bullet,' he said. 'There may be fragments of bone as well as hair and dirt from the battlefield.'

He asked for some saline solution to rinse out both wounds.

'Isobel, can you pour some into this bowl for me?'

Isobel was very careful not to touch the edge of the bowl with the bottle as she poured. Captain Clift used swabs to wash the wounds out.

After a few moments he said, 'Right, I think we've completed this part of the procedure but I want to put in a couple of drains to keep the pressure down.'

Charlotte looked around the operating theatre for drains.

'They're up there,' he said, pointing to the corner of the room. Charlotte looked up at the shelves and saw several glass jars filled with liquid. One had some tubes floating in it like giant worms.

Isobel took the jar down and, as instructed, removed the lid. Charlotte reached in using a pair of large sterilised forceps, removed a tube from of the liquid and put it in one of the many dishes on the trolley.

'Thanks,' she said.

'This smells of disinfectant. Does it need to be rinsed before you use it, Captain?'

He nodded. 'Yes. And then cut it in half and make some small holes along each side to help with the drainage.'

'Right. Isobel, will you get some boiled water for me and pour it into the dish over the drain?'

'Yes, Sister,' said Isobel, forgetting it was Charlotte beneath the theatre gown.

Charlotte laughed. 'Thanks for the promotion.'

She cut the pliable rubber drains. When the tubes had been rinsed, she passed them to Captain Clift so he could insert them into the wounds.

'Not too bad,' he said. 'They're not as good as Sister Duke's, but they'll work, I think, nurse.'

When the surgery was complete, Macdonald's head was bandaged.

Captain Clift said, 'Right, call for the orderly and get him back through to the ward now.'

He removed the ether spray that was keeping Macdonald asleep. As he was taking off his theatre gown, he said, 'Ensure his head is checked every hour, Nurse Robertson. Keep an eye on the drainage and let me know if he complains of a headache again. The good news is that most of these procedures have a satisfactory outcome, particularly since the bullet didn't penetrate the deeper aspects of his brain.'

'Yes, of course, Captain,' said Charlotte. She felt pleased that she had remembered how to handle sterilised theatre instruments.

Isobel went with Sandy as he took Macdonald back to the ward but then returned to help Charlotte clear up.

Charlotte was careful to make sure everything was left just as she had found it. She even added a replacement drain into the jar on the shelf. She didn't want to be in trouble with Sister Duke or Matron, especially as this was their domain.

It felt quite familiar to her to wash instruments, dry and then wrap them in preparation for sterilisation. When she had worked in an operating theatre, this was the final task of most working days, even though Charlotte had grumbled that it was not a nursing job. The operating room experience had been enjoyable and she felt that she was beginning to understand how things worked in this ward.

'Thank you for your help, Isobel,' she said.

'I enjoy it, you know. When I return home, I'd like to do this sort of work.'

'Well, I'm sure you'll make a good theatre nurse, having such an expert like Sister Duke to show you how it should be done.'

Isobel was quiet for a moment, then she said, 'You're much more informal than the other nurses. But I hope you don't get into trouble calling me by my first name.'

'I suppose I am,' said Charlotte. 'It's just how we work in my ward.'

Back in the ward she noticed that two of the beds near the ward door were now empty.

'What's happened to Godman and Douglas?' she asked Margaret.

They had been moved into the side room, Margaret said. 'There's nothing more that can be done for them.'

'Can I go in and see them?' asked Charlotte.

'You can. But if you do, I suggest you avoid letting anyone see you. There's a lot of work to be done in the ward.'

'Yes, I understand that. But it seems so cruel to move them out of the way like this.'

Margaret put a hand on Charlotte's shoulder. 'Charlotte, you need to understand that our work here is about getting the soldiers back on their feet. These two men are going to die no matter what we do for them, and it lowers the morale in the ward if the other men see people in this state. That's why Matron was so annoyed that Francis was bang in the middle of the ward when he died.'

This had already been explained to Charlotte by Matron when she arrived and again by Nurse Brook yesterday. But it still felt wrong. She just had to see this 'Darwin's room'.

She walked into the corridor and opened the door to the side ward, stepped inside and quickly shut the door behind her. She didn't want to be seen. The room was once a storeroom of some kind but the shelves had been removed, and it was whitewashed and bare. The floor was tiled, making it feel cold and very clinical. There were no windows but the wall and door had frosted glass panels in them, which let in a measure of light. It was eerily quiet. She wondered where the soldier's possessions were.

The two patients were lying in beds diagonally opposite each other. She walked over to Godman who was further away from the door and touched his hand.

'I've just come in to see if you're comfortable,' she whispered. He didn't respond. His mouth was hanging open and his lips were sticking to his teeth. She wondered whether she could find something to clean his mouth with. She then checked Douglas and repeated the same words. He appeared to be unresponsive but then she noticed his index finger flickered when she said she was there. He half-opened his eyes and, without looking at her, said in a feeble voice, 'Mother, is that you? Thank God you've come to me. I knew you would.'

Charlotte whispered, 'Yes, I'm here.' She took his hand and put it to her cheek. His fingernails were filthy and his hand felt very cold. It was a mottled blue underneath the dirt, an indication to Charlotte that he was nearing death.

'I ... waiting for you. Sorry,' he murmured. 'Let you down ... Just too painful ... than ... must not ...'

His eyes closed again and Charlotte had a sudden rush of pity for this boy. He was about the same age as her cousin. She also felt for his mother who was somewhere at home wondering how her boy was getting on in the army and probably not yet aware that he was in mortal danger. In this situation, on this occasion, saying that she was his mother instantly calmed him. He'd clearly been trying to stay alive while waiting for his mother to come to him.

Charlotte stayed with him for a few minutes, gently stroking his forehead, and told him how proud she was of him. He said nothing more. If this were one of my boys, she thought, I would hope someone would comfort him like this so he would know he was not alone. She felt horrified that someone could experience such a lonely death. Her tears fell onto the soldier's arm.

Come on, pull yourself together, she told herself. This isn't pity for him; it's about you and your situation. Focus on providing comfort to this poor young lad who needs your attention. She stood up, wiped her eyes with her hands and resolved to come back to see him again later when she had a free moment. She left the room and went to see if she could find anything to clean Godman's mouth.

Margaret was in the treatment room when Charlotte walked in. 'I thought you would find that difficult,' she said. 'That's one of the reasons we don't go in there.'

'I'm more upset that they've been abandoned,' said Charlotte. 'I'd like to give Godman's mouth a clean. Tell me, what do you use?'

'Does he have sordes?'

'I'm not sure,' said Charlotte, uncertain what she had been asked.

'Well, once you've inspected it again, use some soft linen soaked in weak Condy's solution to lift the sordes out.'

'Do you mean bits of mucus on the gum?'

'Yes, of course,' said Margaret with a note of exasperation in her voice. 'Then use some glycerine to moisten the lips.' She added more gently, 'I'm so glad you asked, because that was one of my examination questions.'

'Margaret, you're a walking textbook,' said Charlotte.

'Use some of the dishes on the mouth trolley over in the corner. But don't take the trolley in there.' Margaret paused. 'Charlotte, why do you want to do this?'

Charlotte walked over to the trolley. 'Because I just feel it's the right thing to do. I can't leave those boys entirely alone. One of them was calling for his mother.'

Margaret shook her head. 'Well, when the ward's very busy, you have to prioritise your duties and if they're not going to survive, then we can't give them additional care over the others who might. You'll be in serious trouble if Matron becomes aware of what you're doing.'

Charlotte looked at her. 'I'll find a way, you know.' Her certainty and self-confidence surprised her. She felt like she was a student nurse again, with all the enthusiasm she had experienced when she started her career.

She slipped back into the side-room and again walked over to Douglas's bed. She didn't consider this in any way to be additional care. It was the very core of nursing for her. She spoke softly to him but this time he didn't respond. She touched his hand. It was colder than before, although he was still breathing, gently if erratically. It won't be long now, she thought.

She turned to attend to Godman. She looked at the 'mouth tray' Margaret had told her to use. There were gallipots, sticks around which someone had wound bits of cotton wool, a bottle of antiseptic mouthwash and a bottle of glycerine. She used the sticks to lift out the sordes, as Margaret called them. The glycerine provided a coating on his lips, but Charlotte thought it might just make them drier. Hadn't she been told that recently? Either way, she was sure she was making him feel more comfortable and she told him what she was doing as she wiped his lips with the swab.

Would any of it make any difference? He was going to die soon and it wouldn't increase his chance of survival one bit. But it might just ease his suffering a little and that mattered to her.

When she had finished, she cleared away the evidence that she had been in the room. She heard voices outside in the corridor. She stopped but the shadows passed the frosted windows and she left the room unseen. She disposed of the used items on the tray and replaced it ready for the next patient.

When Charlotte was finally able to stop work to go and eat, she walked into the mess hall where she found Sarah, the VAD, sitting at a table. Had she been crying? Charlotte sat down opposite her. Sarah looked up and blushed. She had been reading a letter and as Charlotte sat down, she folded it up and put it away in her pocket.

'Do you want me to move?' Sarah asked.

'No, please stay. I wanted to have my meal with you.'

'Oh?' Sarah sounded surprised.

'So, what have you been doing all day?'

Sarah frowned as if she was unused to someone striking up a conversation with her.

'Well, I've been trying to sort out all the laundry and that seems to have taken me quite a while.' She leaned forward. 'Matron is so particular about how the linen is stored and I never seem to do it properly.'

Charlotte nodded. 'Yes, I've noticed that she's rather hard to please.'

'I always seem to miss a repair that needs to be done or I don't return the uniforms to the soldiers once they come back from the laundry – and she always seems to spot it.'

'I know what you mean. She has a really keen pair of eyes.'

Sarah smiled. She was a beautiful girl, about twenty years old, with big hazel eyes and long auburn hair swept up into a bun. She reminded Charlotte of women in the lovely Edwardian advertising posters she'd seen in books and could imagine her in a wide-brimmed hat, walking along a promenade in a striking gown, carrying a parasol.

'Where are you from, Sarah?'

'Moseley. It's a small suburb near the centre of Birmingham.'

'How have you ended up working here?'

She had wanted to do her bit, and the summer before she had volunteered for the VAD. 'But to be honest, my preparation didn't ready me for the sort of work I'm doing here.' She laughed. 'I can see I've lived a very sheltered life up until now. I went to some first aid classes in the local scout hut thinking I would be all geared up. But learning how to bandage a friend is rather different from bandaging the poor chaps upstairs.'

Charlotte nodded, which encouraged Sarah to keep talking.

'It's alright for you trained nurses, but for Isobel and me it's hard to witness some of the injuries. I have to stop myself gasping out loud sometimes – I can almost feel their pain. Then that makes me feel really light-headed and I'm relieved to know I'll be spending time in the linen cupboard or making up the swabs for theatre.'

She ran a forefinger round the rim of a cup on the table. 'Then I find myself wondering what will become of the ones who are so badly hurt. And that keeps me awake at night. I fear their lives will be so uncertain.'

Her eyes filled with tears.

Charlotte said, 'That sounds overwhelming, Sarah.' She was quiet for a moment then said, 'I don't know if it's of any consolation but I share many of your concerns. I find some of the injuries tough to look at, too. And like you, I worry about the treatment we offer. Sometimes it seems to just cause more pain. In fact, if I'm honest, I feel completely out of my depth here, too.'

Sarah fixed her eyes on Charlotte's. 'Do you mean that? Or are you just trying to be kind to me?'

'I really mean it, Sarah – probably more than you could ever imagine.'

Sarah sat back. 'I appreciate you speaking to me, you know. Most of the trained nurses seem to resent us being here.'

'Why's that?'

'I don't really know. But my mother tells me that she's seen some letters in the newspapers at home about how we're taking on the responsibilities of the trained nurses – you may have seen them yourself – but I don't agree. And I keep telling Isobel it can't be because we don't work hard enough. I seem to be busy all the time – that's how I cope with it all. But I do find it rather difficult.'

Sarah stood up suddenly. 'I've been away from the ward too long. I'd better get back to the linen cupboard. I've a few things I must finish off this evening.'

Nurse Brook was coming down the stairs.

Charlotte said quickly, 'Sarah, if you and Isobel need someone to speak to about how you're feeling, please come and find me. I often think talking through a problem can lessen its effect.'

Sarah said, 'Gosh, that is kind of you. I'll tell Isobel. I believe it's jolly unfair how Nurse Brook and Matron treat you, too.'

She hurried away leaving Charlotte to think about how hard it must be for these girls who had been thrown into the midst of such a brutal situation. 'Doing your bit' must have seemed so romantic in a way, when viewed from the safety of a scout hut in a leafy suburb in the Midlands. She wondered if Sarah had seen the famous VAD poster that was hanging in her own kitchen. Its portrayal of the war was unrealistic and it contained none of the gruesome detail about the conditions they would encounter, nor about the apparent resentment that would be shown to them by some of the qualified nurses. It made Charlotte wonder how many of those volunteers returned home before they had completed their 'bit'. She would have to ask later if she remembered.

Daisy and Margaret joined Charlotte for supper and later, when they had all finished, they returned to their room. The lack of any post for Charlotte was again commented on but a small package Daisy had received from home provided a pleasant diversion.

She unwrapped a packet of Fuller's peppermint lumps and some Huntley and Palmer biscuits. 'Oh, delightful,' she said with relish. 'This will top up my supplies.'

Daisy had a very sweet tooth and received a constant supply from one of her many friends at home. Her mother had also sent her an artist's pad and some charcoal sticks for her sketching. 'How lovely. I've almost filled my other sketchbook so this is most welcome.' She reached for a piece of paper to write a note of thanks.

Something more mundane was on Charlotte's mind. 'Do either of you have such a thing as shampoo?' she asked. 'My hair needs a wash.'

Margaret said, 'I would usually use shampoo powders but I've run out. When that happens, we usually go and ask Cook for a lemon and mix that with some egg. It gives your hair a lovely shine.'

'Do you think I could do that now?'

'Of course. If you make up a mixture in a dish, I'll use it too. I haven't washed my hair this week and I can wrap it in rolls to help it dry overnight.'

'I think your short hair is so modern, by the way, Charlotte,' said Daisy, laughing. 'If you let me, I'll do a sketch of you and enclose it in a letter home so my mother can see it.'

'That would be fun,' said Charlotte.

'Right then. I'll do it tomorrow.'

Charlotte set off for the kitchen and returned with her egg and lemon mixture in a small bowl.

'I'll leave it beside the bath for you, Margaret,' she called as she put her night things under her arm and headed down the corridor to the bathroom.

This time she used the shower, and tentatively applied a small amount of the yellow mixture to her hair. It had a refreshing smell but unlike her usual shampoo there was no lather so it didn't feel the same. Oh well, she thought, wrapping her hair in a towel. I'll see the results when my hair dries.

This was her moment to think again about her family. They'll be so worried about me, she thought. They might have reported me as a missing person. She just wanted to hug them and tell them how much she loved them. She felt the pain of separation again. It had become a constant ache in her chest. But somehow it was making her love for them stronger.

She wiped away the steam and looked at herself in the mirror. 'I just want to know that I'll be home soon to see them,' she said out loud. But she felt powerless to make it happen. This uncertainty was so tough. She was usually in control of situations.

She cleaned her teeth and returned to her room. Before long, everyone was settled in bed.

'Can I ask a question?' Charlotte said.

'Of course,' said Margaret. 'Anything,' said Daisy.

'Why do we only have officers in the ward?'

Margaret said, 'It's a strict army regulation that officers and men are kept apart. It's to do with maintaining order and discipline so we'll only admit officers here.'

'Oh, I see,' said Charlotte. 'Do the other soldiers have good care as well?'

'Of course they do,' replied her room-mates in unison.

She had a lot more questions to ask, especially about the VADs, but could tell that Margaret and Daisy wanted to sleep.

'Sleep tight, everyone,' said Daisy.

And just as she had done the previous night, Charlotte crossed her fingers and hoped that in the morning she would be back in her real life.

CHAPTER 8

Charlotte woke suddenly, covered in sweat. In her dream she had been running, trying to catch up with a car with her family in.

'Don't leave me! Please. Please wait for me! Don't go.'

She was screaming but they couldn't hear or see her.

She sat up quickly, feeling breathless and sick. Margaret and Daisy remained fast asleep. She mopped her brow using the edge of the sheet and tried to take some deep, calming breaths but it took her a while to settle down again and drop back off to sleep.

The dream seemed very fresh in her mind when she awoke again in the morning and she shivered at the thought of it.

She had her morning routine worked out now and got dressed as fast as her roommates. The skin on the back of her neck was not quite as sore as it had been yesterday but she still put a layer of cream on it.

Daisy was working later but Charlotte was relieved that she was on duty with Margaret again. It gave her confidence a small boost. Even though Daisy was having a slower start to her working day, she still got up so she could have breakfast. She didn't want to miss out on any food, she told them.

'I'm going to spend some time with my sketch pad this morning,' she said. 'See you later. I'm sure everything will be in tip-top shape by the time I join you.'

When they arrived on the ward, there was again no sign of Sister Craig but Matron McLean was there and she told Charlotte that she – Charlotte – would be working a split shift. This meant she would be able to have an extra-long lunch break before coming back to the ward at four and working through to ten in the evening. She would also be expected to attend the orientation lecture that was running downstairs in the mess at two.

'Usually this lecture is for the unqualified staff,' Matron said. 'But I want you to attend, Nurse Robertson, because I am going to include the administration of medicines and I understand that your knowledge of medicine administration is sadly lacking.'

It was a barbed comment but in fact Charlotte was glad that she was going to find out more about the work and the unit. Unknowingly, Matron had reminded her about the drug error.

'Thank you for inviting me, Matron. I look forward to it.'

Matron said nothing but glared at Charlotte over her glasses.

There had been six new admissions during the night. This meant that yet again some of the patients were in different places or no longer there. Charlotte wondered what had happened to the two boys in the side room. She had a feeling they were both dead. Her hunch was confirmed by Nurse Collinson who started her report by announcing that Douglas and Godman had died the previous evening. Charlotte was glad she had spoken to both of them, even though it had not changed the outcome. Nobody else reacted to the news.

Nurse Collinson continued her report. Fraser, Parkes, Clifford and Jackson were among the new names, while Cameron, Burns, Murray, Brown, Stills, Sears, Fellows and Beattie were now familiar to Charlotte, and even though some of the soldiers had been moved around the ward, she felt she was now keeping up with the names.

The soldiers who were categorised as 'A' had been kept warm, and given rectal fluid and analgesia to try to diminish the effects of blood loss and shock. Margaret had told her they did this to ensure a greater chance of success if an operation was required.

Matron McLean allocated the day's duties without any mention of Sister Craig. Nobody asked where she was. Charlotte was assigned to 'special tasks' and observations, while Margaret was tackling the dressings. Matron asked Nurse Brook to hold the medicine cupboard keys in the absence of Sister Craig. This implied that Nurse Brook was in charge as the keys seemed to be the marker of authority in the ward. Nothing changes, thought Charlotte. Nurse Brook was also asked to be responsible for the two discharges, with a third likely later in the day.

Although Charlotte had been given a different set of duties and, in truth, did not know what the 'special tasks' entailed, she felt slightly more confident as the daily routine started. Margaret whispered in her ear that the 'specials' included the men who had colostomies, for example, or gastrostomies or catheters.

Before Nurse Collinson left the ward, she took Charlotte aside and said quietly, 'Was it you who went into the side room before you finished your duties last night, by any chance?'

Charlotte hesitated. 'Yes, it was.'

'I wondered because Godman's mouth looked so clean and I've not noticed that happening before.'

'So do you go into the room at night?'

'Yes,' said Nurse Collinson. 'I'm in there much more than they know. I keep the door open so that the boys can hear that someone is around and they're not utterly alone. If the main ward is quiet, I often take a chair and sit in there with them.'

'That's reassuring. I'm really troubled at the thought that they're moved in there and left to die on their own.

'I think we all find that aspect particularly harrowing. As far as I'm concerned, it's the end of the medical treatment, not the nursing care. The alternative is just too overwhelming to contemplate, really. In fact, if you want to know the truth it's why I offer to do night duty so much.' She smiled, then said, 'Right, I'm off to have some sleep.'

Charlotte made a start on the observation round and it was her first chance to speak to the patients today. She made her way around the ward, taking temperatures and pulses, recording them on the charts and noting down the names of the men who had a fever. It took about forty minutes and then she started on the 'specials'.

One of these tasks involved Lieutenant Ellis, who had suffered both back and abdominal injuries and was paralysed from the waist down. He had a urinary catheter, which surprised Charlotte as she assumed they were a more modern development, although this catheter was made of whalebone and glass. The thought of it made her shudder. What damage it would do if it shattered, she thought.

While she was checking that the catheter was draining properly, Captain Graves arrived at the bedside on his ward round. Charlotte stepped aside and observed the brief but friendly conversation that ensued.

'Now then, how are you this morning, Ellis?' Captain Graves asked.

Ellis said, 'I'm all right, Captain. But I'll be happier when I'm back up on my feet. When do you think that will be?'

Within the next few weeks or months, Captain Graves told him. 'We'll be sending you back to Blighty in the next few days for you to start your recovery.'

The injured man took the news well. It was evidently what he had hoped to hear but it left Charlotte feeling very uncomfortable. This poor man had no sensation or movement in his lower legs, had a dropped foot and no urinary or bowel control. And yet he was being given an assurance that all would be well and even that he would walk again.

'That's encouraging news, isn't it, Nurse Robertson?' Ellis said, looking directly at Charlotte.

'Yes,' she said. She smiled at him. 'Yes, it is.'

Captain Graves moved on to the patient in the next bed while Lieutenant Ellis continued to outline his hopes for his recovery. 'I'm looking forward to when I'm better and I can play cricket again down on the village green.'

Charlotte felt she was in one of the most difficult situations a nurse could face. If she agreed with him, she would be colluding with the probable untruth of the situation. But if she disagreed, then she was shattering his illusion about the future. Did she know all the facts? And anyway was it her place to tell him the 'truth'?

As she had done before in similar situations, she tried to remain neutral and just listen to what he was saying.

'I hope you can play cricket again,' she said, trying to sound confident. 'How long have you been playing?'

'Since school,' Ellis said. 'I love playing and watching it. I was lucky enough to see a test match in London a few years ago. I saw "the Master" playing against Australia.'

Charlotte laughed. 'Sorry. I don't know very much about cricket. Who's "the Master"?'

'The great Jack Hobbs. He's the best opener I've ever seen. He plays for Surrey.'

'And did England win that match?'

'Yes, it was wonderful!'

'Did England win the Ashes that year?'

'It wasn't the Ashes I saw but the Triangular Tournament which included matches against South Africa as well. But we did win in the end. The game I saw ended up as a draw due to the rain but I still saw Hobbs get a hundred and seven runs.'

'That must have been a special event,' Charlotte said. 'It's wonderful when you can see a sporting hero. Tell me, do you live in London?'

Ellis shook his head. 'No, my brother and I went down from Newcastle on the train and stayed in a hotel. It was rather expensive at the time but I'm glad we did it.'

'Well, that's a wonderful memory to have.'

She finished all her checks and left him, seemingly content with his thoughts.

Charlotte was in the preparation room when Captain Graves came in.

She cleared her throat. 'Captain Graves, please can I ask you about Lieutenant Ellis?'

'If you feel that you have something important to say, Nurse Robertson.'

'I was wondering if you think he will regain any function in his lower limbs?'

'No,' said Captain Graves firmly. 'He'll be like this for the rest of his life.'

'Will you tell him?'

'What and remove all his hope? Why on earth would I do that? In my experience, he will come to accept the truth himself in time. He certainly doesn't need to know such information at the moment. It will hamper his recovery. Now, I'm not sure why you're asking me, and I think you're rather presumptuous, but please be careful not to say anything to him that will push him to face the reality of his situation before he is ready to cope with it.'

'Yes, Captain,' Charlotte said. 'I will be careful what I say.'

The second of the 'special' tasks was with Lieutenant Stevenson, in bed eleven, who had undergone abdominal surgery two days earlier. He had been hit by shrapnel, which had damaged his bowel, and he needed help to manage a colostomy formed on the lower left side of his abdominal wall. Unlike the modern adhesive patches used to secure the thin plastic bags, this device involved a belt and a pad. Charlotte had been told to attend to the skin around the stoma and she was to use boracic ointment. Luckily, the stoma and the surrounding skin looked pink and healthy. The stoma sat to the lower left of a long, central abdominal wound that ran vertically and was covered by a dressing.

Lieutenant Stevenson seemed quite resigned to his situation and said he was grateful to be alive. 'This is the type of wound that other chaps dread,' he said. 'Especially when one's guts appear.'

'That does sound gruesome,' Charlotte agreed.

Stevenson said, 'But I had no idea that such remedies were available. It's remarkable what modern medicine can do.'

'Yes,' said Charlotte. 'Remarkable.'

'Do you think it will be regular and I'll be able to know when it's working, so to speak?'

'Well,' said Charlotte, 'in my experience, your bowel should have some regular functioning, but it might take a while to establish a routine. At the moment, we need to make sure that when the colostomy works, it doesn't contaminate the surgical wound you have.'

'I don't know if I like the sound of that, but right-ho – I'll stay alert to the arrival of the first deposit, as it were.'

'Yes, please give me a shout when that happens.'

Charlotte finished the skin care around the site of the stoma. 'Right, that's you all sorted for the moment.'

She thought about Lieutenant Stevenson's remarks about modern medicine as she cleared up her tray. Perhaps every generation considers itself to be so advanced. None of the 'special tasks' she had undertaken was, in principle, any different from the treatments on offer in the modern world.

As she came back into the ward, she stopped by Beattie's bed to see how he was. His dressing had already been changed but Charlotte had noticed when she took his temperature it was steadily climbing. This was not a good sign. Any infection would increase the chance of a bleed. His was one of the names she had written in the temperature book.

'How are you feeling now, Padre?'

Without turning his head, Beattie said, 'Not too bad, thank you, nurse.'

'Can I offer you something to drink?'

'Yes, some water would be most welcome. My mouth feels rather dry.'

'I'll pop down to the kitchen to see if there's any ice. That might be more refreshing for you.'

Charlotte was back within a couple of minutes. She put the iced water into a feeding cup. 'I think this might make it slightly easier to drink, rather than straining your neck.'

'It makes me feel like an old man,' he said with a sigh.

'I apologise,' said Charlotte. 'That's not my intention.' She helped him to take a few sips and noticed how pale he looked.

'Is there anything else I can do for you at the moment?' she asked.

He leant back on the pillows. 'I wonder if it's not too much trouble whether the curé would be able to visit me again. I felt so uplifted by his visit.'

'Why don't I go and ask Tom? He'll be going into Albert this morning to take the patients who are leaving us to go to the station. I'm sure he'd be happy to call in at the church for you.'

'I would appreciate that. Many thanks.' He closed his eyes.

As she walked out of the ward door, Charlotte saw Tom in the yard below once again working on the ambulance. She tapped on the window but he didn't hear so she hurried downstairs and out the back door.

'Morning, Tom. When are you going into Albert today?'

'Howdy, Nurse Robertson, you are in a rush. I'll be leaving just after eleven. Why do you ask?'

'Is there any chance that you could call in at the church to see if the curé is free to come and visit Padre Beattie today, please?'

'Of course. That would be no trouble at all.'

'You're a star!' Charlotte said, heading back inside. 'Thanks.'

'Why have you left the ward, nurse?' A disembodied voice called out as Charlotte was walking quickly around the balcony at the top of the staircase.

Matron McLean was standing by the door to the ward.

'I was just asking Tom if he would ask the curé to come and visit Padre Beattie, Matron.'

She glared at Charlotte. 'That sort of small talk can wait until the ward is quieter. Get back to your duties immediately.'

Charlotte stood her ground. 'Sorry, Matron, but with the greatest respect, I feel that meeting a patient's request is part of my duties.'

Matron said nothing but continued to stare at Charlotte.

Charlotte wondered how Matron managed to spot everything that went on. It was an incredible skill to have.

As she went back into the ward, a trolley passed by bearing Cartwright. He was on his way for surgery. She could see the empty bed was ready to be prepared for his return so she made it up as a 'theatre bed', ensuring that the pillowcases were facing away from the door. As if this is the marker of quality care, she muttered to herself. Yet she had conformed to the petty rule.

As she finished, she noticed Fellows grimacing as he tried to make himself comfortable. She walked over to his bed.

'Has your dressing been changed already this morning?' she asked.

He grimaced again. 'No.'

'Very well. Let me see where we are with the dressings and perhaps I can ask Nurse Wishaw to do yours now. You look like you're in pain again.'

'Well, actually it is rather dreadful,' he said. 'But I don't want to make a fuss.'

'Perhaps it would be better if I could give you something to ease the pain before your dressing is changed.'

Charlotte looked at the chart above his bed to see whether any analgesia had been administered recently. This was Matron McLean's system of recording when medicines had been given to a patient and it worked well in a situation like this when there was such a limited range of medications. There was no record of analgesia being administered so perhaps she could give him some. She would have to ask Nurse Brook as she had 'the keys' this morning and was, effectively, in control of the medicines. Charlotte was not optimistic but to her surprise Nurse Brook agreed. Perhaps it was because one of the doctors was in the ward at the time, Charlotte thought. But no matter what the reason, it meant that the soldier's pain would not be ignored.

Charlotte watched as Nurse Brook gave Fellows an injection. It was about fifteen minutes later that Margaret began to renew his dressing. Charlotte came over to the bedside as Margaret began. The wound site on his abdomen was red and inflamed. This is not looking good, she thought. As with many of the procedures in the ward, there was a 'dressings book' and Margaret noted down her findings as clearly as she could, highlighting colour, swelling and the pain that Fellows was experiencing. Charlotte was used to reporting changes directly to the medical staff, but here there was a clear hierarchy and the senior nurse was the one to say such things. She was beginning to find this frustrating. She mentioned it to Nurse Brook, who was standing over Margaret as she sat at the table writing. Both Charlotte and Margaret were describing the change to Fellows's wound.

'It sounds like you two are playing at being doctor,' said Nurse Brook.

Charlotte and Margaret exchanged glances.

'Really?' said Charlotte. 'I rather thought it was a nursing role to ensure that we report any changes we observe in our patients. So will you report this or shall I?'

'I shall report it as I am in charge. Now finish your work, Nurse Robertson.'

'Of course. Is there anything outstanding that I should be doing at the moment, Nurse Brook?'

'Have you completed the observations?'

'Yes.'

'Have you seen to the colostomy?'

'Yes.'

'Is the catheter running freely?'

'Yes.'

'Is the theatre bed ready?'

'Yes.'

'Well then, you could assist with the remainder of the dressings before lunch. Speak to Nurse Wishaw here about whose are still outstanding. Oh, and check that the discharges are ready.'

'I thought you were tasked with their preparation,' said Margaret.

'Well, I've been far too busy,' Nurse Brook retorted. 'Sister Craig has left so much paperwork to complete that I can't possibly do that as well.' She walked away before anything else could be said.

'She tries my patience,' said Margaret.

Charlotte sighed. 'Mine too.'

She went to make sure that the two officers who were being discharged, Jones and Wright, had their papers pinned to them and all their possessions packaged together. They were ready to leave when Tom and the orderlies arrived just after eleven. Their laundered uniforms had been returned to each man and they had changed into them. Charlotte wished them a safe journey and a speedy recovery.

Even though some had life-altering injuries, there was an uplifting, positive atmosphere when men were discharged back to Britain. She wondered how life would treat them outside the safety of the hospital setting where it was unusual to see someone with extensive disfigurement.

When the fitter patients were discharged in the morning, it meant that the VADs had to take on the role of setting the dining table and serving out the food, as well as washing down the beds and re-making them in preparation for the next admissions.

Charlotte busied herself with a few more activities before the men's lunch arrived. She was relieved that she had managed to keep up with the morning's ward work that morning and had really quite enjoyed it.

When her lunchtime finally came round, at about half past twelve, Charlotte made her way down to the dining room where she had a welcome bowl of soup and a thick slice of bread. Tom popped his head round the door.

'Good, I wondered if you'd be here. Just to say I called into the church and the curé will be most happy to visit again later on today.'

'Thanks for doing that, Tom. It will really cheer him up. I'll tell him when I go back on duty.'

'No need,' Tom said. 'I went upstairs to let him know. That's why I knew you were here. By the way, where's Daisy today?'

'She has a later start. When I last saw her she was doing some sketching in our room. Shall I tell her you were asking after her?'

'That would be grand,' said Tom with a grin. 'You enjoy your break now, Nurse Robertson, and no doubt I'll see you later.'

He whistled as he left the room. That sounds like *If You Were the Only Girl in the World*, thought Charlotte. Perhaps I should tell Daisy that, too.

She helped herself to a cup of coffee and sat down again to look at a magazine lying on a small table. It was the *British Journal of Nursing*, edited by Mrs. Bedford Fenwick, someone Charlotte had studied in a history of nursing class when she was a student. Wow, fancy seeing an original copy of her journal, she thought.

The contents were formal – very different from her own colourful weekly journal. There were lists of appointments, committee memberships and presentations, as well as a roll of honour identifying nurses who had been killed in action. A linked item mentioned a memorial to Edith Cavell, another reminder to

Charlotte of her potentially dangerous predicament. I'd rather not think about that, she decided.

She had some free time until the lecture and the second half of her shift so she decided to go and have a lie down on her bed and read one of the books that had been in her suitcase. She made her way upstairs back to her room where she found Daisy.

'Have you had a lovely morning with your sketch pad?'

'I have, thanks,' Daisy said. 'Although I've eaten my way through a bag of peppermints in the process.'

Charlotte took her shoes off and lay down. She picked up the book on surgical nursing. It had been published in 1915 and there were chapters on inflammation, wounds, surgical procedures and bandaging.

'By the way, Tom was asking where you were as he hadn't seen you this morning.'

'Oh, that is kind of him,' said Daisy.

'And then he started whistling *If You Were the Only Girl in the World.*'

Daisy giggled but said nothing.

Charlotte turned back to her book but her eyes grew heavy and she dozed. When she awoke and looked at her watch, it was just after half past one. It's a bright day, she thought, and I've got time for a short walk outside.

Daisy had left the room without waking her.

CHAPTER 9

This time, Charlotte took the opportunity to explore the estate further. A little two-room cottage was situated about fifty yards from the walled garden behind the kitchen of the main house. As she approached, she saw Monique playing with a doll. She was sitting beside her mother and an old woman dressed in black.

'*Bonjour*,' said Charlotte.

'*Bonjour, mademoiselle*,' replied the mother.

Charlotte, trying out her rudimentary French, discovered the mother's name was Huguette.

The little family had lived on the estate for many years, working in the gardens and kitchen of the house. The house had belonged to a wealthy family before it was sold as a hotel about twenty-five years earlier. The war meant there was no business, and the arrival of the army to turn the building into an officer's hospital had provided the family with much-needed work. Hugette's husband was in the French army but he had not been home for many months. He had been fighting in Verdun. The nearest relative was in Albert, the nearby town. They had always been reluctant to leave their home and as the front line had got further away over recent months, living there had become less frightening than earlier in the war. The old woman was Huguette's mother, who had lived with them for a long time following the death of her husband.

'We pray that we will continue to be safe here,' said Huguette. 'It's kind of you to come and speak to us. We like to meet the nurses, but little Monique is scared of the large nurse so that is why she appears shy.'

Charlotte bent down beside Monique. 'I like your doll. What's her name?'

'Brigitte,' said Monique.

'Oh, that's a lovely name for her.'

'Do you have a little girl, nurse?'

'Yes, I do. Her name is Anne and she's a bit older than you.'

'Does she have a doll like Brigitte?'

'No, she doesn't.'

'Does she have long hair like me?'

'No. She has short hair, like mine.'

Huguette interrupted. 'Enough of that, Monique. The nurse doesn't want to know about your hair.' She turned to Charlotte. 'May I offer you a cup of coffee or a little cognac, nurse?'

'Thank you, that's most kind. But I've to go to a talk by Matron and I mustn't be late. Perhaps another time?'

'*A bientôt*,' called Monique as Charlotte turned away.

She walked back to the hospital thinking about the civilians who found themselves in the middle of war zones. What would she do in that situation? Run away, perhaps, but that wouldn't be easy if you had to try to make a living to keep a roof over your head. How frightening for them, she thought – more people who faced uncertainty in their world. Speaking to the little girl had also reminded Charlotte of her own children and she felt incredibly sad again to be separated from them. This time, however, she was not gripped by panic. Instead, the encounter had made her thankful that her life was so tranquil and safe. Why had she let herself become so concerned with little things in daily life that didn't matter? Giving the children a safe, loving and secure environment in which to grow was so important and it had taken her short visit to this little French family to understand that fully.

Coming into the hall, she saw Nurse Brook sitting on one of the small sofas drinking a cup of coffee.

Nurse Brook looked over at her. 'Had a nice walk before your remedial class?' she called. A barbed comment, Charlotte thought. But she had heard it all before and was not going to let Nurse Brook affect her.

'Yes, thank you. Actually, I was just getting some air and looking around the estate while I had some free time.'

'Can't see the point of that as there's not much here. It's very dull.' Nurse Brook sipped her coffee. 'I saw you talking to the Frenchies.'

Charlotte walked over to her. 'Do you have a problem with that?'

'No, but I'm keeping my eye on you. There's something about you that doesn't ring true. I find it hard to believe that you need to attend a lecture designed for the unqualified staff.' She put her cup down. 'By the way, Matron has asked me to be in charge later on today as she's been called to Albert for a meeting after your talk.'

'Sorry to disappoint you but I'm quite happy to go to the lecture. And where is Sister Craig anyway? Why is she not in charge of the ward?'

'She had to go with Matron.'

Charlotte folded her arms. 'Well, I'm sure you'll enjoy the responsibility of being in charge, Nurse Brook.'

'I couldn't do a worse job than Sister Craig.'

'I disagree. I think you could.'

Charlotte would not normally have expressed such a strong view and had surprised herself by saying it out loud. She was fascinated by how new authority affected people. Over the years, she had encountered colleagues who seemed to develop an air of superiority when given any responsibility. It invariably led to them being intolerant and critical of other staff. So no doubt she could expect to be 'called to the office' by Matron when she returned to the hospital the following morning for some invented minor misdemeanour that Nurse Brook would report.

Nurse Brook was serving her time as a staff nurse, aspiring to run a ward as soon as she could – so others had told Charlotte. What a nightmare she would be when in charge on a permanent basis. She was a weak leader: very inconsistent in her dealings with other people, reluctant to accept any responsibility and not very competent. Furthermore, she seemed to dislike anyone she worked with or looked after. Charlotte wondered why people like her, who appeared to have such a poor opinion of others, wanted to work in a caring role.

As she left Nurse Brook to her coffee, Charlotte found herself valuing the work she did and thinking she really did care about the patients she looked after. It was a long time since she had realised this.

It was just before two o'clock when she walked into the mess where five other members of staff were waiting. Charlotte had not seen any of them before. Perhaps they worked in the medical ward or on night duty. She nodded and said hello to the people sitting beside her as she sat down at one of the tables. But apart from a quick 'Hello', nobody chatted. A couple were trained nurses like her and the others were new VADs who looked around the room nervously. There was a sense of foreboding in the room.

Matron swept in at two o'clock exactly and everyone jumped up as she passed through the assembled class. Charlotte followed suit as quickly as she could. The smell of violets accompanied Matron's arrival and it seemed particularly pungent this afternoon.

'Be seated,' instructed Matron.

This was not going to be any sort of interactive teaching session, Charlotte thought, but a swift lecture.

'I want to tell you about your role here at Bécourt and what I expect of you while you are under my command,' Matron began. 'The first thing to say is your professional responsibilities include discipline, obedience, respect for seniors and the medical staff, punctuality, cleanliness and trustworthiness. It means, and I include you in this, Nurse Robertson, that you do not fraternise with the patients or staff of other ranks, you report changes to the nurse in charge of the ward, not directly to the medical staff, and you obey instructions. Do I make myself clear?'

'Yes Matron,' everyone said in unison. Charlotte felt the others looking at her.

'I expect you to learn the ward routine swiftly and not to have to be constantly reminded of your duties. Those of you who are VADs need to remember that you are not qualified nurses. Your tasks are to support the work of the qualified staff in the care and treatment of the soldiers. This means ensuring that shelves are re-stocked, lotions made and trolleys prepared, as well as helping to ensure that the ward is clean. At no time should you assume the role of the trained nurse. Do I make myself clear on this point?'

'Yes, Matron,' said the VADs.

'Now, infection is our biggest enemy and I will not have dust and grime in the ward contributing to the development of sepsis. Also it is imperative that you wash your hands in-between every task. Is that understood?'

Another chorus. 'Yes, Matron.'

Charlotte thought she could be sitting in a lecture about infection control in her unit.

'As I have gone around the wards I have noticed slovenly habits in record-keeping and this must be rectified. Now, the doctor does not want to read irrelevant nonsense in records, so do not – I repeat, do not – use empty phrases like "Had a good sleep" in your notes as this is meaningless. The doctor wants to read specifics such as how long the patient slept, whether there were any alterations in temperature, or whether the patient required prescribed medication. Furthermore, the discharge paperwork must be completed before the patient leaves the ward. I also want to ensure you are familiar with the fundamentals of medicine administration because some of you qualified nurses appear to be lacking the necessary knowledge and skills in this area.'

Charlotte, who as usual had her paper and pencil to hand, could feel Matron's gaze fixing on her again but she chose not to return it. Matron could not possibly know how accurate her final statement had been.

'Some of the other casualty clearing stations and stationery hospitals have reported incidents relating to the administration of wrong medicine and I am determined that my unit will not be added to this list. I will not tolerate negligence in this area, so I am going to remind you of the principles of medicine administration. I am indebted to Matron Laurence of the Chelsea Hospital for Women for her wise words on this matter and will base this section of my talk on her work.'

Matron placed a wicker basket down on the table and took from it a small book that had some paper markers identifying relevant pages. She began to read extracts from it.

'You need to know the range of medicines prescribed for the patients, the reasons for their use and the side effects. Furthermore, and this is why this is relevant to you VADs, it is important to know how to store medicines appropriately, so the poisons are kept separately. Poisons have ridges on the bottles. This is often a cause of mistakes. Here is how I complete drug administration. Ensure you follow this approach.

'When reading the prescription, ensure that the dose is checked against the doctor's order book. Remember that there is a difference between fluid and solid measures and that the signs will be written first. Let me start with the fluid measures.'

She explained how sixty minims were equal to one drachm, eight drachms equal to one ounce, and half an ounce was about one tablespoon. 'And twenty ounces equals one pint.'

The only two words familiar to Charlotte were ounces and pints. She had never heard of drachms and only knew of minims in a musical context. She sat up straight and ensured she was attending as Matron held the book open at one of the markers so everyone could see the strange symbols. Charlotte tried her best to copy down the symbols for a minim, a scruple, a drachm, an ounce, a pint. How confusing, she thought.

'When it comes to the administration of medicines, I like to have a basket with me with all the labelled bottles so I do not have to walk back and forth to the medicines cupboard,' Matron continued. 'This basket will also contain some graduated medicine glasses and a jug of fresh water. For those patients who have prescriptions three times per day, they should be administered at ten, two in the afternoon and six o'clock in the evening.' She moved a wisp of stray hair from her forehead.

'Ensure that where a poison or injection has been prescribed that a second person checks the dose. I ask the medical staff to record such a prescription in my poisons book. However, in an emergency, a doctor can order a small prescription of a drug such as morphia and a nurse can give it alone, but as I have just said, this is only to occur in exceptional circumstances and I do not encourage such practice.'

She glared at the nurses then lifted a small bottle out of the basket and began to shake it.

'Always shake the bottle before measuring out the medicine and keep the label uppermost to ensure it does not become obscured and illegible. This will save errors and waste.'

Okay, thought Charlotte, some of that is common sense, but those names and measures are completely foreign to me.

But Matron was now in full flow, pacing back and forth across the room.

'Now to the solid measures. Twenty grains is equal to one scruple, and sixty grains is equal to one drachm which is about one teaspoon. However, although I mention the use of spoons, I prefer you to measure the medicine into a graduated medicine glass as they are more accurate. Now, I'm sure you will know that medicines can be administered by mouth, via the rectum and by injection. It is, therefore, important that you read the prescription carefully to ensure you are using the appropriate route.'

She stopped and glared again. Everyone seemed increasingly terrified as the talk continued.

'We often use the rectal route for those soldiers who are severely injured. If you are preparing a medicine for rectal infusion, ensure that your tray has the following: a Jacques catheter, a lubricant, glass connector, rubber tubing and funnel, clips and a protective mackintosh.' She counted off each item on her fingers as it was mentioned.

'An infusion of one ounce takes approximately fifteen minutes to administer. If a medication is to be administered by injection, sterilise the needle and syringe first by flushing them with carbolic one-in-twenty solution. Make sure the syringe barrel is empty before you draw up the medicine. Wipe the skin with antiseptic, lift the skin and insert the needle at the base of the lifted skin.

'You will also have observed that I have a method for recording the administration of medicines on the observation chart kept at the bedside. Complete the details, writing clearly so it is evident that the medication has been given. You may not have seen this in other wards, but I have found it to be a reliable way of ensuring that a patient has his prescribed medication recorded and duplication is avoided. Is that clear?'

They all nodded. No one dared ask for any further explanation but Charlotte's head was still reeling from the weights and measures. They made no sense to her at all and in a more informal setting she would have asked many questions to clarify things. Surely, though, if there were graduated glasses for liquid measures, then she would manage.

But one thing Matron said made Charlotte think about the practice she had observed and tentatively she put her hand up.

'Yes?' snapped Matron.

'Matron, I heard you say that two people should routinely check a poison. Would that include the rectal administration of morphia?'

'Of course. Were you not listening to what I just said?'

'Yes, but I wanted to double-check that I understood you correctly.'

That's interesting, thought Charlotte. When Fellows was being prepared for his emergency surgery on her first day, Nurse Brook had gone ahead and given him a rectal infusion containing morphia. But Charlotte now wondered who had counter-checked it. It would not count as an exceptional situation, in her opinion. And it had happened again this morning.

Matron pointed at various individuals. 'I also want to remind you of the tetanus policy that was introduced last month and your responsibilities in early detection. I am keen to avoid the unhelpful interference of the unit tetanus officer.'

She outlined the signs and symptoms of tetanus, her presentation continuing uninterrupted for another fifteen minutes and including much about the standards of care she expected. Although Charlotte thought it was domineering in tone, it was fascinating to hear from someone who had such high standards.

Matron had made it very clear what was expected in 'her' hospital. Furthermore she seemed able to keep a close eye on how care was delivered and was very quick to reprimand any member of staff who fell below her exacting standards.

Finally, Matron said, 'Right, I have made it clear what I expect of you so keep working hard to improve. Now, please return to your duties.' She replaced the bottle and book in the basket and hooked it over her arm, ready to leave.

The other staff picked up their belongings and departed without saying a word but Charlotte knew that what she had learned about medicines would be useful so she thanked Matron as she left the room. Matron looked a little surprised.

When Charlotte returned to the ward, there were still some 'special tasks' waiting for her to complete.

The first patient she went to was Lieutenant Brown in bed twelve who had been admitted with a fractured jaw a couple of days before and had been for surgery on Charlotte's first day. He was extremely withdrawn and when Charlotte asked if he would let her check the wound he nodded without glancing up at her. He was another patient who appeared to be in a lot of pain as he was unable to use or close his mouth properly. He was dribbling, which was causing the skin on his chin to redden. But he let her clean his mouth and she applied some petroleum jelly to his lips. He had a bandage that supported his chin, almost like a headscarf, and it was keeping some pads in place over a wound.

'Are you in a lot of pain?' she asked.

He shook his head slowly so Charlotte added, 'Well, please let me know if you are and I'll request some pain relief.'

He didn't make any eye contact as she attended to him and Charlotte assumed it was because he was suffering too much, even though he was trying to be stoical about it.

Her next task was feeding Second Lieutenant Murray in bed eight who had a stomach injury. To Charlotte's surprise, he had a gastrostomy tube in place. She had assumed that, like catheters and colostomy formation, such tube-feeding was a more recent development. But instead of putting up a bag of liquid that contained all the appropriate nutrients and which delivered the feed via a pump, as happened in her ward, she found she was expected to administer peptonised beef tea via a funnel and rubber tubing. She headed to the treatment room to find a colleague to help her prepare it. Isobel, the VAD, was there.

'I have to give Murray his feed now,' Charlotte said. 'Can you help me with it, please?'

'Of course,' said Isobel. 'Give me a couple of seconds and I'll go down to the kitchen to fetch it. I got it ready after lunch so I just need to go and strain it.'

She disappeared and returned a couple of minutes later with a jug on a tray.

Charlotte peered at the brown liquid. 'So what's in it?'

'One ounce of Savoury and Moore's saline essence of pepsin, but this time I remembered to boil it for two minutes,' Isobel said proudly. 'Cook keeps a steady production of beef tea for us which makes life a lot easier.'

'Well, thanks for fetching it for me.'

Charlotte put the jug on her trolley, along with a cloth and a glass funnel.

Isobel said, 'Sarah was right. You don't mind us being here, do you, Nurse Robertson?'

'Not at all. I appreciate the help you've given me since I got here,' said Charlotte. 'You've helped me to settle in.'

She took the trolley over to the bed. 'Here's your afternoon tea, Lieutenant Murray.'

The rubber tube was pinned on the top of his dressing and sealed with a wooden spigot.

'Thanks, nurse. I hope that's a nice pint of foaming ale you've brought me.'

Charlotte laughed. 'No such luck, I'm afraid. The only similarity is the colour. I'm not sure how tasty this would be but it's very nourishing, I think.'

She unpinned the tubing, removed the spigot and attached the glass funnel to the end of it. She was slowly pouring the liquid into the funnel when Nurse Brook came into the ward. She called out loudly, 'Nurse, don't pour it all in at once. You'll cause distension and vomiting.'

'I'm trying to pour it in as slowly as I can,' Charlotte said.

As Nurse Brook turned and left the ward again, Lieutenant Murray said quietly, 'That's rich coming from her. When she did my feed yesterday, she filled the funnel up to the top and sent it all in at once. No wonder I was burping for an hour afterwards.'

Charlotte said nothing but raised her eyebrows and smiled.

The feeding took ten minutes and she allowed the funnel to almost empty before filling it again. While the feed was slowly draining into Murray's stomach, she asked where he was from.

'A little village outside Durham,' he said with pride. 'I joined the Northumberland Fusiliers in 1914, on my twenty-second birthday.'

Charlotte thought he looked much older than twenty-four.

'What about yourself, nurse. Where are you from?'

'Aberdeen.'

'I've never been there. What's it like?'

'Well, it's quite a bustling city.' She was about to tell him it was the oil capital of Europe when she realised that wouldn't make any sense. And when he asked about the city's industries, she had to think quickly about life in Aberdeen before the arrival of the offshore industry.

'Fishing, granite and boat-building,' she said. They were the only things she could think of and she wondered for a moment if she was correct. Never mind, that would have to do, she thought. She had almost been caught out again and she was relieved that the feed was nearly complete. She checked under the dressing to see that all was secure before she left. Where the gastrostomy tube entered his stomach, she could see a silver ring attached to tapes that went around his body, holding the tube in place. She replaced the dressing and spigot, and made sure she pinned the tube back on his dressing in the same position she had found it.

As she was taking the trolley back to the clinical room, she could hear Lieutenant Stills calling out. 'Help me, someone. I need help, please. Can you come and help me?'

She called back. 'Just let me clear this away first.'

When she went over to his bedside. He said he was in a lot more pain and had noticed a bad smell coming from his wound. 'What's happening to me?' he asked, desperation in his voice.

Stills had undergone a traumatic amputation of his left leg following an injury caused by a shell fragment. Captain Graves had tried to fashion a stump from the remnants but it had been contaminated at the time of the damage. There was a sickly, offensive smell coming from the wound, the kind of smell that forced you to breathe through your mouth to avoid gagging.

When did you first notice the bad smell?' asked Charlotte.

'Just about an hour ago.'

'Have you mentioned it to the doctor?'

He shook his head. 'Not yet. I told one of the other nurses but she said it was probably nothing.'

'And how are you feeling otherwise?'

'A bit hot and bothered, if I'm honest. And the smell is making me feel rather sick.'

Charlotte wasn't surprised. She said, 'Please let me take your temperature and pulse just now to see if there's any change from earlier.'

As she was doing so she was again interrupted by Nurse Brook. 'What are you doing?' she demanded. 'It's not the time for taking the observations.'

Charlotte explained the situation as calmly as she could and said she thought it wise to check before reporting the situation to the medical staff. For the moment, she had chosen to ignore Matron's instruction at the lecture, particularly since Nurse Brook was in charge of the ward for the moment.

'Well, what are the findings?' Nurse Brook asked.

'He has a faster pulse now and his temperature has risen since this morning.'

'Nurse, it is not your job to report changes to the medical staff. I am in charge and I will do it.'

Nurse Brook turned abruptly and headed over to speak to Captain Graves who was in another part of the ward. Charlotte heard her tell him she had become concerned about Lieutenant Stills.

The important thing is that the doctor will go and see him, Charlotte told herself as she walked down the ward. It doesn't matter who tells him. Even so, she was annoyed and had to tell herself not to feel so put upon. This isn't about you.

She went into the clinical room and prepared a dressing trolley, thinking Captain Graves would want to look at the wound. She pushed it quickly to Stills's bedside. Captain Graves was already there. 'Think we need to look at your leg, old thing,' he said.

He turned to Charlotte. 'That was efficient work, Nurse Robertson. Well caught.'

Charlotte thanked him and he suggested she should stay to see the wound. 'It might be useful for you.'

Charlotte was not at all sure she wanted to see a putrefying wound. She noticed Nurse Brook was still hovering but had taken a step back and soon realised why.

Captain Graves undid the dressing and was faced with a horrible mess. The edges of the wound were swollen, with the tissue a mixture of black and a colour that was almost purple. The discharge that was causing the noxious smell was yellow, as bright as egg yolk. Now that the saturated dressing had been removed, the smell was so overwhelming that a wave of nausea flooded over Charlotte. She started to breathe through her mouth again and distracted herself by focusing on the more worrying and ominous feature – the crackling, bubbling sound that occurred when Captain Graves put his stethoscope on the wound.

'Right, I think we need to set up a Souttar's infusion,' he said.

'Yes, Captain,' said Nurse Brook. 'Nurse Robertson, you heard what the captain said. Go and set the trolley for that immediately.'

'Certainly,' said Charlotte, not wanting Nurse Brook to know she had no idea what was required.

Back in the clinical room, Margaret again came to Charlotte's rescue.

'Margaret, thank goodness you're here' she said urgently. 'Captain Graves has asked me to set up a Souttar's infusion and I have no idea what it is. I didn't want to let on to Nurse Brook so I pretended that I knew.'

'How interesting,' Margaret said. 'We haven't used one of those for a while and I doubt Nurse Brook would know what it is either. I'll have to have a quick think about what we need on the trolley for that one.'

'Is it another of those irrigating systems?'

'Well, yes. It's a way of rinsing out a wound using saline. The saline solution can do a couple of things. It can help remove the microbes that have invaded a wound, and it also encourages the arrival of lymph. It's quite a lot of work but can be very useful. Who's it for?'

'Lieutenant Stills, the chap with the amputation. His wound is putrid. I was almost sick when Captain Graves took the dressing off.'

'Oh dear, that doesn't sound right. This probably won't do any good if there's a deep-seated infection but I suppose they have to try something.'

Margaret opened a cupboard door and lifted out some equipment that she placed on a trolley. 'I'm sure that if Captain Clift were in charge of his case, he wouldn't attempt this.'

The equipment included something that looked a bit like a Thermos flask and some rubber tubing.

'So this apparatus provides a continuous flow of warmed saline over a wound,' Margaret said. 'Could you put some sterile gauze in a dish on the tray and fetch some saline solution which we can warm?'

Charlotte reached for a bottle marked 'Saline solution' on the shelf of lotions.

'Now, get some hot water and the ratio is one part of the saline solution to six parts of water. That will give you a five per cent solution. Why don't you make up the dressing trolley with a one-and-a-half-inch bandage and some pins.'

Charlotte was grateful for Margaret's friendly advice and when everything was ready, she added the equipment to the trolley. As she left the room Margaret, added softly, 'It would be very useful if we had some sort of tape as well, wouldn't it? Like Micropore.'

'Yes,' said Charlotte. 'It would certainly save us having to use pins all the time.'

Pushing the trolley along the ward she stopped in her tracks. She was sure she had heard correctly. Margaret had definitely said 'Micropore'. But how on earth could she know about a type of adhesive tape that would not be invented for many decades?

Charlotte's heart began beating faster at the mention of something from home. If the dressing had not been so urgent, she would have gone back to speak to her. She turned to look but Margaret was now busy with a patient. It would have to wait.

She helped Captain Graves set up the infusion. She placed a sheet of mackintosh under Stills's leg and a bedpan to collect the drained saline solution that would be dripped over his contaminated wound.

'I say, this looks rather advanced,' Lieutenant Stills muttered.

Charlotte was not sure whether Lieutenant Stills understood his predicament. He had developed gas gangrene in the wound and was facing last-resort treatment before surgery – or perhaps death from septicaemia.

Captain Graves covered the wound with a single layer of gauze. He said, 'Yes, this is one of our newer techniques and I've had some success with it. The problem is that the French farmers fertilised their soil so well before the war, using manure, so any injury can set off a sapraemic problem like this.'

Sapraemic? She had never heard the word before and had no idea what it meant. But there was no time to ask.

'Nurse Robertson, the saline should be infusing at about two pints per hour,' said Captain Graves. 'And please ensure the saline levels are topped up regularly and the bedpan emptied. If things are settling down by this evening, then we will pack the leg with carbolic. Otherwise, my only course of action will be surgery. You could also try to reduce that fever. I shall prescribe three grains of Antifebrin to see if that has any effect. Record his temperature and pulse every hour.'

'Yes, Captain, of course.'

Charlotte took Stills's pulse and temperature again and recorded the results on the observation recording chart hanging above his bed. His temperature was a hundred and one degrees Fahrenheit, which she knew was high even though she worked with Celsius.

In the sluice Isobel, the VAD, offered to clear the dressing trolley for her.

'Thanks, Isobel, but this container holds a really horrible-smelling dressing. I wouldn't want to inflict it on you.'

'Please don't worry,' said Isobel. 'I have a strong stomach, Nurse Robertson.'

So Charlotte let Isobel dispose of the revolting dressing, which gave her time to prepare a cold compress and return to the bedside to put the flannel on Lieutenant Stills's forehead.

'I'll do this each time I check your temperature and wound and we'll see if it helps to bring your fever down a bit. Would you like me to go and see if I can find some ice chips for you to suck?'

Still nodded weakly. 'Thank you, nurse, that would be rather refreshing. I feel parched.'

Nurse Brook stopped Charlotte as she was leaving the ward in search of ice. She was unimpressed with the suggestion that it would refresh a patient's mouth.

'I've heard it can make a mouth drier,' she said.

Charlotte tried to be patient. 'I'm not sure why that would be the case. In my experience, patients find it soothing and it's a little bit of comfort for them.'

'Well, tell one of the VADs to go. You shouldn't waste your time on something so menial.'

Isobel had overheard this exchange and volunteered to fetch the ice.

Charlotte mentioned the Antifebrin to Margaret who was busy administering the prescribed medicines. She gave it to Lieutenant Stills and noted it in small, neat writing on his chart.

At least Charlotte had a little more understanding of what 'grains' were following Matron's lecture.

As the day went on, it became clear the medicine was having no effect on poor Stills. The fight he was having with the advancing septicaemia meant that each time Charlotte returned to his bedside, he seemed to be in more pain. By the third check, he had begun to vomit. More than that, his temperature had dropped by only half a degree in two hours. The signs did not look good. He had an episode of shivering as well, which Charlotte recognised as his body trying to self-regulate its temperature in the face of overwhelming infection.

Towards the end of the day shift, Sister Craig and Matron McLean returned from their meeting. Sister Craig looked extremely upset and Charlotte wondered what had happened. Matron, meanwhile, seemed to be very involved in the review of the beds, and patients were shuffled around again.

By seven, Lieutenant Stills's fever was, if anything, getting worse. At the final check before Charlotte went off duty, it looked as though his condition was deteriorating. He was increasingly thirsty, felt 'hot and bothered', and said he had a bad taste in his mouth. His tongue was coated. As Charlotte, for the final time, replaced the bedpan, which was full of offensive discharge, she thought she noticed faint red lines appearing on what remained of his leg. She passed Captain Graves on her way to the sluice and reported what she had seen.

He frowned. 'Don't like the sound of that. In spite of our best efforts, I'm not sure he's going to make it.' More brightly, he added, 'Still, tomorrow's another day, and there's always a chance that we'll win this one. It's happened before.'

They had been so busy for the whole shift that Charlotte hadn't had a chance to think about home and as she left the ward she felt a little guilty because she had, for a few hours at least, forgotten about her normal life.

She tried to work out if Colin and the kids would still be in Braemar or would they have gone home? How lovely it would be to phone and see how they were, and let them know where she was and that she was safe. But what sort of conversation would follow if she told them she was in France and it was 1916? They would have as many unanswerable questions as she had.

She also wanted to speak to Margaret. What she had said earlier – about Micropore – how had that been possible? Charlotte's head was spinning. She hoped that when they sat down for supper there would be an opportunity. They could talk then.

The split shift she and Margaret had worked meant they didn't finish their duties until ten. The overlap with the night staff gave everyone a chance to complete their tasks, settle the patients for the evening and give a proper handover, which tonight included the instruction about Lieutenant Stills. The Souttar's infusion would continue overnight.

Daisy was finishing her meal in a hurry when Charlotte and Margaret finally arrived in the mess.

'Remember to leave room for the pudding,' she said between mouthfuls. 'This custard is sublime, by the way.' She stood up. 'Please don't think I'm rude but I want to go and finish a sketch I started this morning. See you upstairs.'

Charlotte had noticed Tom walking through the hall and thought perhaps that was the reason Daisy suddenly needed to leave. She had been sitting in a position that gave her a good view of the hallway.

The meal consisted of roast chicken, potatoes and cabbage, and the recommended stewed plums from the orchard. But Charlotte was almost too tired to eat and anyway going to bed on a full stomach was never a good idea.

They sat drinking hot chocolate, an alternative to the strong coffee on offer. The other day staff drifted off to their rooms, leaving Margaret and Charlotte alone.

This is my chance, thought Charlotte.

CHAPTER 10

'So, Charlotte, how do you think you're settling in with us?' Margaret sipped her drink.

Charlotte spread her hands round her cup. 'Well, I feel I'm finding my feet at last, mainly thanks to your help. And Matron's lecture also cleared some things up for me. But I'm still a bit puzzled about all those weights and measures.'

Margaret smiled. 'It will come – don't worry about it.' She paused. 'Charlotte, please don't take offence, but are you a qualified nurse?'

'No offence taken at all. And yes, I am.' Where's this going, she wondered.

'The thing is, I can't understand why you don't know anything about the administration of medicines and other things like fomentations and bandaging.'

Charlotte put her cup on the table. 'I can understand your confusion, Margaret. All I can say is that my training was very different from yours. And we use the metric system all the time.'

'Hmm.' Margaret sounded unconvinced. 'The other thing that's puzzling is why you don't have any post. I don't mean to pry but I wonder if perhaps you've run away from home?'

Charlotte laughed. 'No. No, I haven't run away from home. But it's true to say that my family has no idea where I am.'

Keen to deflect Margaret's questions, Charlotte seized her opportunity.

'Margaret, can I ask you something?'

'Of course.'

'Why did you mention Micropore, the adhesive tape, when we were in the clinical room earlier?'

'Micropore?' Margaret wore a quizzical expression. 'Have you ever used it, then?'

'Yes – for securing dressings. Have you?'

Margaret shook her head. 'No, but I've heard that's what it is for. But how on earth could you know that, Charlotte? I've mentioned it to every new nurse I've worked with since I discovered it but you're the only one who has known what it is.'

Margaret hesitated for a moment before continuing. 'I don't think you'd believe me if I told you.'

'Try me.'

Margaret leaned closer. 'Can I trust you not to tell anyone else what I'm about to share with you?'

'Absolutely.'

Margaret's eyes were fixed on Charlotte's. Then she said quietly, 'I have a lovely friend called Gillian. We did our training together in Newcastle. And during our second year, something very strange happened to her.'

She hesitated. 'Oh, I can't say any more. It's so unbelievable you'll think I've gone completely mad if I tell you. I promised Gillian I would never speak about it.'

'Margaret, I don't think I will. In fact, I wonder if your friend and I share something in common. Please – tell me what happened to her.'

Margaret took a deep breath. 'She was on the train going from Newcastle to London to visit her aunt and she fell asleep. When she awoke, she was on another train, but unlike any train she had ever been on. It was nearing Edinburgh, so going in the opposite direction ...' She paused again.

'Go on,' said Charlotte gently, leaning forward in her chair.

Another deep breath. 'She told me she found herself in a different time. A time in the future.'

Margaret said the words quickly, as if she didn't believe them herself. 'She had a note in her bag to say that she was expected for a surgical placement at a hospital in Leith as part of a student exchange. The strangest thing was that her clothes, bag, even her purse had money in it although she didn't recognise any of the things. There was even a reference from a woman at our hospital in Newcastle whom neither of us knew. She was given instructions on how to find the hospital and the particular ward she had to report to. She had an allocated room, as well as a uniform.

I thought at the time it was a tall tale and she made me promise I wouldn't tell a soul. She said it felt like the most vivid dream she had ever had.'

Charlotte was stunned. She leant back. 'Wow, that's an amazing story.' She thought for a moment. 'But why are you telling me now?'

'It's just something about you reminds me of her description of the other students and trained nurses she met when she was there. Your manner, your confidence, the way you stand up for yourself.'

Margaret's eyes were wide. She seemed excited. 'Charlotte, you're so different to most of the people here. There are so many things that you should know about but don't – and some of the things you talk about just don't fit. But what you just told me about temperatures and weights and measures – that reminds me of what Gillian said as well. So my third theory is ... Oh, I can't believe I'm saying this. It's so far-fetched ...'

She looked around, as if checking that no one was listening. Then, in a voice barely above a whisper, she said, 'Charlotte, tell me ... Are you are from the future?'

There was silence for a moment. Then Margaret, her face slightly flushed, straightened her uniform and brushed some imagined crumbs from the table. 'Oh, just listen to me,' she said, looking away. 'It's too ridiculous to contemplate. You must think I'm completely deranged for even suggesting such a thing.'

Charlotte hesitated. 'Margaret,' she said. They looked directly at one another. 'I know this seems completely unbelievable ...' She gave a little dry laugh. 'But yes, I am from the future. And like your friend, I was on a train when I fell asleep. It was going to York from Aberdeen and ... Well, when I awoke, I found myself here. And just like her, I had papers in my bag, a suitcase with a uniform. And if you remember that evening, you were expecting me. You can probably guess how confused I was.'

Margaret put her hand over Charlotte's. 'Daisy and I thought you were just homesick. But it does all make more sense now.'

Charlotte started to cry. Margaret held her hand tighter.

'Are you alright?'

Charlotte nodded. Then, with tears welling, she said. 'It's such a relief to tell someone – to know I'm not ... lost.' She wiped her eyes. 'I can't describe what that feels like. And knowing this has happened to someone else as well – that's comforting for me.' Her tears were flowing freely. 'I've been so frightened – terrified – that I'm completely stuck here and that I'd never see my family again.'

Margaret tried to comfort her. 'Look, if it's any consolation, Gillian felt so scared, too. She thought she had been – I don't know – *transported* permanently. But once she found out it was only going to be temporary, she said that she was able to enjoy it. Perhaps you can, too.' She spoke eagerly, trying her best to encourage Charlotte. 'You'll see – suddenly you'll find yourself back in your own time. It's just something you don't appear to have any control over.'

'But I don't understand. How did Gillian know it was only temporary?'

'One of the other nurses who'd been assigned to look after her took her aside during the experience and confessed that she too had been on a train to Newcastle from Edinburgh, fell asleep and woke up in Belgium in 1915 for three days. She thought then that it might only be temporary and that gave her a bit more reassurance.'

'How long was your friend there for – before she ... came back?' Charlotte asked. She wiped her eyes again.

'Well, she said the experience lasted about four days. But the strangest thing was, once Gillian did return, no time had passed at all.'

'None at all? Really?'

'When she awoke again, the train was just south of Peterborough. It was just as if she'd been asleep for a couple of hours.'

'So how did Gillian get back then?'

'She was told to escort a patient down to some hospital in the Scottish Borders somewhere and had to get a bus back to Edinburgh. That was a frightening experience for her as the bus seemed to go so fast and she was sure it would go off the road. But somehow, she managed to fall asleep on the bus, and when she awoke, she realised that she was back on the train she'd been on originally.'

'What year did Gillian find herself in?'

'1977. July.'

'Did you say that it was a hospital in Leith? The weird thing is that I was there as a student nurse that year. Just think – I could have met Gillian as well.'

'I think I have a photograph of her in my album so you can check.'

Through her tears, Charlotte said, 'Margaret, this is so amazing. I've found someone I can confide in.' Her voice cracked as she spoke. 'But more importantly, you've given me hope – hope that I'll get home again. Oh, I've been so frightened I'd be trapped here and that my family would be so worried about what had happened to me. Honestly, it's such a relief to know that if time isn't passing at the same rate while I'm here, then I don't need to worry. I must still be on the train ...' Her voice trailed away.

She hesitated, then pulled herself upright. 'I'm sorry for that little outburst, Margaret. It seems so selfish of me, but I can't tell you what a relief this is. But go on – please. I'd love to hear more about Gillian's experience.'

'"Incredible" was her description,' said Margaret. 'Like you, some of it was so familiar, but most of the time she felt like she was in a foreign country. All the talk around her was about things she didn't understand or know about, so she said she had to keep asking questions. Because she was a student nurse, no one had high expectations of her ability so she managed to go along with it all. Tell me, is that what it's like for you?'

Charlotte nodded eagerly. 'Yes, exactly like that. As you've seen, some things are familiar to me but the equipment, the treatments, the options for medication – they're all completely different. That's why I have to keep asking questions. And you've been so kind and patient with me – I'm really grateful to you.'

Margaret smiled. 'Well, there was something so friendly about you from the moment we met you at the station. But you know, most of all, it's your approach to life that I notice, Charlotte. At first I thought you were nervous about working here. But I've heard you mention things that we don't have, like house alarms. And as a qualified nurse, you really should know more about the medicines and treatments we use – fomentations, for example.'

'Oh, yes, I know,' Charlotte said. 'I was really tripped up by that alarm incident. And I have to admit that Matron's lecture was very useful – even though I think she saw it as some punishment exercise.'

'Also,' Margaret went on, 'you hesitate whenever you're asked about your home life.'

'You're right. I was caught out by Matron when I first met her and she asked me when I qualified. I was rapidly trying to work out what twenty years before 1916 would be, but couldn't do the sum fast enough. I was just in such a state of shock about my surroundings. I should've just said 1979 to see her reaction.'

'That's such a long time in the future for me – 1979. It seems strange even to say that number. So, tell me, who are you and what do you do in your normal world then?'

'Well, I'm married with three children and I work part-time in a palliative care ward.'

Margaret held up her hand. 'Charlotte, stop. You're talking about things I don't understand again. I think you mentioned it when we met but what do you mean by a "palliative care ward"?'

'We provide care for people who are approaching the end of their lives – people for whom there's no cure. Quite often our patients have cancer but some have other conditions.'

'That sounds like the work I was doing before I came out to work in France. Most of the illnesses that we see have no cure, you know.'

'Yes, I suppose that's right. I'd never thought of it like that.'

Margaret said, 'It just sounds like good nursing care to me. But it does explain your eagerness to look after the men in the side room, doesn't it?'

Charlotte nodded. 'I find the thought of leaving them alone to die completely alien when I compare it to our work at home.'

'That will make this experience difficult for you. As you've seen, our mission is to return men to service again, and that takes up so much of our time that the dying are seen as "surplus to requirements", so to speak.'

Charlotte thought about it. 'I suppose I can see that. But I still find it difficult to accept.'

Margaret said, 'Tell me, do many married women work?'

'Yes, it's common – and usually a necessity because it helps bring in some extra money. In fact, all my friends work at least part-time.'

'That's unheard of for us. In my family, it would be seen as a loss of status for a man if a woman worked. If I were to marry, I'd have to give up my career.'

'I'd find that tough – although sometimes it's hard to juggle work and home life. That's why I was on the train. At times, it all just becomes a bit overwhelming so my husband and children agreed that I should go and spend a few days with my family in Yorkshire.'

'And do you have help with the children?'

'No. Because I work part-time, I have to be there for them coming home from school. That's what causes the most stress for me, if I'm honest. I'm always looking at the clock. I can't tell you how many times I have had to run down the road from work to make sure I'm home in time. Honestly, I often feel like I don't do anything particularly well because I'm spread so thinly.'

'Yes, that sounds like a challenge.' Margaret thought for a moment. 'I have so many questions to ask you. Perhaps when we have our half-day off we could go to Albert and find a café and sit and have a real discussion about it all. But I've got two more questions to ask, then we really must turn in or we won't be up in time for work tomorrow. The first question is, will you promise me that you won't mention a word of this to anyone else?'

'Of course,' Charlotte said. 'And the same goes for me, by the way. What's the other question?' She was expecting to be asked when the war would finish.

'What year have you come from?'

'2001.'

Margaret gave a little gasp and put her hand over her mouth. 'Next century! Oh, that is truly unbelievable!'

They left the mess and headed wearily for the stairs. It had been a busy day – but so illuminating, Charlotte thought. As they were passing the front hall, she noticed the seat that Sister Craig usually sat in was empty.

'Where's Sister Craig's room?' she asked Margaret.

'Upstairs in the main hallway, near the ward entrance.'

'Do you think I would be able to knock on her door and speak to her?'

'Why would you want to do that?'

'Well, I'm concerned about her. She looked so upset when she came into the ward with Matron earlier.'

'It would be a rather unusual thing to do.' Margaret laughed. 'But then we're talking about you, Charlotte.'

As they walked round the balcony on the first floor, Margaret pointed to a door. 'There it is, but don't be surprised if she doesn't answer.'

'Thanks, I won't be long. See you in a minute.'

She knocked on Sister Craig's door.

'Yes, who's there?'

'It's Nurse Robertson, Sister Craig. I was just wondering if I could have a word with you, please?'

There was silence for a moment, then, 'Give me a minute.'

A couple of seconds later the door partially opened and Sister Craig was standing there in her dressing gown.

'What can I do for you, Nurse Robertson? This is rather irregular, you know.'

'Sorry to disturb you, Sister Craig, but I wanted to ask if you're alright. I couldn't help but notice that you looked rather upset when you came into the ward earlier.'

Sister Craig looked Charlotte in the eye and said, 'Come in from the corridor.'

The small room had a homely feel. There were some photographs in silver frames on the mantelpiece and dressing table. The wardrobe door was open and Charlotte could see a bag on the floor with folded-up clothes in it. She said nothing for a moment as she felt Sister Craig was about to speak.

'That's kind of you to come and see me – but you surprised me.' Sister Craig hesitated before saying, 'Can I confide in you?'

'Yes, of course.'

'Sit down, Charlotte. You don't mind if I call you by your first name, do you?'

'Of course not.'

Charlotte sat on the little bedroom chair by the fireplace. She didn't know that Sister knew her first name.

'It's been a terribly stressful day.' Sister Craig perched on the edge of her bed. 'You may have heard at morning orders that I was summoned to a meeting with Matron at the Divisional Headquarters in Albert. The Matron in Chief herself was there.'

'Goodness,' said Charlotte. 'That sounds intimidating.'

'There've been some complaints about the state of the men on their arrival at the base hospitals near the coast and over in England.'

'What sort of complaints?'

'Well, on a few occasions the required paperwork has not accompanied the soldiers as they've left here. And there have been some soldiers leaving the ward unwashed.'

'Have these things been happening regularly? Or do they relate to one particular period?'

'Gosh, I don't know.' Sister Craig thought for moment. 'That's right – they relate to the time since August mainly.'

'Sister, when did you start in your post on the surgical ward?'

'The beginning of August.'

'Was there a gap between the previous Sister leaving and you starting?'

'Yes, I do believe they were without a Sister for about three weeks. I'm not sure what that's got to do with anything, though. The reality is that I feel overwhelmed with everything at the moment and I'm beginning to wonder if I'm suited to this sort of work.'

Charlotte persisted. 'Have you been a Sister in another ward or is this your first promoted post?'

'Actually, I was a Sister in a surgical ward in Bristol– a rather busy place.'

'And did you manage that work?'

'Well, yes, but I had a lovely team. I wish they were here as well.'

'It sounds as though you've been through the mill with all of this. What do you think Matron McLean is thinking?'

'Actually, she's been more supportive than I expected she might be, even though, as you know, she is very hard to please. After my meeting had finished, I had to wait while she spoke to the Senior Matron alone. She was almost sweet to me on the way back here. The recommendation is that I spend a couple of days at another unit, starting tomorrow.'

Sister Craig stood. 'Now, I do appreciate your concern but think I've said enough for now.' She looked directly at Charlotte. 'I am relying on your discretion.'

'Of course, Sister.'

'Thank you. I'm hoping for a better sleep now that the meeting is over. Good night to you.' She tied her dressing gown tight around her. 'By the way, I'll be recommending to Matron that Nurse Wishaw takes charge in the ward tomorrow.'

Charlotte crossed to the door, then turned. 'Well, I'm glad to have had the chance to speak to you tonight, Sister.'

* * *

'Where have you been?' said Daisy. She was putting the finishing touches to the sketch she had done of Charlotte.

'Oh, I bumped into Sister and was catching up on the ward news.'

'I say, Charlotte, please would you let me send this one home to my mother?' Daisy held up the sketch. 'I'm sure she doesn't believe I'm sharing a room with such a modern girl.'

Charlotte laughed. 'Of course you can if you wish. You've captured a likeness of me.'

Margaret smiled.

Charlotte felt in need of another soak in the bath. She gathered her things and walked along to the bathroom, locking the door behind her. She turned the taps on and when the bath was full she climbed in and lay back.

What a difference that conversation with Margaret had made to her whole outlook. She was neither missing, nor trapped here in this foreign land. This whole experience had given her an opportunity to rekindle her love for nursing work and, more importantly, helped to re-build her confidence. She had witnessed uncertainty in so many of the people she had met that it helped put her own life into perspective. She felt gratitude for the life that she had in comparison to Sister Craig, who was so stressed, and the patients with life-altering injuries. Even if this is all a dream, I can learn from it, she thought. And what a remarkable coincidence that one of Margaret's friends had been on a similar adventure, even if it was into the future. I wonder if I did meet her. If I did, I do hope I was like Margaret, not Nurse Brook.

Perhaps she would recognise Gillian in a photograph. She tried to remember when exactly she had been at Leith Hospital during 1977.

She began crying again but this time she shed tears of relief. She was overjoyed that, as far as everyone knew, she was still on the train to York.

She got out of the bath, dried herself and put on her nightdress. When she walked back into the bedroom, Margaret was looking at a photograph.

'This is Gillian, who I told you about,' she said, handing the photo to Charlotte. It showed a pretty dark-haired girl leaning out of a window, waving a handkerchief.

'Oh I do remember her!' Charlotte said. 'She was so quiet and we all encouraged her to ask questions as we thought she was shy. When she didn't come back after the escort duty, we thought she had decided to finish her placement early.'

As Daisy was in the room, Charlotte was reluctant to say more, even though she could see that Margaret was desperate to ask further questions.

Later, climbing into bed, she felt a kind of lightness in her spirit. She knew she had a good chance of returning to her normal life at some point, even if she didn't know when. She was also consoled by knowing that she wasn't a 'missing person'. That possibility had troubled her and it was a great relief to know she could stop worrying about it. Now she could focus on absorbing every ounce of this experience. She didn't even notice the lumps in the mattress as she lay there, slowly becoming sleepier. She had no need to cross her fingers tonight.

She was awoken by a sudden exchange of artillery fire and a shell landing on one of the outbuildings in the hospital grounds – a rude reminder of the reality of being so close to the front line. The scudding, screaming noise of the impact was terrifying and so loud that everyone was instantly awake. Even the main hospital building seemed to shake.

'What in the name of the Lord was that?' cried Margaret. Her bed was closest to the window so she was able to peer out. 'A shell's hit the cottage! Oh dear God. Quick, we must go and see if Monique and her family are alright.'

In an instant the three nurses were pulling on their dressing gowns and shoes.

They fumbled their way along the dark corridor, ran around the balcony and down the main staircase, along the hallway past the kitchen and out into the courtyard. They saw Tom, Sandy and Captain Clift who were all heading in the same direction.

As they approached the cottage, they could see it had taken a direct hit and was in ruins. Little Monique stood amid the rubble, distressed, but not evidently injured.

'*Monique, où sont ta mère et grandmère?*' called Charlotte, trying to keep the panic from her voice.

'*Ne sais pas.*' The little girl sobbed. Charlotte took her hand and held it tightly. She had never been in a situation like this before and had no idea what to do. What was left of the building looked precarious. She didn't want to start moving anything in case doing so made it more dangerous for the little rescue party.

She heard Captain Clift issue issuing instructions. 'Let's see if we can find the mother. Does anyone else live here with them?'

'Just the grandma,' Sandy called.

They began carefully looking through the ruins in search of the two women. An arm was sticking out from under some fallen masonry. It was in a very unnatural position and with some desperate manoeuvring of the rubble, it soon became evident that the person lying under all the wood and masonry was dead.

'That's the grandmother,' said Tom quietly. 'But where's the mother?'

They kept looking and calling. Ten minutes later they found her, pinned under a large oak dresser that had fallen on her.

Daisy crouched beside her. 'I think she's still alive.'

There was blood on the floor. 'She must be severely injured,' said Captain Clift. 'We've got to move this dresser.'

It was huge and heavy but between them they managed to lift it.

'Is there anything we can do for her?' Margaret asked.

'Well, strictly speaking, we aren't meant to treat civilians,' Captain Clift said. 'But as she's part of the hospital staff, let's take her over to one of the assessment rooms and see what can be done.' More quietly he said, 'I'm not hopeful.'

Tom had found a stretcher and carefully they moved Huguette on to it. Tom and Sandy carried her over to the hospital.

'Monique, will you come with me, please?' said Charlotte, still holding the girl's hand. Monique had found her little doll and was clutching it tightly with her other arm.

When the rescue party returned to the hospital, Tom asked if there was anything else he could do.

'Perhaps you could go to Albert to find her uncle and ask if they'll take Monique to be looked after,' Margaret suggested. 'She can't stay here.'

Captain Clift said, 'Good idea, Nurse Wishaw.'

'I think I know where they live,' said Tom. 'It's on this side of the town so it shouldn't take me too long.'

'I'll come with you, Tom,' Daisy said. Charlotte smiled at her, admiring her bravery. Tom looked pleased and he and Daisy set off across the yard towards the ambulance.

Margaret asked Charlotte if she wanted any help with their latest patient.

'No, I'm happy to stay up,' Charlotte said. 'Why don't you go back to our room? It won't be long until we're all back on duty and it might be better if at least one of us has some sleep.'

'Well, if you're sure. Good luck.'

As they were crossing the courtyard towards the back door, Charlotte glanced up and saw Fiona Collinson wave to her. She had been watching the unfolding events from the hall window outside the ward. Charlotte thought about the soldiers up there in their beds and how terrifying the noise must have been for them. It must have felt as though they were in the front line again.

Captain Clift and Sandy had managed to get Huguette into the assessment room on the ground floor where they could examine her properly. Charlotte cut open the woman's clothing so Captain Clift could assess her injuries and found a sheet to cover her. It was obvious from her breathing that she was fatally injured.

Captain Clift spent several minutes examining her, and then said quietly, 'I don't think there's much we can do for her. She has a flail chest. Look how it's moving in different sections. Her breathing is laboured and her pulse is thready. I don't think she'll survive very long, certainly not the night.'

'Well, I'll stay with her,' said Charlotte. 'But first, I'll bring Monique in to see her.'

Captain Clift said, 'No, no, I don't think that's at all appropriate.'

Charlotte protested. 'But Captain Clift, Monique needs to know that we're going to look after her mother. It'll be the last time she sees her, and if we don't allow her, she'll wonder what's happened to her.'

But Captain Clift was adamant. 'It's just not done, Nurse Robertson. I refuse to have anything to do with it. You do have some very strange ideas. I can't imagine where on earth you learned this one.' Then his tone softened. 'I should probably report you but are you willing to take responsibility for your actions?'

'Completely.'

He nodded. 'On your head be it, then.'

Charlotte put Huguette's arms into a theatre gown and tidied up her face and hair, wiping the marks off her face. While Captain Clift was putting away his examination equipment in the corner of the room, Charlotte went out into the hallway and found Monique sitting on a chair, still clutching her doll.

'Come with me, please, Monique,' Charlotte whispered in French. 'I want to take you in to see your mother.'

They walked back to the assessment room. Charlotte opened the door and ushered the girl in.

'Look, here she is. She's not very well because of that loud explosion, but we're caring for after her as best we can.'

Monique said nothing but reached out and touched her mother's hand.

'*Mama?*' she said, starting to cry again.

Charlotte took the little girl back to the front hall, where they sat and waited until Tom reappeared.

He said, 'I've found Monique's uncle and he's come to take her back to his farm.'

'Thanks, Tom.' Charlotte felt relieved that Monique wouldn't have to stay in the room too long. She turned to the girl and said, 'Monique, your uncle has come to take you to Albert. I think it'd be good if you would give your mother a kiss goodbye.'

She led Monique back to where Huguette lay and lifted up the little girl so she could give her mother a last kiss. Monique then placed the doll's face against her mother's cheek too, as though she was also kissing her.

'That was a sweet thing to do for her,' said Charlotte.

As they left the room, she noticed that Captain Clift's back was turned to her but she distinctly heard him sniffing and the sound of him blowing his nose.

They walked out through the kitchen into the yard where Monique's uncle was waiting.

'Do you speak any French, *mademoiselle*?'

'A little.'

'Did the old lady survive?'

'I'm sorry, but no, she didn't. She was dead when we arrived at the cottage after the explosion.'

'And the mother, Huguette, how badly is she injured?' he asked slowly.

'I'm so sorry but she's been very badly hurt.'

'I see.' The man shook his head sadly. 'Will she ... survive?'

Charlotte was aware of the enormous impact her answer would have. 'One of our doctors has examined her and I have to tell you that we don't think she will – I'm very sorry.'

The man looked at his feet.

Charlotte said, 'But I want you to know that we're looking after her as well as we can. Do you wish to see her?'

He shook his head again then lifted Monique on to the back of the small cart. He offered her no words of consolation.

To Charlotte he said, 'No. It's more important to take the child to our home. Huguette is my wife's sister so we'll take good care of her, you know.'

'Thank you. I'll tell Huguette when I go back inside,' said Charlotte.

'Come on, child, let's get going now.' As they turned to leave, the uncle leant down from the cart and said to Charlotte, 'Please make sure she doesn't suffer.'

Charlotte held out her hand to him and nodded. 'I'll stay with her. She won't be alone.'

She watched as the cart rolled out of the yard, Monique huddled on the back, clutching her doll and crying silently. Charlotte blew her a kiss and thought how small and abandoned the girl looked.

Sandy had been back to the ruined house and had managed to pull the old woman's body from the rubble. She was lying beneath a sheet on a trolley that he was wheeling across the courtyard.

'I wouldn't look if I were you. Her face was severely injured,' he said. 'But I couldn't leave her there like that. We can arrange for her to be buried in the morning.'

'What on earth will happen to that little girl?' Charlotte asked.

'Hard to say. But at least she has some family who can give her food and shelter.'

'What a traumatic experience for her, though. In the space of a couple of hours, her world has turned upside down. Her mother and grandmother are gone, as well as her house, and now she's being taken to live elsewhere.'

'Aye, it's one of the many awful consequences of this war,' Sandy said.

'Poor wee mite. I just feel so sorry for her.'

Tom and Daisy had come back out into the courtyard to see Monique depart with her uncle. Tom had his arm around Daisy's shoulders. Well, thought Charlotte, perhaps something positive might come of this suffering.

Back in the assessment room, Huguette was alone. Even in the short time Charlotte had been out of the room, her condition had changed. Her breathing was worse – it was starting and stopping now, and there was a rattling noise coming from her throat. She had also developed a deathly pallor. Charlotte touched her hand – it was cold and mottled – to let her know she had returned. If I were at home, thought Charlotte, I would be asking one of the doctors if we could prescribe something but that's not going to happen here.

A few minutes later, Captain Clift returned.

'How is she?'

'I don't think she has long now,' said Charlotte softly. 'Her breathing's very laboured and she has a noisy rattle in her throat. I'm glad the little girl didn't have to hear that.'

'Quite,' he said. 'I'm going to see the patients in the ward but I'll be back shortly. I'll bring some atropine down with me to see if that allays the secretions at all.'

Charlotte leant over and said in broken French, 'Huguette, I want you to know that we have called for your brother-in-law and he has taken Monique away to Albert to be looked after at your sister's house. He has promised to take care of her and I said that I would tell you.'

Shortly after, Huguette's breathing stopped and Charlotte could see that she had died. She straightened out her arms and covered her with a sheet. When Captain Clift returned, he confirmed the death.

'So what do we do with her now?' asked Charlotte.

'Well, let's ask Tom to call the local priest and she can be buried along with her mother in the graveyard in the village.'

And that was how the evening ended, with the two bodies being taken to the local chapel by Sandy and one of the orderlies working on night duty.

Charlotte knew that her mind was too active to allow her to go back to bed immediately and she didn't want to simply lie awake in the dark. Instead, she went to the kitchen to find something to drink. She didn't hear Captain Clift enter the kitchen behind her and turned round with a start when he said, 'I've never seen anything like that. Who taught you to involve children?'

Charlotte hesitated. 'It's our regular practice at work. We try to do it if we can.'

Captain Clift was looking at the floor with his arms crossed. 'My mother died when I was a child,' he continued, almost as if he hadn't heard her reply. 'I longed to say goodbye to her but I wasn't allowed. I was always told that it would be harmful, but having seen what you did tonight, I'm sure you'll have helped that little girl in the long run.'

'That must have been tough for you.'

He nodded. 'Bloody awful, as a matter of fact. It's always there at the back of one's mind – that I was not able to say goodbye to her.'

He was fighting to maintain his composure and Charlotte was astonished to see him push his feelings away and return to the present and the mundane task of making coffee. She wondered how he managed it.

'Right then,' he said. 'Think I'll turn in now.'

'Yes, no doubt it will be another busy day tomorrow,' Charlotte said. 'Good night.'

She finished her drink and made her way upstairs. But instead of going to her room, she went to the ward instead. As she had expected, the door to the side room was open. She could see Fiona Collinson sitting at the desk in the centre of the ward, bathed in low lamplight. She became aware of Charlotte's presence and came over to the door to speak to her.

'Hello, Charlotte. What are you doing here?'

Charlotte smiled. 'Well, my mind's racing after what happened this evening and I'm not ready to go to my bed yet so I thought I'd come and see how everyone is. I saw you looking out of the window watching that awful event.'

'That's thoughtful of you. But don't let Matron know. You're not allowed to be in the ward if you're off duty, you know. What happened to the mother?'

'I'm afraid she died about an hour ago.'

'Some of the men got a real fright and poor Brown wet the bed with terror. It's the only time I've heard him say anything, and even then it was more of a loud groan.'

'Poor things. It must have been very scary for them. Is anyone in the side room tonight?'

'No,' said Nurse Collinson. 'But it wouldn't surprise me if Fellows and Beattie are moved through later as neither are doing well. Now, I suggest that you try and get some sleep. It's three in the morning and you'll be back on duty soon.'

Charlotte yawned. 'You're right. I'll head off and try to still my mind so I can sleep. See you in the morning.'

As she walked along the corridor to her room, she could hear the strains of Beethoven coming from one of the other bedrooms. She wondered if it was Captain Clift who found solace in music.

Her roommates had managed to get back to sleep but had left the lamp on for her. She climbed into her bed, dimmed the light and lay back. She wondered why Matron McLean, Sister Craig or Nurse Brook had not put in an appearance during the entire disturbance. She would have expected Matron to take command of such a commotion and everyone in the building must have heard what was going. Rather strange, she thought.

But what a day it had been. The elation she had felt following the conversation with Margaret was now replaced with a tremendous sense of sadness for Monique who had witnessed the deaths of both her mother and grandmother.

When everything was put in perspective like that, it confirmed Charlotte's own thoughts that her own problems were not quite so bad.

She closed her eyes.

CHAPTER 11

Charlotte managed a few hours' sleep and when she woke was relieved to have had some rest. She often had trouble getting to sleep or she would wake early, especially if she had things on her mind. She would often lie awake at home, worrying about the uncertainty of the future or her perceived failings as a wife, mother and nurse. So it puzzled her that she had slept after such a traumatic evening.

Daisy was still fast asleep so Margaret and Charlotte got dressed quietly. Charlotte's neck was now raw from the starched collar, despite her best efforts to soothe it using cold cream. Her skin stung as the collar came in contact with it.

Down in the mess, the other staff were discussing the previous night's events over their bread and coffee.

'I heard the mother was killed as well,' someone said. Charlotte could have explained in detail what had happened but she had neither the inclination nor the energy. Instead she sat quietly and ate her bread, dunking it carefully in the bowl of warm coffee.

Margaret said, 'Right, I suppose we should go up and start our day.' Perhaps she felt the same way about reliving what happened.

'Sounds like a good idea,' said Charlotte. Then she added, 'Margaret, I have to say that with each day that I'm here, I feel more confident about the work. And that's largely down to your kindness towards me, you know. When your friend Gill was on her placement in Leith, did she say if there was someone who took her under their wing?'

Margaret thought for a moment. 'Yes, there was a senior student called Louise who didn't let Gill out of her sight. Gill said that she was incredibly knowledgeable and was so patient with her, even though she knew so little. That seems just like you, Charlotte.'

'It does help though, doesn't it?' said Charlotte. 'I find it amazing to think that there's a person who's not only willing and able to mentor a colleague like me who has arrived out of nowhere, but always seems to be there at the right time. I can't imagine how I would have managed without you. I would have been in pieces.'

Margaret smiled. 'That's kind of you, Charlotte, I appreciate it. And I think you'd do the same.'

Sandy was in his usual position, mopping the upstairs hall. 'That was a bad business last night, wasn't it?' he said. 'I made contact with the priest a couple of hours ago and he's taken the bodies to the churchyard already.'

'That was good of you, Sandy. It's a shame there's no time to go there – I would've liked to go and pay my respects,' said Charlotte.

Margaret said, 'Charlotte, if you went to every burial, you would never be on duty.'

'If it's any consolation, I was there,' Sandy said. 'It's kind of you to thank me but I would say the same to you quines. It was good of all of you to help last night as not everybody chose to, so I admire your bravery.'

The two nurses thanked him and went into the ward.

'Do you understand his accent?' asked Margaret.

'Of course. Why do you ask?'

'What was that word he used? "Quines"? What did he mean?'

Charlotte laughed. 'That's Aberdonian for "girls". How nice it is to tell you something for a change!'

They were surprised to find Matron sitting at the desk in the ward. Sister Craig was nowhere to be seen and Charlotte remembered what she had said to her, in confidence, last night. She felt disloyal saying nothing about it to Margaret but she had given her word to Sister and didn't feel she could betray her trust. The previous night's events had distracted her so much she had forgotten a lot of the conversation.

Fiona Collinson was ready to present the review of the night and Charlotte noticed that she said nothing about Brown in bed twelve being incontinent as a result of the shelling. How discrete that is, she thought. That's the sort of information that doesn't need to be reported.

The report followed the pattern of the previous days. There had been two new admissions overnight after Charlotte had visited the ward and probably as a result of the artillery strike. That meant Captain Clift must have been up to the ward again.

Curiously, Matron McLean made no mention at all about last night's incident. She seemed more annoyed about the admissions again but for a different reason today.

'I don't understand why we have had admissions overnight. We were not on "take" last night. I'm going to follow this up this morning.'

As before, there were some new names to add to Charlotte's list who would be going to the operating theatre today. One of the men sounded as though he had a particularly nasty wound on his buttock. The condition of a few patients was deteriorating, including Brown, with the fractured jaw, Fellows, Beattie and Stills.

A couple of issues stood out over and above the planning for the patients who were due to go for surgery, treatment or discharge. One was that Matron thanked Nurse Collinson for ensuring the proper order of the ward overnight – and by the expression on Nurse Collinson's face, she was amazed as well. 'Thank you, Matron McLean,' she stammered.

Matron then said, 'In the absence of Sister Craig today, I am assuming command of the ward. If I am called away, Nurse Wishaw, you will deputise for me?'

'Of course, Matron,' said Margaret. Charlotte noticed that Nurse Brook looked irritated not to be selected but Matron's choice of leader was a relief for the whole team, all of whom admired the quiet confidence of Margaret, although she herself was uncertain of her leadership skills.

'Nurse Robertson, you will attend to the dressings today,' Matron went on. 'Nurse Brook, please complete the observations and the specials, and Nurse Wishaw, please attend to any admissions, discharges and medicines. I will leave the remaining planning in your capable hands.'

The other issue Matron raised concerned Lieutenant Brown. She announced that special attention must be given to him to ensure he didn't develop a wound infection. It appeared that he had attempted to remove his dressings overnight and Charlotte wondered whether he had already begun to become septic if he was doing that. Furthermore, based on what Fiona Collinson had told her about the aftermath of the artillery strike, the poor man seemed to be incredibly scared about his injury.

With morning orders complete, the rhythm of the ward day began and the chatter of voices as the breakfasts were served. Charlotte reviewed the dressings book and counted twenty-four she had to do. She considered the order in which she should do them so she would lessen the risk of passing on an infection. However, her plan to start with the cleanest wound first was thrown into disarray because she had to attend to Lieutenant Stills who seemed extremely restless.

As she approached his bed, she could see his temperature chart hanging above it. His fever was still high, at one hundred and two degrees.

'Good morning, Lieutenant Stills.'

He clawed at his sheets. 'Where am I?'

'You were injured and are in the hospital. Do you remember?'

'When am I due back at school?'

'No, you're not due at school. Do you remember, you were injured in the fighting and you are now in hospital?' she said calmly.

'Where am I? Is it time for prep?' He tried – and failed – to get up.

'You're not at school,' Charlotte repeated. She then explained again where he was.

The Souttar's infusion had been ongoing overnight but the wound looked as revolting as it did the evening before. If anything, the tissue looked soggier. And the contents of his bedpan were enough to make the strongest stomach turn. Charlotte started mouth-breathing again to lessen the stench of rotting flesh as she removed it. The instruction had been to stop the infusion until the ward round, which she now did, and she wondered what would happen to him today. It would not be long before he was moved into Darwin's room.

She covered the bedpan and took it to the sluice. Sarah, the VAD, was there and as Charlotte and the container entered, she started retching.

'Sorry, Sarah.' Charlotte laughed as she emptied the contents into the washer and quickly flushed the chain. 'At least I lifted the grate so nothing got stuck.'

Her attempt at humour simply made Sarah vomit her breakfast into the sink.

'I'll never get used to this,' she said, groaning.

'Sorry,' Charlotte said again. 'This stuff is especially grim.'

'How do you manage not to vomit?' Sarah was still leaning over the sink.

'I try to breathe through my mouth, which makes it just bearable. But to be honest, I'm only just holding on to my breakfast too. When I first started nursing, I spent a lot of time either being sick or fainting. It takes some getting used to.'

Back in the ward, she noticed Stills was trying to get out of bed again. He clearly had no understanding of what was happening to him. What did they use here to treat patients with delirium? She needed to tell someone. Margaret was nowhere to be seen but Matron was at the other end of the ward, looking out of the window. Charlotte walked over to her.

'Excuse me, Matron, but please could I speak to you about Lieutenant Stills?'

Matron turned to her. 'Yes, Nurse Robertson, what is it?'

'I'm concerned that he's becoming delirious. He has a fever of a hundred and two, he's disorientated and now he's trying to get out of bed. The exudate from his wound is still extremely offensive in spite of the Souttar's infusion, which has been running overnight.'

'Right,' said Matron. 'I thought this might happen. I will inform the doctor. Thank you, nurse, that was most comprehensive. Now get on with your duties.'

Wow, thought Charlotte. That was almost a compliment.

As she turned away, she saw that Lieutenant Brown had removed his dressing again. She went over to his bedside and asked if he was in pain. He tried to say something, but she couldn't quite make it out, so she went to the clinical room to set a trolley to re-do his dressing. Her schedule was not going to plan but that was the nature of this kind of work.

Back at his bedside, she noticed that the edges of his wound were slightly red and inflamed. His temperature was normal, however, as was his pulse.

'If you tell me why you're removing your dressing I'll try to replace it in a way that makes you a bit more comfortable.'

He lay still but his eyes were downcast. She stood in silence for a few moments but he didn't speak so she began replacing the dressing. Then he let her clean his mouth again. He had a spit mug with carbolic lotion at the bottom to act as a disinfectant and he made an attempt to spit out the Condy's solution that Charlotte used to clean his mouth but most of it simply dribbled down his chin.

She felt a sense of unease around this man but didn't know why. She thought she might ask others if they felt the same.

'I haven't had much to do with him,' said Margaret, who was in the preparation room when Charlotte was clearing the dressing trolley. Matron McLean came in having overheard something of their conversation. 'I can tell you why he is continually pulling at his wound,' she said forcefully. 'He is a coward.'

'A coward?' Charlotte said. I'm sorry, Matron, I don't understand.'

'His wound is self-inflicted and he is hoping that by introducing some infection into it, then it will absolve him of having to face up to his actions.'

'Face up to his actions? What does that mean?'

'A court martial followed by execution, I would imagine.'

Charlotte was shocked. The reason behind the extra attention the staff had been instructed to give Lieutenant Brown was now apparent.

'So let me see if I understand this situation,' she said in a clear, confident voice. 'We have a severely injured man who may well die as a result of his injuries, and we have to do our utmost to keep him alive so he can be taken back to his unit and shot for cowardice. Have I understood you correctly?'

Margaret looked at Charlotte with an incredulous expression. No one ever spoke to Matron or any other superior like that. Matron closed the door and then turned to face Charlotte.

'No,' she hissed. 'You are completely wrong, Nurse Robertson. We have a man who might encourage others to neglect their duties if such behaviour is condoned. So I repeat, the closest observation must be made of him so that justice can be served. I expect you to do your duty. And how dare you speak to me with such impertinence, Nurse Robertson. I will be putting you on a report and, believe me, you will hear more about this.' She spun round, opened the clinic room door and walked off.

Charlotte had never encountered anything like this. Her heart was pounding; she could feel her face flushing and her whole body shaking with a sense of injustice for Brown. She hoped he would succumb to a wound infection and would not have to be dealt with by the military. Her real world had clashed completely with this Edwardian, military one. She suddenly felt a flood of compassion towards that poor man. No wonder he was so withdrawn.

A short while later, Brown removed his dressing again and Charlotte saw him do it. She went into the clinical room to set up yet another tray so she could replace it. Nurse Brook was there, preparing a tray for some other procedure. She said, 'The sooner they take that man away and deal with him the better. He's taking up time and a bed that could be given to someone more deserving.'

Anger surged through Charlotte. 'Do you know, Nurse Brook, I think you are one of the most heartless people I have ever met. Why on earth did you become a nurse?'

She walked away, not waiting for a response.

Back at Brown's bedside, she decided to say something to him but kept her voice low.

'Tell me, what's your first name?'

No answer. His gaze remained fixed on his hands lying in his lap.

'Please tell me what your first name is?'

'Gilbert,' he whispered.

'I hope it's alright if I call you by that name.'

He gave a small, slow nod.

'I just wanted to say, Gilbert, that I think what you did took enormous courage, especially if you knew the potential consequences.'

He glanced briefly at her and then looked down at his hands again.

'I assume you know the likely consequences of your actions?'

He nodded once more, without raising his eyes. A drip of sputum dropped onto the sheet from his mouth. He whispered something. Charlotte had to concentrate hard to hear him over the noise of the ward,

'Just wished it had worked.'

'Is that why you keep on removing your dressing?'

Again he nodded.

'I feel so sorry for you. I know I can never understand what you've witnessed but for you to take the action you did, I think it must have been awful.'

'All my friends have gone, all six,' he said, his words still a whisper. 'We joined up together and I'm the last one. I just couldn't face it anymore. I've been here since the start. We all came out together.'

His gaze was still fixed on his hands.

'Last month, Bob was killed when he was out on patrol and his men brought his remains back in a sandbag. The final straw was last week, seeing Jack being blown up and then ... his boot ... dangling on the wire in front of me. That was all that was left of him.'

Charlotte swallowed. Her mouth was dry. 'That's dreadful for you. I can't imagine what that must be like. So you tried to shoot yourself? In the mouth?'

Slowly he raised his eyes to hers. 'Well, you can't change what's happened.'

His eyes fell again. 'Get on with whatever it is you have to do,' he muttered.

'I'll replace the dressing and clean your mouth for you again.'

'Just the dressing, nurse, then leave me. Please.'

Charlotte did as he asked but didn't secure the bandage very tightly over his head. She noticed that there was more discharge on the dressing he had removed and wondered if this and the slight changes she had seen around the edge of the wound heralded the start of an infection. In a way, she hoped they did. She saw, too, that his spit mug was empty.

'What happened to the contents, Gilbert?' she asked, pointing at the mug.

'It spilt,' he said, not looking up.

'Do I need to replace the sheet for you?'

'No, there wasn't much in it. Just leave me now.' Then he added, 'But thank you for offering.'

'If that's what you prefer.'

Charlotte returned the dressing trolley to the clinical room, feeling tremendous sadness, because of Brown's desperation and the lack of care shown by Matron McLean and Nurse Brook. But she hadn't disobeyed the order she'd been given. The dressing had been replaced even though her instinct was to leave it and encourage infection. She wondered how often this happened and what her roommates thought about such actions.

She continued with her dressings and noticed that Lieutenant Stills seemed to be less restless. As she passed his bed she saw he now appeared unaware of anything happening around him. Charlotte noted from his medical card that he had been given some chloral hydrate, which had sedated him almost entirely. His pulse rate had slowed which, according to Margaret, was a bad sign and during the ward round a decision was made to move him into the side room later in the day.

Beattie was still in a precarious condition. Charlotte was unsure if the curé had managed to visit again and wondered whether Beattie knew what was happening to him. Like Stills, he seemed to be sleepier today. Was his wound still leaking under the dressing?

In fact, Beattie did appear to know that he was in a perilous state. When he awoke as Charlotte approached his bed to attend to his dressing he was distressed. He understood from his work as a chaplain that because he had not been moved down the ward his condition remained serious. How quickly patients learn the routine, thought Charlotte. Just like staff. We signal their condition to them without any words at all.

Captain Graves felt it would be for the nurses to change Beattie's dressing if his wound had soaked through the bandage. Charlotte was nervous in case she dislodged something and caused a severe bleed but she was in luck. When she took off the top layer of padding, there was no staining on the inner gauze dressing.

'I can just leave this alone at the moment, Padre,' she said. That didn't comfort him at all.

'I should be able to face this with more courage but it's deserted me,' he said sadly.

'What do you mean?' Charlotte was re-padding the top layer of his dressing.

'I'm the one who's meant to have an intact faith, to be strong for others, but I feel terrified about what might happen to me.'

'Is that why you felt you wanted to speak to the curé again?'

'Yes, he's one of the few people who might have some understanding. I couldn't discuss such a thing with you, nurse, with all due respect.'

'Of course, I respect your wishes. I wish I could do more to console you.'

A set of folding screens had been placed near Beattie's bed and when she had an opportunity Charlotte asked Margaret about them.

'It's more because of what might happen to him,' Margaret said. 'He's likely to have a significant bleed and Matron won't want that happening in front of all the other soldiers. It's not good for morale.'

'Well, at least he's staying in the ward,' Charlotte said. She thought whatever happened to the padre, it couldn't be worse than seeing a friend's remains dangling on barbed wire like poor Brown.

Margaret said, 'We did have a chap a couple of months ago who had a major bleed in the side room. It was all rather ghastly to clean up afterwards.'

'That must have been awful. God, you must have seen some terrible sights while you've been here.'

Margaret sighed. 'The German artillery makes a terrible mess of bodies at times. I try to put such things to the back of my mind but it can be hard.'

Charlotte went to change the dressings on Thomson's legs. Even though he was still on the fracture bed, which must have been so uncomfortable to lie on, his mood was positive. He was reading a copy of a newspaper from home and catching up on relatively recent news.

'Good morning,' Charlotte said brightly. 'And how's my favourite Scottish Canadian doing today?'

'Chipper,' he said. 'I think I might be on the move soon. The doctor thinks I'm almost ready for my trip back home.'

'It'll be good for you to spend some time nearer your family before you go back to Canada,' said Charlotte.

He smiled. 'I'm looking forward to getting there.'

Charlotte began cleaning around his wounds but the skin was tense and rigid. She had been told about tetanus at Matron's lecture and wondered if he might have early symptoms.

She didn't want to worry her patient but thought she should mention it to Captain Clift in case it was a complication.

The next time Captain Clift appeared she mentioned it to him.

He said, 'I doubt it but it's possible, Nurse Robertson.'

He went and checked the wound and when he returned to the desk, he said, 'Yes, I think you're right. We might be seeing early tetanus. Let's have an anti-tetanus 500USA units injection and I'll notify the authorities. It'll undoubtedly mean a visit from the anti-tetanus officer so that will lessen my popularity with Matron. Do we know if he had his first anti-tetanus serum?'

Charlotte checked Thomson's card. There was a date, dose and signature recorded against the first injection.

'Well, it can happen even if the first anti-tetanus injection was given,' Captain Clift said. 'Hopefully, by acting on the early symptoms, full-blown tetanus will be avoided.'

Once there was a lull in the work, Charlotte was spared from her duties to go and have a cup of coffee. She took her cup and sat in one of the corners of the main hall for a change, mainly because the chairs looked so comfortable and she was now beginning to feel the effects of the night before. Sarah, the VAD, saw her and shyly made her way over.

'Hello, Nurse Robertson. Please, would you mind if I asked you a question?'

'Of course not. Why don't you get yourself a drink, then come and join me?'

'Are you sure?'

'It will do you good to have a soft seat for five minutes.'

When she returned with her coffee, Sarah sat down opposite Charlotte, who said, 'You had a question for me?'

It wasn't the work in the ward that Sarah wanted to speak about but news from home.

'I don't think I've told you that I have a younger brother. Please, can I ask your opinion about something my mother has written – in connection with him?'

Charlotte wondered what was coming but said she would help if she could.

Sarah said, 'Well, Simon is only twelve and he developed diabetes a few months ago. Poor thing, he was so thirsty all the time. The thing is he's not well and Mother tells me he's losing weight. She's read something about a special diet based on oats and she wants to know what I think. But I don't know anything about diabetes. What should I say to her?'

Charlotte had no idea how to answer. She knew, of course, that left untreated, diabetes mellitus would cause death. But she also had a feeling that 1916 was before the development of insulin. Again, she found herself caught between two worlds.

'I'm sorry to hear about your brother's illness, Sarah, but I'm not up to date with the current treatments, I'm afraid. I wonder if you should speak to one of the other nurses about it.'

'Oh, I couldn't possibly bother them with it,' Sarah said. She looked down. 'I'm sorry, I shouldn't have bothered you with it.'

Charlotte took no offence and was secretly pleased that Sarah had approached her.

'Would you like me to speak to one of them on your behalf? I'm sure they wouldn't mind.'

Sarah looked immediately more cheerful. 'Well, if you think that would be acceptable, then thank you, I'd be grateful. But only if it's not an imposition. My mother seems to forget I've only had two weeks' training.'

'I can imagine that suddenly you've become the family expert in all things medical,' said Charlotte. 'Leave it with me and I'll see what I can find out for you.'

Sarah stood up. 'I'd better return to the ward now. They'll wonder where I've got to. And we're not supposed to sit here so I'd better dash.'

'What have you been doing this morning since I caused you to be so ill?'

'Restocking the linen cupboard and preparing more dressings.'

'Well, I'm grateful to you because I seem to be going through the stock quickly today with all the dressings I've had to do.' She finished her coffee. 'I suppose I should get back too. But to be honest, I'm enjoying this comfortable seat a bit too much.'

'Let me take your cup through to the kitchen for you, Nurse Robertson.' She took Charlotte's cup from her.

'Please, Sarah, call me Charlotte.'

'Oh no, that would not be proper at all,' Sarah said.

Charlotte was surprised. She'd forgotten again how formal this world was.

CHAPTER 12

As Charlotte walked through the hospital again, she thought how in her modern world, patients newly diagnosed with diabetes would be established on insulin and able to live a full, normal life. Sarah's brother sounded like he was terminally ill. It reminded her of a time when she nursed a young student who had been admitted in a life-threatening diabetic coma. He'd gone on a camping holiday with his friends and didn't want them to know he had anything wrong with him so he had decided to leave his insulin at home. He was almost at death's door when he was brought to the hospital by his friends, who had known all along he had diabetes. He was lucky to survive but did so thanks to modern treatment. Sarah's brother had no medication to help him.

She would try to remember to seek advice from one of the doctors or her roommates later.

She went back to the dressings. One of her tasks was to change the facial bandage of Bremner who had been blinded. Charlotte was careful to ensure that he knew she was approaching his bed. The bandage covered both his eyes. As she replaced it, he said, 'Do you think they'll send me to St. Dunstan's?'

Charlotte was not sure what he meant. 'Gosh, I don't know. I've not heard that name before. Tell me, what is it?'

'It's a place where they send blind people,' he said in a matter-of-fact way.

'I don't know what the plan is. Perhaps for the moment you should concentrate on regaining your strength.'

'So you won't tell me then?'

'Tell you what?'

'If I'll be blind forever.'

Charlotte stopped what she was doing. 'I don't know the answer to your question so I'm unable to answer it, I'm afraid.'

He sighed. 'What kind of nurse are you anyway, to keep me in this dreadful state?'

She finished tying the bandage. 'Well, it seems you don't think I'm much of a nurse at all. But I can't give you the answer if I don't know the facts.'

'Get out of my sight,' he barked.

How ironic that he used that phrase, thought Charlotte as she pushed the dressing trolley back to the preparation room. It was understandable that he was angry. He was young and frightened, and uncertain of his future. But it always stung when patients took out their anger on her. She wondered what she would be like in the same situation, especially if she thought she was not being told the truth.

It was now late morning and Charlotte still had sixteen or more dressings to complete. She had managed to say goodbye to Macdonald before he left and had a quick word with Tom when he came to collect the men. He was wondering how his favourite 'gals' were after the terrible events of the night before.

'We're all safe and we managed to get back to sleep eventually, thanks, Tom. But I don't suppose you slept much, did you?'

'No, I was out on duty again but I couldn't get that little girl out of my mind. I just feel so sad for her. If I have any free time over the next few days, I might drop by to see how she is.'

'I'm sure she'd be glad to see a familiar face,' said Charlotte.

Lunch came but she kept going with her work. A couple of men only required wound checks, which meant the trolley didn't have to be cleaned in between. She was concerned about Pritchard, though. He had sustained a deep wound to his buttock and was lying on his front following his operation.

'Are you alright there?' she asked.

'I don't suppose I have much choice, do I, nurse?' he replied. He sounded sleepy.

'Yes, you're right. Apologies, it was a silly question.'

'How long do I have to lie on my front?' he asked.

'I'm not sure. Let me find out for you.'

Just as she was finding some confidence, these two patients had left her feeling uncertain again. But she consoled herself more quickly than before. Don't lose your nerve, she thought – they're asking you specific questions about two situations you've not encountered before.

She moved on to the next few patients, replacing a soiled bandage on Fraser's leg in bed five and then attending to Cameron's chest wound in bed six.

One of the last patients she had to see to was Fellows in bed thirty. He was the first person she had helped to admit to the ward and for that reason she felt a small sense of connection with him. He had a severe abdominal injury and although the surgeon had done what he could, his condition was deteriorating. He was in a lot of pain and it was agony for him to move. He was unable to eat or drink, his gut had stopped working and was distended again.

'How are you doing, Captain Fellows?' she asked as she removed his bandage.

He grimaced. 'Trying not to move too much.'

His wound was tense and the edges were very red.

'Can I re-apply your dressing, please? I'll try not to hurt you as I do it,' Charlotte said, as kindly as she could.

'Yes, go ahead.'

'Is there anything I can get for you?'

'Well, I wonder if you could reach into my diary and give me the photograph of my little one to hold.'

'Of course.' Charlotte picked up the black leather-bound diary that contained some letters and a few photos. She handed it to him but he said, 'Please look for it for me. I think it should be towards the back.'

Charlotte did as he asked and found a little picture of a young woman holding a tiny baby. She handed it to him.

'This will give me strength, nurse. The thing is, I've not yet met my little girl.'

'How old is she?'

'Just three months. We called her Maisie. We decided on names while I was on leave in the spring.'

'Maisie Fellows. What a lovely name that is.' Charlotte found this little conversation moving. Fellows's condition was deteriorating and that there was a good chance he wouldn't survive. She wondered if he knew. It seemed so poignant that a photograph was giving him such inner strength.

'I could help you write a letter to them later, if the ward's quiet.'

'Yes, I'd appreciate that. I'll think about what I want you to write.'

She knew she might have no time at all if the work didn't let up. But she also felt she should honour such a small but important task for a patient and decided that if she had to she would stay on after her shift to do it.

As it turned out, it was only after all the daily tasks had been completed that she was able to go back and help him compose the letter.

'You'll have to forgive me. I'm not much of a secretary,' she said.

Fellows gave a little laugh. 'Don't worry, nurse. I'm not going to dictate *Bleak House* to them.'

'Just as well. I don't have enough lead in my pencil to cope with that. But, that's my favourite book!'

He smiled. Charlotte laid a piece of paper on the bedside table and said, 'Okay, fire away.'

She immediately regretted using such an inappropriate phrase. 'Oh, I'm so sorry. How thoughtless of me. I meant to say I'm ready to start.'

He didn't appear to take offence and began slowly dictating his letter.

Dearest girls, You won't recognise the hand that is writing this letter but the contents and sentiments are from me. I'm a bit laid up at the moment but wanted you to know that I send my love to my best girls from France.

I've been in the hospital for a couple of days but am now on the mend and hope to be coming home for a bit of rest and recuperation soon. I must say that my team looked after me so well the other night and I am very proud of them. Carroll even gave me his last cigarette which was jolly decent of him.

I hope Maisie is a good baby for her Mummy and I can't wait to meet her.

I will sign off now as the nurse has plenty of things to do.

My love to you both from across the sea.

'Would you like to sign it yourself?' asked Charlotte, trying her best not to cry.

'Yes, that would be good to do. Thank you, nurse.'

Charlotte placed the piece of paper on top of his observation chart and gave him a pencil. He managed to scrawl his first name at the bottom of the page.

'I'm happy to put this in an envelope for you and add it to the mail collection when I go off duty if you like. What's your wife's name?'

'Thank you. That would be kind. My wife's name is Grace.' He kissed the photo he was clutching then told Charlotte the address. She wrote it on the envelope and put the letter in her pocket.

The day had been so busy it had taken nearly the entire shift to complete her work. She saw the night staff were arriving and that was her cue to finish, much to her relief.

She found herself thinking about Sister Craig and hoping everything was alright with her, wherever she had gone. Matron McLean had not re-appeared in the ward either but Margaret had everything running like clockwork. She will be a super Sister when she's promoted, Charlotte thought. She had dealt efficiently with the arrival of the tetanus officer who had spent some time looking at the medical notes of Thomson as well as those of other patients. He had also spoken to Captain Clift who told Margaret that a report would be forthcoming the following day. 'Matron and the CO will not be very happy with the situation but that's not my concern,' the captain added.

She had not had time to speak to Daisy who had started work at midday and was about to finish as well. She was, as usual, 'famished' and looking forward to a well-earned meal.

Charlotte was putting on her little cape at the door when she remembered the precious letter in her pocket. She popped it in the post-box, knowing that it would be winging its way to England the following day. She was relieved she had helped the young father write it – he might have died without his family knowing how much he loved them.

She also remembered that she had promised Sarah she would find out more about diabetes and mentioned the conversation to Daisy as they were walking down the staircase.

'Yes, I've heard about that oat diet,' Daisy said. 'I seem to remember reading about it. But I'm not so sure it will make a lot of difference, to be honest. What a shame for them. Although the diet is probably not harmful either so she could reassure her mother that it won't make things any worse.'

'Thanks, Daisy,' Charlotte said. 'It's just that I've not heard of it.'

'Diabetes is such a cruel disease. I just wish there was a way it could be cured and that fewer young people succumbed to it. When I was working on a medical ward, we lost five in the space of a month.'

'How awful that must have been. That sounds like my ward at home.' Charlotte could think of nothing else to say in reply. She decided to change the subject. Yet again she was out of her comfort zone and into uncertain territory. It would be so easy for her to talk about modern diabetic medicine.

'Did you manage to see Tom today?'

'Not really,' said Daisy. 'Did you?'

'He popped into the ward earlier to find out how we all were after last night. He's such a kind person.' Daisy stopped and gripped the banister as she continued to talk.

'You know, he's like that with everyone. He's told me that he always feels a sense of guilt if a soldier doesn't get to the hospital in time and he finds dealing with dying men almost impossible.'

At the bottom of the staircase she paused again and touched Charlotte's arm.

'He told me about one particular event which stuck in his mind. Not long after he came here, he was sent to pick up an officer who had been carried to a first-aid post by his men. He was badly injured but it had been decided to transfer him to the hospital. Tom had been told to get there as soon as he could in case he could be saved. He loaded the man into the ambulance as gently as possible and cranked the engine. He then climbed into the cab but was stopped by some of the captain's men. "Don't go yet," they told him. "We're just putting the captain's belongings in with him." For a moment, Tom lost his cool. He said, "Hey, I've been told to get your captain to the hospital as soon as possible and I really shouldn't wait a moment longer".

'But of course, he did hold on, and after a couple of minutes the soldiers banged on the side of the ambulance and called that he could leave. As usual, the journey was full of bumps and jolts, even though Tom was trying to pick the smoothest route through the mud. It took half an hour to reach the hospital because of the poor state of the roads.

'When Tom got out of the ambulance, he noticed that the sides of the vehicle were covered in flowers and then he realised that this must have been what the soldiers were doing. He knew what he'd find when he climbed into the back. The captain had died on the journey and the soldiers had known it would happen, so the ambulance had been adorned rather more like a hearse.

'Tom felt so sorry that he had been bad-tempered with the men and he told me that from that day on, he would never show his impatience like that again, no matter the situation. Those soldiers had shown their devotion to their officer. Tom even helped with the funeral to show his respect for their camaraderie. The captain was buried in the small graveyard that had been created at the back of the outbuildings. And, unusually, he had flowers on his grave. Isn't that just incredible that he would do that?'

Daisy was now gripping Charlotte's arm tightly.

They were both quiet for a moment. Charlotte said, 'Gosh, that's quite a story. You've got yourself a fine man there, you know.'

'What do you mean by that?' asked Daisy angrily, letting go of Charlotte's arm.

'Daisy, it's just as clear as anything that you're in love with Tom.'

Daisy's reaction surprised Charlotte. 'No, no. You're quite wrong, Charlotte. Please don't say things like that.'

She turned abruptly and ran back up the stairs.

'What have I said?' Charlotte called.

But she decided not to go after her. She obviously needs to be on her own for a while, Charlotte thought. Instead she went into the mess to have her dinner, wondering what she had done to offend her roommate.

When Charlotte got back to their bedroom later, having eaten her supper alone, Daisy was asleep, or pretending to be, with her back turned. Charlotte had brought with her a small plate of stew and potatoes because she thought Daisy would need some sustenance after such a long day. Margaret was nowhere to be seen.

Charlotte was keen that the day should not end like this so she took a deep breath and said, 'Daisy, I'm so sorry if I spoke out of turn downstairs. I didn't mean to offend you.'

Daisy didn't move.

'Please speak to me. Look, I know you aren't asleep. And I've brought a peace offering.' She put the plate of food on the bedside table.

Daisy turned. She looked at Charlotte with red-rimmed eyes. After a moment, she said quietly, 'The thing is, Charlotte, I'm promised to someone at home. And anyway, why did you say that downstairs?'

Charlotte said, 'You always brighten up the instant he appears. And you blush if his name's mentioned. I couldn't help but notice how you offered to go to Albert with him last night. And I also saw he had his arm around you.'

'Oh my, I was unaware of that,' said Daisy, blushing again. 'The thing is, I thought it was you who had fallen for him.'

'Me?' said Charlotte, amazed. 'Why would you think that?'

'Well, I've found you in the courtyard speaking so informally to him. And in the ward. I just assumed you had ... feelings for him.'

'No, honestly, Daisy, I think he's a wonderful person who's very easy to speak to, and I admire him for being a volunteer. But nothing more. I'm happily married with a lovely family. I can promise you that I'm not hunting for a new man.'

Daisy sat up. 'You say that, but it's strange to me that you have no photographs of your family. And you get no post. That suggests all is not well in your life.'

Charlotte didn't know what to say. She sat down next to Daisy on the bed.

'I can understand that. I can't explain why no letters have arrived yet. And yes, you're right, I have mislaid my photographs. But that doesn't alter the fact that I'm not interested in Tom in the slightest. So, did you get upset because I had said something that was true?'

Daisy turned away. 'Oh, Charlotte, I'm not sure. I can't stop thinking about Tom and I love it when he's nearby. But I'm so torn about the chap at home. I hate the thought of letting him down, too. And anyway, perhaps Tom has a girl waiting for him back home in America.'

'Have you asked him?'

'Of course not. That would be too forward.'

'I don't agree,' said Charlotte. 'At least then you would know where you stand if he is single.'

'But the thing that's so confusing for me is that I'd be so upset if I found out he did have a girl at home. I'd rather not know.'

'That seems strange, if you ask me. Tell me, how formal is the arrangement between you and the man at home?'

Daisy sighed and rubbed her eyes. 'Well, our mothers have been friends for years and they seem to think we'll be married when I'm home again. My mother's always talking about it in her letters.'

'And is that what you want?'

'Oh, I don't know, Charlotte. I'm unsure if what I want matters. I don't have much choice as far as I can see.'

'I'm not sure that's true. But if you had to choose between Tom and ... what's his name?'

'Stuart.'

'So who would you choose – if it was left to you?'

Daisy hesitated. 'Tom,' she said finally, then, 'I can't believe I just said that. But it's the truth.'

'Well, perhaps you should do something about it then. I suggest the first thing you need to do is to find out if he's free.'

'Oh, no.' Daisy looked shocked. 'Anyway, how could I do that?'

'Well, I could find out for you if you like.'

'I couldn't ask you to do that.' She paused, then whispered, 'Would you really?'

'Leave it with me,' Charlotte said. 'Now look, here's some supper for you by way of a peace offering. After your busy day, you need to eat, you know. Am I forgiven?'

'Yes, of course you are, you silly goose!'

'And I'm sorry if I hurt your feelings earlier. It wasn't intentional, you know.'

'Thank you for saying that. And you're sweet to have brought me some supper as well. Please, can we keep this to ourselves?'

'Of course,' said Charlotte. Another secret to keep, she thought.

The door opened and Margaret came in.

'What have I been missing then?'

Daisy glanced at Charlotte who said, 'I thought I would treat Daisy to supper on a tray instead of having it in the mess tonight. What have you been up to?'

Margaret sat down on her bed. 'I went to have a cup of tea and a catch up with one of the nurses in the medical ward. Because of our working patterns, I haven't seen her for a couple of weeks. She was filling me in on all the news. And guess what's happened?'

'What?' said Charlotte and Daisy together.

'Well, it appears that the CO complained about Matron to the matron-in-chief. That's why she was trying to be nice yesterday. Matron McCarthy told her to be more supportive to Sister Craig as well instead of over-riding her decisions all the time.'

'Do you know why Sister Craig hasn't been on duty for a couple of days?' asked Charlotte.

'Matron McLean has arranged for her to visit another surgical ward to gain some insights into running a ward in war conditions. And then she's spending a night at a hotel near the coast to have a bit of peace and to regain her composure.'

Charlotte said, 'How do you know all this, Margaret?'

'Oh, this is a small unit. Any news travels fast,' Margaret said. 'I do hope she comes back to us soon. She's such a good Sister.'

She stood. 'Right, I think I'll go and have a bath. Oh, by the way, my friend was asking about you Charlotte. It seems that people have been talking about your bravery – asking Matron a question at her lecture.'

Charlotte smiled, 'I suppose it is time to settle down again. Let's hope we have a quieter night than last night.'

She was relieved that Margaret and Daisy knew what was happening to Sister Craig and that she hadn't been the person who disclosed the information.

She climbed into bed and picked up the nursing textbook lying on her bedside table. She flicked through the pages and again stopped at the chapter entitled 'Surgical nursing'. She was able to read about the procedures she had been using over the last few days and it helped her understand the logic behind them. Before antibiotics, it made sense to try to wash the 'bugs' out of wounds to prevent them becoming infected. If that happened, then it was up to nature to run its course.

Later, when Margaret returned from the bathroom she stood in her dressing gown looking out of the window at the ruins of the farmhouse. 'I wonder how little Monique is today,' she said. 'I hope her father is still alive. Perhaps Huguette's family will try and contact him. Wouldn't it be dreadful if he came home on leave and found this devastation?'

'Or perhaps she's now an orphan,' said Charlotte. 'I think Tom was going to try to see her when he's en route to the station in Albert in the next couple of days.'

'Oh, sometimes this is all too much, you know,' Daisy said. She began rummaging in her suitcase for a biscuit tin. 'No wonder I need the comfort of food all the time.'

They switched off the lamps and settled down to sleep. Charlotte closed her eyes and thought about her family, sending them all her love. She hoped her children would not have to experience being left like Monique. She was less worried now about being trapped here – but she did still want to be back in her real world.

CHAPTER 13

Charlotte woke up in France again. While she was brushing her hair, after the others had left the bedroom, she looked at herself in the mirror. Her sense of uncertainty had returned. What would happen if her experience was different from that of the other two people Margaret had told her about? What if she didn't get home again? Had they really travelled through time? It seemed so unlikely. This was the beginning of her fifth day – but for the others, their adventures had lasted only for two.

She began to feel shaky again. Although the story Margaret told her suggested that at home time wasn't passing at all, that might be untrue. If so it would mean that she had disappeared for nearly a week. She tried to imagine what she would do if one of her family vanished suddenly. She would be frantic with worry.

There was another issue Charlotte was concerned about. If she was 'here' permanently, what would happen to her? When her service was completed, where would she go? She didn't know anyone other than the staff she had met in the hospital. Would she have to go to another hospital or would she be sent back home to work? But then where would she live and how would she manage? She would be alone and that thought scared her.

She tried to push it to the back of her mind but she had a nagging sensation in her stomach. As she brushed her hair, she glanced at her hands.

'Where are my rings?' she said out loud.

She had put her uniform dress in the laundry basket outside the room last night and had forgotten to unpin her rings and wear them overnight.

She yanked open the door, hoping the basket was still there. She was in luck. The orderly had not yet been to collect it. She put her hand in the pocket of the first dress she saw in the basket – but the rings weren't there.

'Where are they?' She started to cry. Her hands were shaking now. She began pulling the laundry out of the basket and then saw there were some more dresses in a pile on the floor. She had put her hand into someone else's pocket, which she would have realised if she hadn't been in such a panic. Her dress was there, and she found the rings immediately. A sense of calm flooded over her as she was reunited with the only tangible link she had with home. She wondered how she could have forgotten about the rings.

'How careless,' she muttered. What a bad start to the day. She was a bundle of nervous uncertainty again.

Let's start this morning again, Charlotte, she told herself. Take a deep breath, calm yourself down and go for some breakfast.

She went downstairs to the mess where Daisy and Margaret were finishing their coffee.

'What took you so long?' said Daisy. 'We thought you were right behind us.'

'I thought I'd lost my rings and had to rake through the laundry basket for them.'

Margaret said, 'You must be relieved to have found them.'

'Yes, I got myself into a real panic.'

On the ward, Charlotte noticed that a few of the patients due for transfer home were already getting ready to leave. Even though everyone knew that Sister Craig wouldn't be on duty this morning, Matron McLean didn't join the ward orders either. She must have gone to one of her regular meetings in Albert, Charlotte thought. She knew she would have to face the consequences of her verbal volley later.

Fiona Collinson expressed surprise about Matron's absence and about her friendly disposition the previous day. She was uncertain whether she should go ahead with the morning orders and was reluctant to start without her. Nurse Brook didn't want to risk incurring Matron's wrath and said, 'You must wait for her.'

They all sat in silence, looking at each other. After a few minutes, Margaret said, 'Nurse Collinson, just make a start with the handover. I'll update Matron when she arrives.'

There were lots of changes to remember. The good news for Charlotte was that today she understood everything, which was progress. She listened as the range of injuries sustained by the soldiers were listed. She had already seen wounds from head to toe in the short time she had been here.

Fiona continued with her report, noting that Swann, McConnell and Pritchard had survived their first night after surgery. Brown, Stills and Fellows were continuing to deteriorate, Beattie seemed to be the same, and eight patients were scheduled to be transferred to base hospitals. Some of these were the first patients that Charlotte had looked after when she arrived, including Thomson with the broken legs, as well as Evans, Inglis and Stevenson.

The staff were reluctant to start work. Without a senior nurse, some didn't seem confident to plan the day ahead. Nurse Brook remained silent so Margaret took charge.

'Right, it looks like we're going to have a busy day with so many of the men moving on. Let's focus on that first. We have eight going onwards to the coast today. I need to confirm with Captain Graves whether Stills will be moved into the side room, so we can swap the remaining men around the ward after everyone else has left. Once they've gone, we'll have twelve empty beds – very unusual. If you remember the last time that happened, we had an influx of admissions and that may happen again.

'Nurse Robertson, please will you be on dressing duty once you have completed the observations? Nurse Brook, will you see to the medications and discharges? Sarah and Isobel, can you help with the dressings and discharges as well?' She looked at her watch. 'Our target time for the discharges is ten o'clock.'

Everyone nodded except Nurse Brook who said, 'I wouldn't plan the day like that.'

Daisy, in her soft voice, said, 'Nurse Brook, Nurse Wishaw is in temporary charge, and I think it's confusing to have more than one plan, so let's just get on with the work as suggested.'

Nurse Brook sighed and shook her head.

There was going to be a lot of upheaval in the ward during the morning and there was a buzz in the air as people collected possessions and paperwork that had to accompany the men as they left.

Charlotte recorded the observations for the patients who were staying and carried out the first-day post-operation wound checks on Swann, McConnell and Gilbertson. There didn't appear to be any immediate complications following their surgery but McConnell had been very sick overnight. She had a word with Ellis and Wilson and helped to lift them off their beds so their skin got some relief from the pressure of lying still.

She also continued to speak to Brown in bed twelve who now had a fever. His mouth was coated and unclean but he refused to let her clean it. A nasogastric tube had been passed during the night to ensure he continued to have fluids. But it seemed a futile act given his deterioration. Whoever had ordered it had felt he still needed to receive active treatment but Charlotte was more inclined than ever to let nature take its course. She would have to follow orders, though, however half-heartedly. She wondered whether anyone else felt the same way about Brown's situation and how often something similar had happened before.

At nine-thirty, Tom and James appeared to see if any of the men were ready to go. Both were always very efficient but were willing to help prepare the men if needed. James was whistling *Pack Up Your Troubles in Your Old Kit-Bag*. Charlotte managed to say goodbye to Inglis and Cameron, wishing them luck.

Stevenson, with the colostomy, called her over. 'I wish to report a movement and thought you would like to know.' He laughed. 'Better out than in, I say.'

Charlotte smiled. 'Thank you for telling me.' She admired his attitude.

'Rather glad it's happened before I leave.'

'I agree,' she said. 'But perhaps I should give you something in case it happens again on the journey.'

She went and found some supplies for him which he put in his bag.

'There, that's you all sorted. But where's your envelope?'

'Don't know, nurse.'

Charlotte could see a pile of papers on the desk and wondered if the other men who were about to leave had their paperwork.

To Tom she said, 'Hold on a minute. I need to check you have all the paperwork the men need for their discharge.'

The relevant papers had been gathered but they were all together in a pile, not sorted into the individual envelopes and not recorded in the ward register, although it didn't take long to re-arrange everything and ensure the right paperwork went with the right patient. But the men also needed tags attached to the front of their uniforms to indicate their destinations. She was annoyed it hadn't been done. Nurse Brook seemed to be walking smartly around the ward but not doing very much. I hope she's given out the medications correctly, Charlotte thought.

She felt relieved that Bremner was going. His anger towards her yesterday had been unfair. But she made herself say goodbye. She hoped he would apologise but he didn't.

The discharged men had all left the ward a few minutes after ten, which gave the nurses and VADs plenty of beds to clean and remake. After the doctors had finished their ward round, it was decided to move Stills into the side room. The smell from his leg was revolting and it pervaded the whole room. Someone had placed a little pad containing lavender on his pillow. Captain Graves had increased the dose of morphine and chloral hydrate, so perhaps the poor man would now be unaware of his situation and relieved of his pain and distress. He certainly appeared oblivious and was barely rousable. Charlotte wondered who a letter of condolence would be sent to. It felt as though it would have to be written soon and she would be comfortable to write it, if needed. She wondered whether she could ask him if he could share any words he wished to send home. But it was probably too late for that now.

Poor Brown was dying as well but the plan was for him to stay in the main ward so he could continue his treatment. Charlotte noticed that after Stills had been moved to the side room Margaret and Captain Clift were deep in conversation. Margaret then came over to speak to her.

'You were looking after Brown yesterday, weren't you?'

'Yes, he kept removing his dressing and I replaced it a few times over the day.'

'Did you do anything else for him?'

'I just tried to clean up his mouth a couple of times. But the last time I tried, he refused to let me near him.'

Margaret said, 'Did you notice anything unusual about his mouth when you cleaned it?'

'No, not really. Why?'

'His lips and gums are looking like they've been burned. They've turned white.'

'Burned?' said Charlotte. 'How on earth could that happen?'

'Well, his spit mug is dry, and Captain Clift and I are wondering if he's drunk the disinfectant in the bottom of it.'

Charlotte thought for a moment. 'Now you say that, his spit mug was empty yesterday and he said he'd spilt it but didn't want me to change his top sheet. Oh dear, have I missed something?'

Margaret shook her head. 'You weren't to know he'd do something like that.'

'What's at the bottom of the spit mug?'

'Carbolic.'

'That sounds terrible.' She hesitated. 'So what will happen to him now?'

'It depends on how much he's managed to swallow. Captain Clift says that if he's ingested enough, it will kill him. He'll become giddy, then delirious.'

'Is there any antidote?'

'Not really. He could have his stomach pumped but Captain Clift thinks it's too late for that so he's decided to move him into the side room. He feels he can do no more.'

Charlotte had secretly hoped that Brown would succumb to a wound infection. Somehow this act of self-harm seemed a harsher way for his life to end. Brown had decided to act in a way that would ensure his death would occur in the ward. She felt nothing but pity for the man. Other people could view him as a coward but she was certain he wasn't.

Pritchard was the other patient causing some concern. He was in bed number three, still lying face down because of the wound on his buttock but this morning it had been decided to turn him on to his back. It took three of them to do it and as they did so he became aware, for the first time, of the extent of his injuries. All that was left of his genitals was a raw wound. A catheter had been inserted directly into his bladder to drain urine.

The whole ward heard his screams.

No one knew what to say to him. Captain Clift decided to prescribe a sedative to calm him but also to lessen the distress of the other soldiers.

'This is the injury all the men dread,' Daisy said. 'I hate it when we have a soldier like this.'

Charlotte was lost for words. She tended to the dressing that surrounded the catheter but could think of nothing to say that didn't sound trite. So, like everyone else, she stayed silent and simply explained to him what she was doing. What made the situation worse was that the poor man had not sustained any life-threatening injury – but Charlotte knew that for him everything about his life had changed.

She completed her task as quickly as possible so she could get away. But he was weeping uncontrollably and she felt that she had to do something. She touched him on the arm, knowing it was inadequate, and said simply, 'This must be so difficult. I'm so sorry for you.' He made no response.

As she was setting up her next dressing trolley, she said to Margaret, 'That was much harder to deal with than the men in the side room.'

'I agree,' Margaret said. 'I suggest we put some screens around his bed.'

Charlotte did so but wondered whether it was to give the man some privacy or put his distress out of sight. His sobs still echoed round the ward.

Nurse Brook went behind the screens and Charlotte heard her say, 'Stop wailing like a baby. Grow up, you're disturbing everyone.' Charlotte shook her head. Such lack of compassion amazed her.

Beattie's condition, by contrast, seemed to be improving. Nothing was soaking through his dressing and his temperature had returned to normal. His mood was brighter too. He had managed to sit out of bed for a while first thing that morning, enabling him to stretch his legs.

'Maybe they'll let me move on to a hospital at home soon,' he said. 'Each day I'm feeling stronger, you know.'

'It'd be nice if that could happen soon,' Charlotte said.

Captain Sears in bed twenty-four had sustained a bad head injury and had now been in the ward for six days but his condition was deteriorating. He had been to the operating theatre to have the wound cleaned and fragments of bone and earth removed.

Margaret had prepared Charlotte before she went to change his dressing.

'Make sure that you avoid putting any pressure on the dressing over the entry wound on the scalp and, if possible, try to sit him up. It's a different approach to the boys who have abdominal injuries.'

'Right,' said Charlotte. 'Thanks. I hadn't thought about that but the lack of pressure makes sense now you explain it.'

Sears had been unconscious since the original injury and for the first twenty-four hours after his operation. He had then started to wake but only when pressure had been applied to his breastbone or earlobes. The following night, however, he was more awake but had started to complain of a severe headache and seemed disorientated. He was now lying in a foetal position and he shielded his eyes from the light on the rare occasions he opened them.

Charlotte knew that she wouldn't be able to get him into a sitting position. She turned his head so he was facing her and then removed his dressing. She gasped when she saw what was underneath. Brain tissue was protruding out of his wound. She'd never seen anything like it before. She applied the new dressing as lightly as she could and reported her findings to Margaret. She now understood why she had been instructed to apply the dressing without any pressure.

'That was horrible, Margaret. I wasn't expecting to see his brain.'

Margaret said, 'When his wound was inspected by Captain Clift two days ago, that had started to happen. He told me it was a bad sign and asked for the Red Cross to become involved so that his parents had time to come over. I put a call through to HQ and they sorted it all out.'

'His parents are coming over? I had no idea that could happen during the war. Do you know, I'm beginning to question whether anything we do in my world is that new.'

'It's something we can't do very often,' Margaret said. 'But in a situation like this, it's only a matter of time before they die. In a way, it's fortunate he can stay here. Sometimes when we've been busy and short of beds, even in the side room, we have to send them on to the base hospitals when they're as bad as this, and I suppose a few of them must die on the way.'

'That's a horrible thought as well. Thank goodness he can stay here with us then.'

'Yes, I suppose that would appeal to you, Charlotte.'

Margaret was quiet for a moment, then said briskly, 'Now we have some space in the ward, I think we should move his bed nearer the main door. Let's swap his bed position with Beattie's.'

Charlotte said, 'Okay, I'll get Sandy to help me do that now, if you like. I'm sure it will help Beattie as well. I know he's wondered why he's not been moved yet.'

Beattie said he felt as though he had been promoted when they wheeled him along the ward to his new bed space.

Charlotte had initially been surprised that Sears wasn't being moved into 'Darwin's room'. But it made more sense to her now she knew his parents would be arriving. Perhaps moving patients into the side ward was the option when there wouldn't be time to call for family. But she felt a sense of injustice for the soldiers who had been moved and for the lack of opportunity for them to be visited – although she could see it would take a lot of organisation and when she thought about it further, she knew it was both unrealistic and time-consuming. Besides, the side room would not be a pleasant environment at the moment because of the smell coming from Stills's leg. Perhaps it was better that he stayed in the main ward.

Forty-eight hours after a telegram was dispatched to Sears's parents in London, they arrived at the hospital and were ushered into the ward by Sandy.

Mr. and Mrs. Sears were a smartly dressed couple. He wore a three-piece suit and a wide-brimmed hat, with a gabardine overcoat over his arm. Mrs. Sears had a black belted suit on and a felt hat. Charlotte took the opportunity to speak to them at the ward door and prepare them for their son's condition.

'Thank you for coming over so quickly,' she said. 'I'm afraid your son is not doing so well today. Unfortunately, he's not awake and his condition is continuing to deteriorate.'

'We're just desperate to see him,' said Mrs. Sears.

They were trying to control their emotions but Charlotte could see their distress.

She accompanied them to his bedside and Mrs. Sears let out a stifled cry when she saw him. 'My poor darling boy. What has happened to your beautiful hair?'

Charlotte had forgotten to tell them his head had been shaved before his operation. Mrs. Sears stepped forward and took hold of her unconscious son's hand.

'Eddie, Eddie, I'm here.' He was unresponsive.

Charlotte said, 'My advice is to keep talking to him. He may still be able to hear you even though he can't speak and is deeply asleep.'

'I do hope he's not feeling any pain,' said Mrs. Sears.

'I hope so too,' Charlotte said. 'I think he looks quite settled today. The doctor has prescribed pain relief for him and it's given as and when he needs it.'

'Is there ... anything more that can be done?' Mr. Sears asked very slowly.

Charlotte straightened the bedclothes. 'Well, we're aiming to keep him comfortable and prevent any further infection. But I'm afraid he doesn't seem to be responding. 'Would you like to have a word with the doctor in charge of his case?'

'Yes,' said Mr. Sears. 'That would be useful – to help me understand his situation.'

Mrs. Sears was sobbing into her lace-edged handkerchief. 'What a sorry state of affairs all of this is.'

Charlotte said, 'I'll let Captain Clift know you have arrived. In the meantime, let me get a couple of chairs for you so that you can sit with Eddie. When you're ready to have a little break, please go and sit downstairs in the hallway and we'll make you a drink. I'm sure this has been a real shock for you.'

'Thank you, nurse. That would be kind after our long journey,' said Mr. Sears. Mrs. Sears took hold of her son's hand and pressed it against her cheek.

As she walked through the ward, Charlotte could hear her softly singing *Aye Fond Kiss* and she had to fight back her tears. *Aye fareweel and then forever ...*

Captain Clift saw the couple at their son's bedside and went over so there was no need for Charlotte to tell him they had arrived. After sitting with their son for twenty minutes, Mr. and Mrs. Sears left the ward and went downstairs to the front hall.

Charlotte followed and collected a pot of tea and cups from the kitchen. She poured them both a cup. Mrs. Sears was probably not much older than Charlotte.

'I was so proud of Edward when he enlisted last year,' she said. 'But I had such a horrible feeling this would happen. You only need look at the daily casualty lists to know that it would come to your door at some point. I know he's given his all for King and country but I'm so frightened for him.'

She pulled a small blue book out of her bag. 'I'm trying to comfort myself with this new book.' It was called *The Adventure of Death*. A curious title, Charlotte thought.

'The thing is,' Mrs. Sears went on, 'the good doctor who has written it suggests that death is not to be feared. But I'm so frightened – for Eddie and for us.'

Mr. Sears muttered something under his breath, got up and disappeared down the corridor that led to the back door.

'My husband tells me I shouldn't be so emotional about all this but I can't help it. He's my only son and so young – just twenty. Oh, I had so many hopes for his future.' She was crying 'Do you think I'm unpatriotic for feeling like this?' she asked Charlotte.

'I don't believe you're unpatriotic at all. It's only natural to be upset about your son, especially when he's been so badly injured. It must have been a difficult time for you and your husband after Eddie joined up.'

'Yes, it has. And to be honest, I've felt a sense of fear almost every time I've seen the telegram boy cycling through our neighbourhood. I tried to make Eddie join one of the territorial regiments so that he could serve in England but my husband wanted him to be a "proper soldier". I often felt that we would be in this situation. Many of my friends have had to face this. So many of them still wonder whether their sons are dead. I suppose we're fortunate to be able to come over to see him ...'

She stopped, took a deep breath and whispered, 'Even though ...' She paused again, apparently unable to say out loud that her only son was dying.

'At least I'll be able to look my neighbours in the eye now.'

She sobbed into her handkerchief again, finally taking a couple of deep breaths. 'Thank you for your attention, nurse, but please would you give me a few minutes to let me gather my composure.'

Charlotte, who was becoming upset as well, witnessing this mother's distress, stood and said, 'Of course.'

She went in search Mr. Sears who was outside having a cigarette.

'Hello there, can I fetch you a cup of tea?'

'No, thank you. But it's kind of you to offer, nurse.'

'How are you?'

He drew on his cigarette. 'Well, I'm very proud of my boy for serving his country. I thought it was the right thing for him to do. Tell me, nurse, do you have any family?'

'Yes, two boys and a girl. But they're young so I can't imagine what it must be like for you – and I'm sorry this has happened to your son.'

'You are fortunate indeed,' he said. 'I hope the war will be over before they have to enlist.' He ground the cigarette end under his shoe. 'The thing is I wish it were me in that bed. He's so young and hasn't yet had his life and now it looks as if it's all over. I was the one who encouraged him to join up and now I'm full of regret about that.' His eyes were fixed on a point in the distance. 'But I can't admit that to anyone else and I don't know why I'm telling you. I trust you will keep this conversation to yourself.'

'Of course. You have my word.'

Charlotte wanted to say more but a voice was calling.

'Nurse Robertson, come back to the ward this instant.'

'I'm sorry, Mr. Sears. I have to go. Please come up when you're ready.'

Charlotte hurried back inside, thinking there was a universal link between parents who suffer the pain of losing a child, whether from injury or illness. How awful it must be – something you would never get over. She hoped she would never have to face it herself.

She was unprepared for the torrent of anger that Nurse Brook directed towards her as she made her way upstairs.

'How dare you take it upon yourself to talk to those parents in that way,' she snapped.

Charlotte stood her ground. 'I don't understand what you mean. *Those parents* have had distressing news and have travelled for two days to reach their only son's bedside, so the least we can do is show them some compassion. What exactly have I done wrong?'

'It's not your job to instigate such conversations, even in the current situation,' Nurse Brook said. 'You should have made them wait downstairs and then found Matron to speak to them.'

'Well, I apologise if I haven't followed protocol. But at home I would be expected to do this as part of my duties as a qualified nurse. Furthermore, Matron is nowhere to be found, as you well know. So would you have just left them to wait in the hall for an indefinite time, knowing how distressed they are?'

'I would have waited for a superior to bring them to the ward. But that doesn't matter, you are under Matron McLean's command here and you will do as she says. This sort of thing sets a bad example. We can't have the ward overrun with tourists from England.'

'Tourists?' said Charlotte, aghast. Then, in a tone that was quiet but determined, she added, 'That's a cold and bizarre way of describing parents who are about to lose their only son.'

Nurse Brook's mouth moved as though she was about to say something but then she hesitated. An inner strength was surging through Charlotte. She was determined not to be intimidated.

'Get back to your work,' Nurse Brook hissed. 'But rest assured, I shall be informing Matron about this.'

This time Charlotte didn't hold back the frustration that had been building since she and Nurse Brook had met.

'Please go ahead, if you think it's necessary. But you do not threaten me in any way if that's your intention.'

Nurse Brook said nothing but turned abruptly and walked away.

Charlotte felt calm despite their confrontation, although was unsure where her resolve had come from. She usually found any situation like this very unnerving and would often be reduced to tears. She walked back to the ward reflecting on her newfound certainty.

Stills and Brown had been moved into the side room. In Matron's absence, Charlotte went to see them, this time feeling no need to sidle in. Stills was very settled but unresponsive. Brown shut his eyes as she approached.

'Gilbert,' she whispered, 'are you aware that you've been moved?'

He nodded.

'We're going to look after you here in this quieter room now. You'll not be moving anywhere, you know.'

He didn't open his eyes.

'Are you in any pain?'

He shook his head slowly but said, 'I feel sick and my head is spinning.'

He took hold of his nasogastric tube, opening his eyes and staring at her as he pulled it out.

'I'm assuming you don't want that to be replaced now.'

'Correct,' he whispered.

'Okay, I'll not mention what's happened to anyone. Is there anything else I can get for you?'

He looked at her again, 'I would like to speak to a padre if possible.' He closed his eyes again.

'Let me see what I can arrange for you.'

Charlotte left the room wondering how she would contact a padre. She then had a thought. Perhaps Beattie could speak to him. It might do both of them some good.

CHAPTER 14

Charlotte approached Beattie's bed and explained the situation, then asked if he felt well enough or able to offer the dying man any words of comfort.

'I realise you've been badly injured yourself but I'm not sure how much time we have and Gilbert wishes to speak to a padre. The other man in the room won't be able to hear so you would have privacy.'

Beattie thought for a couple of seconds. Then he said, 'Do you know, Nurse Robertson, it might be very useful for me to do a bit of work for a few minutes. I think I feel strong enough.'

Charlotte was relieved. 'Thank you, Padre. I know this will give him such comfort. Let me check with Nurse Wishaw who's in charge of the ward today and if she agrees, then I will come and collect you in one of the wheelchairs in a couple of minutes.'

Charlotte found Margaret who was dubious about the merits of the unorthodox proposal but agreed.

'If you can, try and make it appear that you're taking Beattie to look out of the hall window or something – so it's not too obvious.'

'You're a star,' said Charlotte. Margaret simply shook her head.

Charlotte found a wicker wheelchair and helped Beattie into it. He asked her to pick up his Bible then she pushed him along the corridor to the side room. Gilbert heard the door open and turned to look.

'Gilbert, this is Padre Beattie. He's agreed to come and speak to you.' She pushed the chair over to the bedside.

Gilbert looked over and started to cry. Padre Beattie held the man's hand and said to Charlotte, 'Thank you, nurse. I'll speak to him in private now.'

'Yes, of course. I'll come back to see you in twenty minutes or so.' She left the two men together.

In the event, Beattie stayed with Gilbert for nearer forty minutes.

'No, please leave me for longer,' he told her when she went back the first time.

Later, as she pushed Beattie back to the ward, he said, 'I'm not sure if your plan was intended to help my recovery but it has in a strange way, so thank you.'

'I'm just glad you're well enough to offer him comfort, Padre.'

The encounter with Gilbert had clearly exhausted him and he soon fell asleep.

Early in the afternoon, both men in the side room died.

She did let Beattie know about Gilbert, though. She hoped Nurse Brook wouldn't write the condolence letter as she would probably let his family know exactly how his wound had been caused.

It was now four in the afternoon and Matron's absence was noticeable to all the staff in the ward but manifesting itself in different ways. There was palpable relief among the VADs but Nurse Brook had lost her authority.

'Where is Matron?' was the question on everyone's lips. Even Sandy, the one other person in the building who knew everything that was going on, had no idea where she was. 'I haven't seen her all day, although she does go to Albert quite often.'

Nurse Brook and Margaret were engaged in a small power struggle.

'I should write the report tonight,' said Nurse Brook.

'I disagree,' said Margaret, who had been in charge all day. 'Captain Clift asked me to do the ward round with him and I have the latest information about the patients. So with respect, Nurse Brook, I will write it.'

The ward was calm now and there had been no new admissions during the afternoon. The two patients who were behind the screens were still there. Sandy and one of the other orderlies moved the two bodies from the side room.

'Does anyone recall Matron saying that she was going to HQ?' asked Daisy. 'It's not like her to disappear without saying anything.' She decided this offered a good excuse to go and find Tom to ask him if he had taken Matron to Albert.

'Go on then,' said Margaret, laughing.

She was back within five minutes. Tom had not driven Matron anywhere.

'I think something must be wrong. This is most unusual for her,' said Margaret.

Charlotte said, 'Has anyone been to her room to see if she's there?'

'No,' said Daisy. 'Entry to Matron's room is strictly forbidden unless you're invited in, like you were the other night.'

Margaret called over to Nurse Brook. 'So, as you feel you should have been in charge of the ward today, are you going to go and find Matron?'

'No, I'm sure there's a good reason for her absence,' said Nurse Brook. 'I think we should leave it and wait until she returns.'

Margaret disagreed. 'I believe we should at least knock on her door and see if she's there. I thought you'd do nothing, Nurse Brook, so I'll go. Charlotte, come with me, please.' Margaret said.

They went downstairs to the front hall and approached Matron's room. Margaret hesitated, wiping her hands down her apron before knocking on the door. There was no reply.

'Do you think we should try it?' said Charlotte.

'Well, if she's out, the door will be locked so there's no harm in it. My heart's pounding, though.' She knocked again, and tried the handle. The door opened.

The room was in darkness. There was a moan from the bed in the alcove. Margaret drew back the curtains a little as Charlotte approached the bed. Matron McLean was lying there, covered in sweat and clearly unwell.

'Quick, Charlotte, go back upstairs and fetch one of the doctors.'

Charlotte hurried out and ran back up the stairs to the ward. Isobel was there. 'Have you seen either of the doctors?'

Captain Graves emerged from the treatment room. 'Yes, Nurse Robertson, I'm here, what's the matter?'

'It's Matron McLean. We've just found her in her bedroom and she appears to be unwell.'

They rushed back down the staircase. Margaret was taking Matron's temperature. 'She has a fever of a hundred and one.' Captain Graves began an examination. Matron's hair was matted and stuck to her head.

'Matron, how long have you felt unwell?'

'About two days,' she whispered.

'Any cough or sore throat?'

'No.'

'Any vomiting?'

'A few times during the night.'

'Do you have any generalised aching? I can see you have a fever.'

'Yes,' she said weakly. 'I feel sore all over. And I have a headache.'

Captain Graves nodded. 'My first impression is influenza as a possible diagnosis.' He turned to Margaret. 'Give her five grains of quinine in a teaspoon of tea and make her comfortable. It should lessen the severity of the infection. Make sure that you wash your hands well when you leave the room. If this is a case of influenza, I don't want it spreading. I'll leave her in your capable hands, Nurse Wishaw.'

To Matron, he said, 'I think you should stay in bed for now until you regain your strength.'

She was evidently feeling too unwell to disagree.

Margaret said to Charlotte, 'You go and get the tea from the kitchen and I'll get the quinine.'

When the two nurses returned a few minutes later, Matron was very drowsy but was able to swallow the medicine. They moved away from her bedside to discuss what to do next.

'She looks like she could do with a wash,' Charlotte whispered.

Margaret hesitated. 'Well, I suppose we should. That's what I would do for a patient with influenza at home. But please, can we do this together?'

'Of course. It always feels strange to nurse a colleague, doesn't it?'

Margaret glanced over at the bed. 'It's because she's so senior and ... well, it's *her*. But it will be a bit easier if we're both here.'

'I'll get some fresh sheets and a jug of warm water, and we can make a start,' said Charlotte. 'And I'll let the others know where we are.'

She was soon back with all the equipment. Meanwhile, Margaret had been finding out more about Matron's illness. Her mouth was sore and she seemed to have an awful lot of saliva.

'What time is it?' asked Matron.

'It's just after four in the afternoon,' said Margaret.

'I seem to have lost a few hours then. But I need to get up as I've so much work to do today.' She tried to sit up but quickly lay back down again, groaning quietly.

'I would advise you to stay in bed for a while, Matron, just as Captain Graves suggested,' Charlotte said. 'You have a fever and we thought you would benefit from a wash to freshen you up.'

Matron didn't object. They lifted her nightdress off and as they did so, a pile of soiled gauze dressings fell onto the bed.

'What on earth is this?' said Margaret.

Charlotte said, 'Forgive me for asking, Matron, but is this why you wear violet perfume by any chance?'

'That's not any of your business, Nurse Robertson. But yes, it is.'

Margaret turned to Charlotte and gestured that they should step back from Matron's bed. 'How did you know?' she said quietly.

'I noticed it that night I went to her office. And I wondered at the time if this was the cause.'

Although a pile of dressing material had fallen away when Matron's nightdress was removed, a few layers remained. They were dark brown and stuck to her skin.

'What is this, Matron? asked Charlotte.

Matron's eyes were closed. 'I have been tending to a small sore myself. But that is not your concern, Nurse Robertson.'

'Matron, I hope you don't mind me asking, but what have you been dressing the wound with?' said Margaret. The question surprised Charlotte.

'I've been using a little perchloride on some gauze.'

'Have you been moistening the gauze before applying it?'

'Yes, it prevents it sticking.'

'I think that might be the reason you've become ill.'

'Why's that?' said Charlotte.

Margaret said, 'The perchloride can cause influenza-type symptoms like this. I've seen it happen before.'

'How can it be treated?' Charlotte asked.

'The first thing is to stop using it and the symptoms will settle quite quickly.'

Matron said, 'That is observant of you, Nurse Wishaw. Now please get about your business. I'm sure you're being missed in the ward.'

'It won't take us long to make you a bit more comfortable,' said Charlotte, wringing out a facecloth.

They washed Matron together. Even though their training was separated by more than sixty years, the procedure for a bed bath had not changed. They took great care to keep their patient covered up. The water was changed three times – after washing Matron's face and neck, then after her limbs and trunk, and again before they washed her back and her 'privates', as the soldiers would say.

Charlotte had also brought the mouth-care tray down with her and they cleaned Matron's mouth and brushed her hair.

'Perhaps we could pin it up out of the way so it doesn't stick to your face,' said Margaret.

'Very well, if you wish,' Matron said.

They managed to change the bottom sheet, which was wet with perspiration, as well as the pillowcases. It all took about twenty minutes and when they had finished Matron was in a clean nightgown and looking less distressed than when they had found her.

'Matron, have you sought help for the lesion on your chest?' asked Charlotte.

'I repeat; that is none of your business, nurse,' Matron said firmly, despite her weakened state. 'I thank you for your assistance but I now ask you to stop speaking about this matter and not to mention it to anyone else.'

'Of course, Matron.'

Margaret said, 'Is there anything else we can assist you with?'

'No, please just leave me to rest.'

'I'm sure Captain Graves will return to see you as he knows you've been unwell today,' Charlotte said. 'But clearly he doesn't know the cause and if you don't want us to say anything it will stay in the room with us.'

They gathered up their things and left Matron to recover.

As they closed the door behind them, Margaret said, 'But should we not tell someone about it?'

'I don't think so,' said Charlotte. 'For all we know, she has spoken to one of the doctors here or perhaps in London about it. I feel this is for her to deal with.'

'Well, it doesn't feel right. But I suppose she has given us a clear instruction.'

'Exactly.'

In the front hall, Mr. and Mrs. Sears were sitting at one of the small tables. The reason why became clear when they went back upstairs to the ward. Charlotte saw that the screens around their son's bed had been closed.

'He died about an hour ago,' said Isobel. She had tears in her eyes.

For the third time that afternoon, Sandy and his colleague had to lift a body on to a stretcher and carry it downstairs. The little cortege walked to the small graveyard at the back of the hospital for the funeral. Charlotte heard the unmistakable sound of a lone bagpiper playing a haunting melody that made the hairs on the back of her neck stand up. The music transfixed her and she could feel her eyes prickling. The tune somehow evoked in her feelings of home, warmth and safety. How ironic that it was being played at a funeral in a foreign country.

She managed to speak to Sears's parents briefly after the funeral when they came back into the building to say goodbye to the staff.

'That was a beautiful piece of music. I could hear it from here.'

'The orderly arranged for someone to play. It was a retreat air from my part of Scotland and very suitable for this occasion,' said Mr. Sears.

His wife said, 'I would like to have taken him home with me. I've heard it's possible, but I know it can't always happen. At least we know where he is. And I have his watch.'

'That's something of a comfort,' Charlotte said. 'Please take care of yourselves and have a safe journey home. I'm sorry that we had to meet in such sad circumstances.'

Mr. Sears held out his hand which Charlotte shook. 'Thank you for your caring attitude to Edward and us,' he said.

They turned and left the ward, clutching a bag containing their son's possessions. But as they were crossing the courtyard to be taken back to the station for their journey home, Charlotte saw Nurse Brook approach them and say something. Whatever it was, it caused Mrs. Sears to become extremely distressed again.

Nurse Brook came into the ward a few minutes later.

'Did I see the Mr. and Mrs. Sears leaving to catch the train?' asked Charlotte.

'Yes, I told them they were lucky to have seen him – unlike so many others who never see their sons again.'

Charlotte was exasperated. 'Oh, Nurse Brook, what in the name of God is lucky about their situation? I think that's insensitive.'

'You're too soft,' growled Nurse Brook.

'And as I said to you the other day, I think you're heartless.' Charlotte turned and walked away, shocked at her sharp retort. It was the sort of remark she often thought but would be reluctant to say out loud for fear of offending someone. But she had no concerns about letting Nurse Brook know how she felt.

Nurse Brook called after her.

'What was wrong with Matron, then?'

'Captain Graves thinks it's probably influenza.'

'Just as well I told Nurse Wishaw to go down to her room then.'

Charlotte spun round. 'Do you know, you are truly unbelievable. You said no such thing. In fact, if I remember correctly, you didn't want anyone to go to her room at all.'

Nurse Brook strode off.

Charlotte went back to the desk, seething quietly. Margaret was sitting there, looking at the daily task books. 'So who still needs attention?' Charlotte asked.

'Please could you see how Pritchard is doing for me?'

Charlotte went into the bed-space behind the screens and could see Pritchard was very drowsy and his breathing laboured and slow. Something about the situation didn't feel right. She lifted one of his eyelids and she noticed how small his pupils were. She looked up at his chart but nothing was recorded on it.

Back at the desk, she said to Margaret, 'He's settled but his breathing is very slow and his pupils are like pins. Has he had an injection of morphia recently?'

'Is there anything on his chart?'

'No.'

Margaret lifted the doctors' order book and looked. 'It says he can have a quarter grain of morphia by injection if needed.'

'It looks to me like he's had a much larger dose than that.'

'I'll mention it to Captain Graves but he's unlikely to do anything about it even if that's the case. In fact, he would probably encourage a heavier hand with the syringe.'

That was difficult for Charlotte to hear. She knew Pritchard had sustained a terrible injury but she also knew it was not life-threatening. One of her colleagues had decided to give him a larger-than-prescribed dose of morphine in the hope that it would cause him an overdose and that he would die. Who would have done such a thing? It reminded her of the drug error she had been involved in at home which, she realised, was not as severe as this.

She tried to busy herself for the rest of the shift with her remaining tasks. Pritchard died about two hours later.

As Charlotte left the ward, she thought about the four patients they had lost today, all in such different circumstances. Two had died in the side room, while the others had died behind screens. Two had died of their wounds, and one had been visited by his family. Poor Gilbert had received comfort from the padre but had a hand in his own death. And now it appeared that Pritchard had died as a result of someone giving him an intentional overdose.

Before she went to bed, Charlotte returned to Matron's room. She knocked and went in. Matron was looking better even though she remained drowsy and didn't react as Charlotte approached her bed.

'Good evening, Matron. I thought I would pop in and see how you were feeling now.'

Matron opened her eyes. 'A little better tonight, thank you, Nurse Robertson.'

'Would you like me to get you a drink?'

'A little brandy. There's some in the decanter on the table over there by the fireplace.'

This was not the answer Charlotte was expecting but she complied. She poured a small measure into one of the crystal glasses on the table and brought it over.

'Help me up a bit.'

Charlotte did so then offered Matron the brandy. She took it but her hands were shaky. 'You will have to help me. I have no strength in my arms at the moment.'

'Yes, of course.'

Charlotte put the brandy glass to Matron's lips and she took a sip. It took about five minutes for her to finish the drink and neither spoke as she did so. When the glass was empty, Matron said, 'That'll be all.'

'Well, I do hope you have a more settled night, Matron. I'll pop in and see how you are in the morning.'

'As you wish, but it won't be necessary. I will be back to work after a good night's sleep.' She leant back on her pillows, then said, 'By the way, Nurse Robertson, don't think that this additional visit with absolve you from facing up to your actions.'

Her comment upset Charlotte. 'Matron, I can assure you that the only reason for this visit was to see how you were. Goodnight.'

She left the room and thought about her reaction to Matron's indifference to the care she had received and her view of why Charlotte had visited again. She felt aggrieved that Matron had not thanked her for looking after her and hurt at being accused of trying to curry favour. It felt unfair. This was the second time she had received no thanks for the care she had given and it affected her. She went back upstairs to her bedroom.

'So how is Matron tonight?' said Daisy.

'I think she's feeling better because she was a bit snippy with me.'

'I'm sure she'll bounce back. She's made of strong stuff.'

'She's determined to be back on duty tomorrow.'

Margaret said, 'You're in a positive mood this evening, Daisy. Would that be anything to do with the presence of our lovely American on the ward?'

Daisy blushed.

'Perhaps,' was all she would say.

'Daisy always likes it when Tom offers to help us move the beds around and sweep the floor for us. Isn't that right?'

Daisy said nothing.

'I've heard him say what lovely eyes you have,' Margaret added.

'From what I've seen, he's one of the world's good guys,' said Charlotte.

Daisy nodded. 'He is, yes. He realised after we'd finished all the ward moves that James had gone out on a call instead of him and he felt bad about letting him go when it was his turn. Honestly, they're such a pair!'

'I bet he's done the same for James lots of times, though,' Charlotte said.

She sat on her bed and unlaced her shoes. Her feet ached and she started to rub them.

Margaret passed her a small bottle. 'Here Charlotte, try this as a foot soak. It's excellent.' The label said 'Permanganate of potash' – another lotion that Charlotte had never heard of.

'Just add a few drops to a basin of warm water and soak your toes for fifteen minutes.'

'I say, would you two like a cup of tea and a piece of my mother's best fruit cake after all your work with Matron?' said Daisy. She was rummaging in a box under her bed. 'I almost forgot about it.'

'That does sound lovely,' said Margaret. Charlotte said, 'Yes, please.'

Daisy got up to go and fetch the teacups. 'I'll be back in a minute.'

When she reappeared with a tray, she cut three generous slices of cake.

'That looks delicious,' said Margaret – and it was.

They began talking about the ward and the day's work.

'Another interesting day,' said Charlotte. 'You did well taking charge in Matron's absence, Margaret.'

'Well, it was clear Nurse Brook was not going to manage.'

'She almost let the men leave without their papers this morning,' Charlotte said. 'I know I have my problems but she's inefficient, and what's more I don't think she cares about any of the men here at all.'

'That's rather harsh,' said Daisy.

'She told that poor man Pritchard to stop acting like a baby. Imagine doing that when he was so badly injured.'

Margaret said, 'You know, Daisy, Charlotte's right. When Matron isn't around to instruct her, Nurse Brook doesn't have any leadership qualities. And we've both said in the past that she won't make a very good ward sister.'

'Well, that may be so but she's had a hard life, and I do think you're a bit unkind.'

'Daisy, I know that you're a gem and you never think ill of anyone,' said Margaret. 'But in this case, I believe you're wrong.'

'What do you mean, Daisy? Why has she had a hard life?' said Charlotte.

'She was orphaned as a young child and had to look after her brothers and sisters, so she was responsible for others at a young age. She had to take on some pretty demanding jobs and only managed to be admitted for training in a local hospital.'

Charlotte said, 'Even so, that doesn't explain the uncaring way she behaves towards the men. I don't know what she said to Mr. and Mrs. Sears as they were leaving but I don't think it was words of comfort.'

'But she hasn't experienced that sense of comfort herself so it's not surprising her manner appears so cold.'

'And,' Charlotte said, 'when Margaret and I came back from seeing Matron, she claimed the credit for us going!'

'I'm surprised you're becoming so heated about her. Margaret, what do you think?'

'Well, I can see an element of truth in what both of you are saying. I find her a person who has been tough to get to know and I suppose that's what I find rather difficult.' She looked over at Charlotte. 'Remind me to stay on your good side.'

'I suppose I have over-reacted a bit,' Charlotte conceded. 'But I still say she's uncaring. And I wouldn't trust her as far as I could spit.'

Daisy put her hand to a mouth. 'Oh, what a coarse thing to say, Charlotte. I'm surprised you would say something so vulgar.'

'Sorry. That's a very common saying at home.'

Charlotte quickly changed the subject.

'So, Margaret, why did Captain Clift move Brown into the side room?'

'Mainly because Matron wasn't around. He didn't agree with the original plan to continue active treatment but he's caught between his old civilian life and the army. He has to follow orders, which he finds hard at times. In a way, I think he's relieved that Brown's wound became infected, that he drank the carbolic – and that he'll no longer have to face the consequences of his actions. That's very different from the view of our colleagues in the army. Matron seems to believe that this sort of action could spread like influenza if men are not dealt with harshly in these situations.'

'I went in to see him in the side room and he pulled out his nasogastric tube in front of me,' said Charlotte.

'Captain Clift thought he might and told me to leave things alone if that happened.'

'Just as well I did nothing about it then. Tell me, do you have many patients who come in with injuries like Pritchard's?'

'Not that many,' Margaret said. 'But Captain Graves told me that on one occasion when a soldier did appear with a similar injury, he begged to be put out of his misery. I think the boys at the advance dressing stations are often heavy with the morphine in such cases.'

'I wonder if that approach has continued in the ward. It probably explains why he died this afternoon.'

'It's hard to know how to care for them when they're injured like that,' said Margaret.

'Or what will become of them,' Daisy added. 'He was engaged to be married, I think, which it makes even sadder.'

Charlotte told them she had been at a loss to know what to say when she looked at his dressing.

'Well, you wouldn't be the only one,' said Margaret.

Daisy said, 'In some ways, it's just as well he died.'

Charlotte thought for a moment. 'I understand what you mean but I can't agree with the way he died. It feels as though he's been put to sleep.'

'Sometimes that's just what has to happen,' said Daisy, but Charlotte shook her head in disagreement.

The subject changed to lighter topics and they continued to chat about the day and their work.

Finally, Daisy yawned and said, 'I think I'm ready to settle down for the night.' The others agreed.

When the lamps were put out, Charlotte lay in the dark going over all that had happened and thinking again about her husband and children.

I hope I'll be able to tell them all about this amazing adventure when it's over, she thought. But will they believe me when I tell them?

Her uncertainty about being trapped had lessened a little during the day. Perhaps, she thought, that means I'm ready to go home and when I next open my eyes, I'll wake up on the train again.

CHAPTER 15

She heard the now-familiar six o'clock knock on the door and immediately felt a sense of disappointment. Here she was, still in this uncomfortable single bed, still a nurse in 1916 France. I'll just have to get on with the day then, she thought.

She said good morning to Daisy and Margaret and began to dress. She had become adept at putting on her uniform now. She checked that her rings were secured in her pocket as she didn't want a repeat of yesterday. They reminded her of Colin and the children and she wondered what they planned to do today. She so wanted to be with them. I need to distract myself again, she thought.

They went down for breakfast and Charlotte wondered how Matron would be feeling but decided not to knock on her door.

As ever, Sandy was cleaning the upper landing.

'Good morning, Sandy. How are you today?'

'Aye, it's another bad business, nurse,' he said.

Charlotte agreed, thinking he was talking about the events of the previous day. But he wasn't. Shortly after morning orders, Tom came into the ward, just as he did every day. His ashen expression heralded bad news. She asked him what was wrong. He could hardly speak.

'It's James,' he stammered. 'He got hit by a sniper when he went out on that call for me last night.'

Charlotte put her hand over her mouth. 'Oh God, no. Is he badly injured?'

'I don't know,' Tom said. 'And the worst thing is I don't even know where he is. I just knew something was wrong when the ambulance didn't return. I heard the news from one of the other crews.'

'Do you know how it happened?'

'All I know is that he went up to one of the advance dressing stations, just behind the front line. It sounds as though someone was lying in wait for them to pass.'

The full details emerged during the morning. An ambulance from another unit had gone off the road, which was why the hospital was called on for additional help. James had willingly volunteered. Tom had not known that the call had come in because he was helping in the ward. No one knew if James was dead or alive so it was a question of waiting.

But there was no halting the daily routine of the ward.

Matron appeared but she ignored Tom as he passed her to leave the ward.

Charlotte thought she looked considerably better. There was still a faint smell of lavender, though.

'Let's start the morning orders and stop this dawdling about,' Matron announced.

Nurse Collinson began her review. Unusually there were nine empty beds. Fellows was still in the ward but his condition was worsening. He had, however, been included in the list of soldiers who were being discharged. Charlotte thought this must be a mistake but no one questioned Nurse Collinson. Five soldiers would be going for surgery today. They had a variety of injuries but had all been categorised as 'B' wounds. Aston in bed one seemed to be the only 'A' wound but Croft in bed two, who also had an abdominal injury, was reported as being still too ill for surgery.

At the end of the report, Matron allocated the daily work. The first task was cleaning.

'As there are so many empty beds at the moment, you all have time to attend to the ward cleaning, before the monthly inspection. You need to ensure that these tasks are completed this morning. There is a reason why we are clearing the ward. I have been notified that we have been allocated at least fifteen admissions today.'

To Margaret, she said, 'Nurse Wishaw, please be in charge of the new admissions when they arrive and the theatre cases. The medical staff will review the other two this morning so continue the resuscitation efforts with Aston and Croft. Nurse Ashville, you can attend to the observations and dressings.'

She turned to Charlotte. 'I have decided that you will accompany the departures today, Nurse Robertson, but it will be later on in the afternoon before they leave and therefore you will report to my office at twelve-thirty exactly. In the meantime, you can help Nurse Ashville with her work.'

'Yes, Matron,' Charlotte said. 'From the morning orders, I understand that Beattie, Ellis, Deans, Paterson and Jackson will be going. Is that correct?'

'Fellows will also be discharged today.'

'Fellows? But is his condition suitable for travel?'

Matron sighed. 'As reported in the morning orders, there will be six of them going on to the coast, including Fellows. There is nothing more we can do for him and it would be best to send him home. Now, make sure they are ready to leave by five this afternoon. You must attend to the discharges properly today as I understand from Nurse Brook there was an unnecessary scramble to collate the paperwork yesterday.'

'Matron McLean,' said Margaret. 'Nurse Robertson was not responsible for the discharges yesterday.'

'That doesn't match the information I was given.'

'I assumed charge yesterday morning and I asked Nurse Brook to do it. Fortunately Nurse Robertson noticed that the papers were incomplete just before the soldiers were leaving the ward.'

'Is this correct, Nurse Robertson?'

'Yes, Matron.'

'That doesn't change anything about the need to ensure that all the men are ready to be discharged.' Matron stood. 'Now, I am returning to my room to attend to some paperwork,' she announced. 'Nurse Wishaw, please be in overall charge of the ward again this morning. Sister Craig will be back on duty later.'

Most of the staff went about their duties half-heartedly while awaiting news about James. An hour later, an ambulance arrived in the back yard and those who saw it pull up had a feeling he might be in it because it was from a different unit. Charlotte and her colleagues watched from a hall window. As the ambulance came to a halt, Tom had jumped up and opened its doors. He quickly climbed down again. He was looking skyward with his hands on his head and an anguished expression on his face.

Margaret, without turning, said, 'Go and comfort him, Daisy. We can manage here for a while.'

Daisy ran off down the corridor and they heard her feet thundering down the main staircase. By the time she reached the courtyard, the body was being lifted out of the ambulance.

Everyone watching was distressed. Tom insisted on being a stretcher-bearer for his friend who was carried into the assessment room where Huguette had died a couple of nights earlier. Daisy, Charlotte, Margaret and the two medical staff were among those who paid their respects. James looked unmarked, apart from a small bullet hole between his eyes. The sniper had been deadly accurate.

'Right, let's get him tidied up before we take him out to the churchyard to bury him,' said Daisy quietly, beginning to cry. 'I can't understand why I'm so upset.' She wiped her eyes. 'We deal with this all the time.'

Charlotte tried to console her. 'But this is so different. Those young men upstairs are strangers to us when they arrive but we knew James. This loss is personal. It feels even worse because he's not a soldier.'

Margaret, who earlier had gone back upstairs, popped her head round the door. 'I know you want to do the best for James but we need you both back on the ward. There's a lot to do before all those admissions arrive. I'm sorry ...'

Daisy said, 'Yes, Margaret, you're right. I just want to make him look at peace for Tom. We're almost finished – a few more minutes. Please.'

They wiped James's face, cleaned his hands and tied his ankles together, then crossed his arms over his chest. That was all that needed to be done.

Charlotte said, 'Why don't you have a quick break before you come back to the ward? Go and see how Tom's doing. I'm sure we can cope for a few minutes.'

Daisy gave a sad smile. 'No, it's probably best to distract myself.'

So they returned to the ward and tried to focus on their work. Just like every day, there were beds to make, medicines to be administered, dressings to be changed, observations to be recorded and soldiers to prepare for discharge. Daisy and Charlotte divided the sixteen dressings between them and it took them nearly three hours to complete their tasks. Charlotte was pleased that she kept up her with Daisy's work rate. She was able to replace the bulky bandages neatly, and the VADs helped with the disposal of the dirty dressings as well as getting on with the cleaning and scrubbing.

The morning passed quickly. It was nearing twelve-thirty. Charlotte managed a quick chat with Margaret.

'I'd better go and face the music. I'm sure I'm about to be severely reprimanded for my outburst yesterday so I hope I see you again.'

Margaret said, 'I don't know what she'll say or do but I don't think you're going to have a very friendly meeting. You'll need courage but for heaven's sake,

Charlotte, don't make it worse for yourself. Please watch what you say. Remember you're not in 2001 – not at the moment, at least.'

Charlotte nodded. 'You're right, but given my situation what can she do?'

'She could dismiss you from the hospital – and if she did send you away from the unit, where would you go?'

Charlotte suddenly felt nervous.

'I did think about that the other day. I promise I'll try to behave in a professional manner, suitable for 1916. Wish me luck.'

Charlotte walked down the stairs thinking about all that had happened over the past five days. It had been an amazing adventure for her, even with all her initial uncertainties about her skills and her fears about being away from her family. She was walking with more confidence but felt she needed every ounce of it now. Perhaps this will prepare me for the disciplinary meeting when I get home, she thought.

Sandy was sweeping the downstairs hall as she passed.

'Aye-aye, nurse, remember to be canny now. Don't make things worse for yeself. You're a good, caring nurse and that goes a long way in a place like this, ye ken.'

'Thanks, Sandy. That means a lot to me.'

She knocked on Matron's door and a voice instructed her to enter. She wiped her hands on her apron before opening the door, just as Margaret had done the day before.

Matron McLean was sitting at her desk with her back to Charlotte. Sister Craig was also in the room.

'Hello, Nurse Robertson.'

Charlotte smiled. 'Hello Sister Craig. It's good to see you again.'

Matron took her time before turning round and Charlotte was left standing.

Finally, she said, 'I take it that you understand why you are here.'

'Yes, Matron.'

'Do you have anything to say?'

'Matron McLean, I feel I should apologise for being rude to you yesterday. I didn't mean to be disrespectful but I was trying to protect Brown from what I consider to be ...'

Matron interrupted. 'But it's not your place to consider anything and you need to learn obedience if you want to work in my unit. If Sister Craig hadn't put in such a good word for you, I would have sent you back home immediately, with no hesitation. She tells me what a valuable contribution you have made to the ward team, which I find rather surprising. But let me make it clear that I have added a warning note in your file and if anything like this happens again, I will not hesitate to dismiss you. Do I make myself clear?''

'Yes, Matron.'

Charlotte assumed she would be asked to leave the room now that her reprimand was over but Matron didn't appear to be finished with her. She turned back to her desk and lifted a piece of paper that had a numbered list on it.

'Consider that matter closed now but please make sure that you watch what you say to senior staff. Believe me, I will not tolerate behaviour like this again. Now, sit down, Nurse Robertson, I wish to ask you some questions on another matter.'

Charlotte sat on one of the little chairs, uncertain what she was about to be asked. She found she was sitting bolt upright.

'This morning, Nurse Wishaw informed me that you had to step in and complete the work of Nurse Brook from yesterday. Is that correct?'

'Yes, Matron. The papers were in total disarray and I didn't want the soldiers to leave the ward without them.'

'Has this happened before while you've been here?'

'Yes, it also happened on the second day as well – if my memory serves me.'

'I see. Can you also confirm whether you countersigned the medication book four days ago when Fellows, who was a new admission that day, was given morphia?'

'No, Matron. I didn't countersign anything because I was uncertain about the medication doses and only administered medication following your lecture.'

'So are you telling me that this is not your signature?'

Matron lifted a ledger and pointed to a row towards the top of the page. There were two signatures. One said 'E Brook'. The other name was hers but it was not her writing.

'It's not, Matron. I can assure you that although it's my name, that isn't my signature.'

'I see. Thank you, nurse.'

Charlotte was still puzzled.

'Please may I ask why you're asking me these questions?'

'No, you may not. Sister Craig, do you have any questions?'

Sister Craig nodded and said to Charlotte, 'I recall that on your first day here, Nurse Brook showed you how to admit a soldier to the ward. Is that right?'

'Yes, Sister, she did.'

'Did she mention the importance of washing the soldiers entirely on arrival and checking that they had been given their first dose of anti-tetanus serum?'

Charlotte was finding the interrogation uncomfortable. She remembered Nurse Brook telling her not to bother washing the soldiers' feet. 'Yes, I believe she did say something about it.'

Matron said, 'Sister Craig, I think that was the morning when I felt the ward was very disorganised and some admissions had not been completed correctly. However, that shouldn't excuse poor practice by a qualified nurse.'

'Yes, Matron, but I do believe this has been one of several deliberate acts to try to remove me from my post.'

'Thank you, Sister Craig, but please say no more at the moment. Nurse Robertson, you can go now but in future, I repeat, show more respect for your superiors.'

Margaret's plea for caution echoed in Charlotte's head. 'Thank you, Matron,' she heard herself say as she walked towards the door.

She went slowly back up the stairs trying to work out what had just happened.

Margaret was waiting for her in the ward.

'Well, are you being dismissed? Oh, do tell me what happened?'

'I've had a caution put on my record and if it happens again I'll be sent home immediately,' Charlotte said. 'But Sister Craig was there and I think something else is going on. They asked me questions about Nurse Brook.'

'Nurse Brook?' said Margaret. 'What's she got to do with anything?'

'Well, she's signed my name in the medication book for one thing. Matron showed me something I'd apparently signed the other day. I think Nurse Brook must have added my name.'

'Oh, that's not good. Did they ask you anything else?'

'Whether I'd admitted anyone on my first day and how I was instructed to do it. I'm not sure if I told you how dismissive Nurse Brook was about the night staff but I didn't say that to Matron.'

'No, I don't think you did. But most of us could give an account of her poor practice. I wonder if anyone else will be called into Matron's room. Perhaps you were asked because they can see you have more confidence in being outspoken than the rest of us.'

'That's not entirely true, Margaret. You stood up for me in front of her at morning orders earlier.'

'That's only because I felt able to do so because you were there. I've learned so much from you, you know.'

Charlotte was surprised and thanked Margaret. 'It's mutual, you know. You've helped me feel so much more certain about my nursing skills.'

'Are you sure about that?'

'More than you'll ever know,' Charlotte said.

None of the expected admissions had arrived yet so Margaret arranged for an early lunchtime so the team would be fresh and ready for a potentially chaotic afternoon.

There was also another reason to finish lunch early. A short funeral had been arranged for James. His body was wrapped in an American flag that Tom had brought with him from home. As the little party filed out of the hospital to accompany the body to the graveyard, Charlotte, Daisy and Margaret were amazed to see an important-looking group of officials waiting at the graveside. Matron McLean and Sister Craig were also there, dressed in their formal uniforms.

It was only now that the full truth of James's bravery became known to the assembled company. The divisional surgeon-in-chief had heard about his death and had come to the hospital for the funeral. James had been cited three times previously for bravery under fire and now he had been awarded the Croix de Guerre. It was pinned on the cloth covering his body before it was placed in the grave. The citation was written in French.

> *James Kenmure was a true 'Good Samaritan', previously mentioned in dispatches. His unending devotion to duty has led the General commanding the division to confer the Croix de Guerre on him.*

There was a note on his grave-marker: 'James Kenmure. An American who died for France.'

As the citation was read out, there were muffled sobs from the mourners standing round the grave. For a moment, Charlotte thought she caught Matron McLean wiping a tear away but then realised that she was merely brushing her hair aside.

She looked around the small congregation. Daisy was clutching Tom's arm tightly. He looked grief-stricken and Charlotte wondered if he was blaming himself for James's death. She imagined that Tom would want to write to James's parents – but what a hard letter to write. For now, though, with the funeral service over, everyone had to resume their work, despite the raw grief they were feeling.

Back on the ward, one of the outstanding tasks was the application of a cold pack to Gilbertson in bed twenty-one who had developed a fever. Charlotte was intrigued to participate in another two-person technique. It involved rolling up a mackintosh sheet and a wet sheet lengthways on the bed under the patient, unrolling it and then wrapping the patient in the cold sheet. Chunks of ice were then placed on top of the wet sheet for about twenty minutes. The patient's temperature and pulse were recorded every ten minutes to see if the fever was lessening and if the procedure was making any difference. In this case, to Charlotte's surprise, it did seem to work. The wet sheet and mackintosh were then removed and the patient lightly covered, more for modesty than anything else.

As Charlotte was clearing all the wet material away, she spoke to Sarah who was making dressings. Sarah was nervous because she had made a mistake a couple of days earlier and the batch of dressing material had to be thrown away.

'What happened?' Charlotte asked.

Sarah explained that she had been cutting dressings into various sizes before putting them in the steriliser. 'I thought you added the idoform before you sterilised them, not afterwards. Unfortunately, if you do it before, it causes the material to disintegrate. But I didn't know that at the time. When I opened the steriliser, there were just threads left.'

Charlotte was just about to offer words of comfort but Nurse Brook was marching towards her along the corridor.

'How could you?' she shouted.

Sarah looked alarmed.

Charlotte stood her ground.

'Excuse me?' she said.

'How could you be so hateful about me to Matron and Sister Craig?'

'No, Nurse Brook, you've got that wrong, I wasn't hateful at all. I gave factual answers to the questions they asked. I could've said a lot more than I did.'

'Well, whatever you said, I'm being moved back to England.'

'As I have just said, I answered their questions factually. Your actions have resulted in this outcome, not my words.' Charlotte spoke calmly, which seemed to infuriate Nurse Brook further.

'You seem so sure of yourself but I can see your game, you know. You're hoping to impress Matron so that she'll promote you.'

'Wrong again, Nurse Brook. I haven't any such ambition. All that matters to me is that we care for our patients well and compassionately. And compassion seems to be a quality you don't possess. And furthermore I will not stand by and watch a senior colleague being undermined. It's happened to me and I won't let it happen to someone else.'

'It should have been me who was promoted,' Nurse Brook said angrily. 'I've worked as a staff nurse for long enough. I've served my time. You people are all the same – smug, certain and working against the likes of me.'

Charlotte was amazed at this outburst. She had never felt she had those traits and was uncertain at first how to respond.

'I think you're wrong, Nurse Brook. I've found this experience to be extremely taxing and, if you want to know the truth, I've never felt more uncertain in my life.'

'You liar! That doesn't help me one bit, you evil bitch.' Nurse Brook was yelling and jabbing her finger into Charlotte's chest.

'Is that the worst you can call me?' said Charlotte. 'Well, all I can say is you're wrong. And I don't think there's anything further to say on the matter.'

Nurse Brook glowered at her then turned and marched back along the corridor.

Margaret, the VADs and some the soldiers had heard this altercation from the main ward. Some had been shocked by Nurse Brook's language but it had had no impact at all on Charlotte, which surprised everyone.

Someone must have reported it to Sister Craig because she took Charlotte aside when she arrived in the ward.

'I'm shocked to hear what Nurse Brook said to you, Nurse Robertson. Are you alright?'

'Yes, Sister. I've been called much worse than that.'

'I can't imagine anything worse ...'

Charlotte cut her off. 'Honestly, I'm fine. I don't think I've ever met such an uncaring person. And Sister Craig, I wanted to say thank you for supporting me as you did with Matron. I was apprehensive about what she would do with me.'

'I'm sure she could have dismissed you for less, you know. In all honesty, I didn't have to say very much. She thinks you're a good nurse. She's admired how well you've adapted to this sort of work. She told me that she didn't think much of you when you arrived but you've impressed her with your ability to learn quickly. The two doctors also gave splendid reports about you. However, Matron still finds you rather outspoken. On the other matter, she has had Nurse Brook ... well, in her sights for a while and her actions this week have been the final straw. I think Nurse Brook underestimated Matron's ability to see beyond what she was being told. The way you've stood up to her helped Matron to see what Nurse Brook has been trying to do.'

'I know Matron wouldn't tell me but are you able to say what else Nurse Brook did?'

Sister Craig paused before she spoke. 'Well, she's been in the habit of falsifying records for a while, both saying that medications have been given when they haven't as well as adding others' names to notes. That's why Matron wanted to ask you directly about the signature in the book. It was your question at the lecture the other day that made her follow that up. It's most likely that she also gave Pritchard a large, single dose of morphia and that's why he died yesterday. The tetanus officer also noted the similarity of the writing on the medical cards and thinks that she hadn't been administering the anti-tetanus medication if a soldier arrived without having the first dose. That's why Thomson developed early symptoms.'

'I only knew about the symptoms of tetanus because of her lecture, Sister.'

'It doesn't matter how you discovered it. Perhaps you don't realise how many men used to die from tetanus at the beginning of the war, so early intervention is critical.'

'All those errors sound serious. What will happen to her?'

'She'll be dismissed from the service, I imagine.'

'Why would someone act in such a way?' asked Charlotte.

'I think she was sure she wouldn't get caught. She seemed so sure that she should have been promoted as well. It's difficult to deal with someone when they have such little insight into their abilities. No doubt she will continue to think it's been a conspiracy against her.'

'I think you're right about that, Sister.'

'But luckily we won't have to deal with it here any longer.' She straightened her cap. 'Now then, I must attend to some work. Without Nurse Brook here, I'm ready to be Sister of this ward again.'

CHAPTER 16

Charlotte was overjoyed to know that Matron thought she was a good nurse. I'll take that as a compliment, she thought.

Later they all managed to sit down for a cup of tea.

'Am I right in remembering that you'd been doing escort duty when we first met?' Charlotte asked Margaret.

'That's right; it's something we do quite often. The fun escort is on the barges but most of the time we go on the trains.'

'I didn't know barges were used for to transport soldiers.'

'It's quite common,' Margaret said. 'And more comfortable for the soldiers, as you saw from your bumpy ride here.'

'Do I need to take anything with me on the train?'

'No, the idea is that you hand them over at the earliest opportunity to let them go on the sea train to Dover and you return on the next train. You should be back by nightfall – as long as the train isn't going too slowly. But you're not leaving till five so you might have another late night. Sometimes I think it would be quicker to walk. It all depends on how often you're shunted into a siding to let a troop or munitions train come in the other direction.'

As the time for departure approached, Charlotte thought about the soldiers she was escorting and what might go wrong. She wondered about Beattie's neck wound and put a couple of packets of swabs in her pocket, just in case. She also thought that Fellows was probably too ill to move.

She managed to have a quick word with Margaret in the ward just before the soldiers were due to leave. She asked if patients were ever left because their conditions were deteriorating.

Margaret shook her head. 'On a day like this when there are lots of admissions due, the doctors will move anyone who has a pulse.'

'I should have known better than to ask, I suppose. I'd better keep a close eye on Fellows, I think.'

'You might not be looking after him though. I'll leave the lamp on for you in case it's late before you return.'

'Thanks, Margaret. See you later then.'

'We have an afternoon free tomorrow, so let's go to Albert and find a cafe so we can discuss our travel adventures.'

'I'd like that very much.'

The orderlies had arrived to start with the transport of the soldiers.

'Right,' Charlotte said, 'it looks like we're ready to go.'

She put her cape on and accompanied Beattie's stretcher down the staircase, across the front hall, out of the large glass doors and down the steps to the line of waiting ambulances. Half an hour later they were ready to start their journey. Just as Charlotte was climbing into the back of the ambulance, Sandy appeared with a newspaper, *The Press and Journal*.

'I've finished with this,' he said, handing it to her. 'It's recent. I thought you might like to read it on the train – if you get a moment.'

'Thanks, Sandy, that's kind. I'll enjoy looking at it.' She waved goodbye to him as they headed down the drive.

Tom was the driver on the short journey to Albert railway station, continuing with his work despite his grief. Charlotte admired the incredible resilience of all the people she had met.

The shutters in the back of the ambulance were open and as they made their way slowly to the station, she watched the hospital and estate disappear from view.

A line of ambulances was going in the opposite direction – at least fifteen. Clearly the busy period of admissions was about to start and she felt bad about missing it. Charlotte estimated that they would have more admissions than beds because there was sure to be more than one man in each vehicle.

She could see now the potholes that had made their journey to the hospital the other night so bumpy. Tom was trying to avoid them so progress was slow. The road was also full of trucks, men and horses – more so than on her arrival – and there was a lot of debris on the verges, as well as dead horses. The decaying carcasses made her stomach heave as they edged past.

The station forecourt and yard were busy, as they had been on that first night, but this time Charlotte felt a lot more confident. Tom helped the station orderlies lift the men and directed them to the right platform. They had to pick their way carefully through the crowds. The news about James had spread and a couple of the orderlies commiserated with Tom.

Charlotte was surprised by the length of the train – fifteen carriages, all painted beige with a large red cross on the side.

The officer in charge checked the men's labels against a list and advised the orderlies where on the train each man should go.

The patients were loaded through the windows of the carriages, which could all accommodate three tiers of wounded men, but it was a difficult job to move the soldiers off the stretchers and on to the beds. Every man had his personal possessions with him, stowed under his pillow.

Tom ensured that everyone was settled, and then he and Charlotte climbed down from the train. He had to shout over the hissing of the trains and all the noise in the station. 'I'll see you later this evening. You're not going that far, so you should get back tonight and I'll come and collect you. The guard will call to let me know when you've returned. Have a safe journey.'

'Thanks, Tom. But judging by that convoy we passed, it looks like you're going to have a busy time for the rest of the day.'

'Yes, I'm going to pick some more men up on the way back. I'd better get on with the loading now. I'll try to say goodbye before the train leaves.'

Charlotte climbed back onboard, noticing how organised the carriages looked. The beds had all been made, everything was tidy and there was a smell of disinfectant.

A nurse appeared and said she was in charge of the train. 'And who have I got with me on this journey, then?'

'I'm Nurse Robertson from Bécourt Hospital and I'm accompanying these men up to the coast today.'

'Good to meet you, Nurse Robertson. I'm Sister Dunsmore. We're off to Étaples this evening. Tell me, have you worked on a train before?'

'No, Sister.'

Here we go again, thought Charlotte, expecting another comment about her inexperience. But Sister Dunsmore said simply, 'Never mind, you will soon get the hang of it. It's really just a ward on wheels. Let me take you to the staff coach where you can leave your coat. I'll give you some equipment to carry with you as you make your rounds – it'll save you a bit of shoe leather.'

As they made their way towards the back of the train, Sister Dunsmore said, 'You can use one of the seats to rest in. But that might not be for many hours, depending on our progress.'

In the staff coach, Charlotte put down her bag and the newspaper Sandy had given her, got off the train again and pushed her way along the platform to where the last few soldiers were being loaded. It was all being done very efficiently, with the train staff checking off the passengers' names.

Charlotte wanted to say goodbye to Tom but she couldn't find him in the crowd. Then, as she climbed back onboard the train, she heard him calling. 'Nurse Robertson, *bon voyage*. I'll see you later.'

She spotted him through the carriage window and waved. 'Thanks, Tom. Take care. Yes, see you later.' He was waving back.

The train whistle blew and the carriages shuddered then started moving. Charlotte closed the window and thought she should familiarise herself with her new surroundings.

There was a small sluice-like room that had a few basins, urinals and bedpans, and some cupboards with dressings and medicines. As most of the carriages had been adapted to take stretchers, there was little room to sit down.

The train crept along and, as Daisy had suggested, there were soldiers walking alongside the line, easily keeping up. She wondered where they were going.

She had about thirty men to keep an eye on in one carriage and a further twenty-five in the next but despite the numbers it was less frenetic than in the hospital. There was a medical officer in her section as well as a couple of orderlies. Beattie and Fellows were in different carriages. The other passengers had come from different units and not all were injured. Some were being repatriated due to illness. She was able to check the men's medical cards to see if any needed medicines, and made sure that all the men who needed pain relief had been given a morphia tablet before they set off.

'Where are you from?' she asked one young man who looked extremely young, lying with his leg elevated.

'Bristol,' he said. 'I was commissioned through the Officer Cadet Battalion in February while I was a student at the university.'

'What were you studying?'

'English literature. I hope to become a teacher once this is all over.'

'Have you been here for a long time?'

'Not really. Only since May, when I finished the training.'

'How did you get injured?'

'The dreaded night patrol, I'm afraid. We go out with our men on working parties. It's safer at night than during the day. You know, nurse, my patrol was so kind to me. After I was hit, one gave me a cigarette and another went and fetched me a cup of warm tea while we were waiting for the stretcher.'

'Where were you hurt?'

'I got most of my right foot blown off. I was more concerned not to show any fear to the men. I hope I carried that off. Do you know, I'm not looking forward to going home. My pals tell me they feel really out of step when they're home now.' He gave a wry smile. 'I suppose that'll be accurate for me.'

Charlotte said, 'I wonder why they feel that way.'

'I think everyone just wants to carry on with their lives and not think about things over here anymore.'

She kept an eye on Fellows as the journey began. She was concerned that his condition would deteriorate with all the movement involved in transporting him from the hospital to the train. But perhaps the thought of going home was giving him a boost. She was so pleased he was on his way back to Britain and would be able to meet his baby daughter.

Three hours into the journey, it had begun to get dark outside. The electric lamps had been lit all along the train and in one of the carriages she noticed a pool of blood gathering on the floor. She followed the trail. It was Beattie's blood. The jostling and movement required to get him on to the train had been enough to make his wound break down and it was bleeding heavily. The blood was dark so she guessed it was not from an artery. Even so she knew it was potentially life-threatening. She reached for the swabs in her pocket.

He looked to be sleeping. She touched his arm. 'Beattie, your wound has started bleeding and I'm going to push on it to try and get it to stop. I'll try not to hurt you.'

He said nothing as she pressed firmly at the base of his wound, hoping the bleeding would stop.

She called out. 'Please can someone ring the bell and ask for the MO to attend?'

After what seemed a very long time but was probably only minutes, the doctor arrived. 'Update me,' he said urgently. She quickly explained Beattie's history.

'Right,' he said. 'We'll just have to continue to apply pressure and hope the bleeding stops. It looks as though you caught it in time, nurse, but it would be wise to sit him up. It should help lessen the bleeding.'

They managed to prop Beattie up using rolled coats and Charlotte spent the next fifteen minutes with her hands firmly pressing on his neck. When the bleeding was under control, Charlotte let go of the padding, which was soaked through with blood.

'Perhaps you should go and tidy yourself up, nurse,' said the doctor who had come back to check on the situation.

Her hands and apron were smeared with blood. She walked along the carriage until she found a tap. When she turned it on, rusty coloured water came dribbling out but it was enough to rinse her hands. She also dabbed at her uniform but it had little impact on the bloodstain. It'll have to do, she thought. She hadn't brought another uniform with her.

In the carriage allocated to staff, she was ready to sit down as her legs were beginning to ache. 'Brew's up,' came a friendly voice from along the corridor. It was one of the orderlies.

'Is there a spare mug of tea for me?' she asked.

'Of course, lass. Come away and have one.'

She walked along the corridor and when she took the mug offered to her by the man making the tea, he said, 'I've put the milk and sugar in for you. And by the way, your ambulance man was very optimistic about the time it'll take us to get to Étaples. The last couple of journeys took twenty-eight hours. Another fifteen miles to go now, I reckon.'

He sipped his tea. 'I'm Deryck, one of the volunteers on the train.'

Charlotte explained who she was. 'Pleased to meet you,' she said.

He told her that he was part of a team of forty volunteers who were Quakers and that he'd been working on the train for nine months. It sounded like hard work most of the time but he said he enjoyed it.

'I'm not doing any fighting but I feel I'm making my contribution.'

It was completely dark outside now. Charlotte looked at her watch. It was already after nine. Margaret was right, it was going to be another long night.

'Go and sit down for five minutes,' Deryck suggested. 'All the men are settled for the moment and I'm happy to keep an eye on them for you.'

'That sounds like a good idea, thank you.' She added, 'How many men are on the train?'

'Probably about four hundred today.'

'Will we return to Albert on this train as well?'

'Yes, and you'll have the pleasure of joining me in scrubbing it from one end to the other.'

She pulled a face. 'That doesn't sound like much fun. We were doing that in the ward this morning as well.'

He smiled. 'Right, you go and sit yourself down for a few minutes – build up your strength for the coming night.'

Charlotte found herself a place by a window, even though there was little to see through it. She put her feet up on the seat opposite, sipping her mug of tea. She found the newspaper Sandy had given her and began to read about Aberdeen in 1916.

The rhythm of the train was soothing. She was exhausted from her week's work and all the emotion – James's death, in particular. Her eyes felt heavy. She would have a nap. Just for a few minutes.

The train stopped suddenly and with a jolt that woke her. She was sure she'd only been asleep for a few minutes. Right, she thought, better get back and see how Beattie is.

As she walked back through the train, she saw that most of the men were settled in their narrow bunks. Do any ever fall out, she wondered, hoping they wouldn't while she was working.

Beattie's wound had stopped bleeding but there were lots of blood-soaked swabs lying beside him. She picked them up and went to look for a waste-bin to put them in. At the end of the carriage was a closed door. She tried the handle, thinking this might be where rubbish was stored. In fact, it was a storeroom, full of scrubbing brushes, buckets, brooms and pails, with a toilet and sink as well. She stepped inside to see if she could find a bin and as she did so the train jolted and the door slammed shut behind her. There was no light in the room and she felt around for a switch, dropping the swabs as she did so. Then the light suddenly came on – and everything was different.

She was in the toilet compartment of a modern train.

What had just happened? How could she have been transported back to 2001 like this? She caught sight of herself in the mirror. She was in the clothes she was wearing when she left Aberdeen. Her handbag was by the small basin. Her watch said 3.05pm. Did that mean she was near York? But where was her uniform and the bloodied swabs? She unlocked the door and made her way back to her seat, feeling dazed and disorientated. Through the windows she could see the outskirts of York and could feel the train slowing down.

'Are you all ready for your weekend, dear?' asked the old lady sitting opposite.

Charlotte stared at her for a moment, trying to gather her thoughts.

'Yes ... erm, yes, I am.' She quickly gathered her bag and joined the queue of people waiting to get off the train.

'Goodbye' she said, turning to the elderly couple.

She was stunned. She felt shaken. It was reality that now seemed like a dream. Her head was spinning.

As she got to the end of the carriage, she turned to wave to the couple. They gave a little wave back. And then she thought she recognised the old man. No, it couldn't be. Surely that would be impossible. She looked again. This time she was certain. She had been sitting opposite Padre Beattie. There was no time to speak to him. She got off the train.

Her mother was waiting for her on the platform. They hugged.

'Hello, darling. Have you had a good journey?' She stood back. 'Are you alright? You look a bit flustered.'

'Hi, Mum, yes, but it's ... oh, it's all so strange. I fell asleep just after Stonehaven and had the most vivid dream.'

'Well, that will have made the journey pass quickly.'

'But it didn't, Mum. The dream, it was so real. I was in a hospital in the war – the First World War – it was September 1916. I met all the staff, I shared a room with two other nurses. I was there for five nights, Mum. I helped nurse the patients, I was in a uniform. It's as if the journey here has taken almost a week ...'

'You've always had such a lively imagination, Lottie.'

'Honestly, Mum, it really was as if I was there. I could describe where I was, who I met, who I helped to look after.'

'Well, perhaps you can share your dream with me later. But for the moment, let's get going so we miss the traffic. You know how busy the road out of York can be.'

In the car park, Charlotte opened the door of her mother's little hatchback and put her bag on the back seat. They turned out of the station, alongside the city walls and on to the road to Harrogate. Even with all the traffic, they were travelling faster than Charlotte had in the ambulance train last night.

Charlotte pulled her phone from her bag – two missed calls from Colin. She rang him.

'Hi, Lottie, have you got there safely? I guess the signal wasn't good over the border and that's why you didn't get my call.'

Tears stung her eyes as she heard his voice. 'Yes, although I felt like I wasn't on the train for most of the journey.'

He was silent for a moment. 'That's a strange thing to say. Are you alright?'

'I suppose I must have been asleep. But honestly, Colin, it didn't feel like that.'

He interrupted. 'Well, you can tell me about it when you get home. I must go. Anne wants to walk up to feed the ducks in the pond at the top of the hill. Hang on; I'll put you on speakerphone so you can talk to the kids.'

'Hello, Mummy!' There were three voices all trying to speak at once. Charlotte was suddenly overwhelmed. The tears were now running freely down her face.

'Hello! Oh, it's so lovely to speak to you all. I've really missed you. I feel I've already been away for ages.'

'Oh, Mummy, you only left this morning,' said David.

'I know, but for me it feels like I've not spoken to you for a hundred years.'

Will said, 'We're having a lovely time. We stopped for lunch in Ballater on the way out.'

Anne chipped in. 'Daddy let me sit in the front. And it was really fun.'

A heated debate followed about who would sit in the front seat next time.

They all started laughing. It was difficult for Charlotte to hear what each one was saying but she was delighted to hear their simple disagreement.

'Okay,' she said. 'Tell Daddy I'll phone again tonight.'

'Bye, Mummy. Love you,' they called. David said, 'Send our love to Nana.'

'And love to all of you, too,' their grandmother called back.

The journey took about thirty minutes. It was much more comfortable than Tom's ambulance. When they reached the house, her mother made tea and produced a coffee and walnut cake.

'Oh, Mum, my favourite. Thank you.'

They sat at the kitchen table. Her mother said, 'Darling, is everything alright?'

'Yes, I'm fine, Mum. Why do you ask?'

'I noticed how upset you became when you spoke to the kids just now and I wondered ... You're not depressed are you?'

'No, Mum. Honestly.' She took a sip of tea. 'It's just that ... Well, I've been a bit stressed recently, especially with that mistake I made at work. But I'm not at breaking point or anything. Work has been so busy and that's why Colin thought it would be a good idea for me to come and see you for a few days – have a break instead of going out to the countryside. But when I was on the train and fell asleep and had that dream ... I felt ... I don't know, so lost and out of reach from everyone. Seeing you and speaking to Colin and the kids has made me realise how much I love them, that's all. I think I feel homesick, if I'm honest.'

Her mother settled back on her chair. 'So tell me what happened then.'

For half an hour, Charlotte recounted her dream, describing the hospital, the staff, Matron, Sister Craig, Daisy and Margaret, Nurse Brook, Tom, James, even Sandy. She explained about the similarities between the nursing work and her training. She recounted stories about the patients, those who died, both in the ward and in 'Darwin's room', as well as the men who survived. She told her mother about sharing a room with Margaret and Daisy, the plight of little Monique and the disciplinary interview with Matron. She mentioned the story about Margaret's friend, Gill, and her encounters with the uncaring Nurse Brook and finally how the old man on the train looked exactly liked Beattie.

Her mother listened intently, asking her questions now and again about the patients and pouring more tea.

‘Well, I’ve never heard such detail about a dream, nor one that has lasted so long. All that reading you’ve done about the Great War must have been well processed by your mind to enable it to come tumbling out like that.’

‘I suppose so, Mum, but it just felt so real and I was certain I was there. At the start, I was really uncertain about everything and as each day went by I felt like I was gaining more confidence, especially after I realised I wasn’t trapped there.’

She paused for a moment. ‘I think in a strange way, it’s helped me regain my confidence.’

Her mother said, ‘I’m glad to know that you didn’t get lost there and you’re safely back with us. I still think it’s a reaction to all the stress you’ve been under recently, you know.’

She had a point, Charlotte thought. But that didn’t explain how she could have had such a detailed, vivid dream. How could she have made up all those names and procedures?

She went up to the bedroom to unpack her things. At least I know what’s in this bag, she thought. She put her wash-bag on the dressing table and noticed a hardback book with a red cover sitting there. She went to the landing and called downstairs. ‘That looks like an interesting old book, Mum – the one on the dressing table.’

Her mother appeared at the bottom of the stairs. ‘Consider it an early birthday present. Lottie. I had a bit of time to kill the other day when I was in town so I wandered into one of the second-hand bookshops and found that one. I wondered if it would be of interest to you. I think it’s another of those diaries you like so much – by a nurse from the war.’

Charlotte said, ‘That’s really sweet of you. Perhaps after that dream I’ll understand what’s written in it now.’

Later, when she had unpacked, she took the book downstairs and sat at the kitchen table looking through it. The author was someone called Campbell and it had been published in 1925. It included diary entries, photographs and some sketches on shiny paper. Suddenly, something about the surname made her turn back to the front where there was a dedication. The book had been written by a D. Campbell and was dedicated to all the staff of the hospital where she had worked during the war at Bécourt, near Albert.

Charlotte squealed.

‘Mum, I don't believe it. Look at this. This is where I was! It’s just as I described it to you. Look, she even mentions Matron McLean and Sister Craig. How could I have known that? The author – Daisy – she's one of the nurses I shared a room with. Although she was Daisy Ashville then. That means that she must have married Tom, the ambulance driver, after all and gone back to America with him.'

Her mother was not convinced. 'You must have read the book before, Lottie. And for some reason, you dreamed about it on the train.'

Charlotte looked more closely at the photographs and sketches. They were so familiar to her and she smiled when she saw a picture of Margaret and some of the other staff.

But perhaps her mother was right and she had seen the book before.

'This is unnerving,' she said. 'I know it seems impossible but I'm convinced it was real. I'm just so pleased to know what happened to Daisy and Tom. In fact, I'd like to think I encouraged her to start her relationship with him. She was promised to someone in England, but after James was killed, she must have changed her mind.'

Her mother smiled. 'Well, personally, I can't see how it could be real but it's certainly clear in your mind.'

Charlotte continued looking through the book. She stopped at one of the sketches and gasped, then laughed.

'Look, Mum, maybe this will convince you.'

She held up the book. There was a drawing of a nurse in uniform. The caption read, 'Nurse Charlotte Robertson, a member of the Territorial Force Nursing Services who worked with me in September 1916.'

NHS Grampian

HR department

Aberdeen

October 10th 2001

Dear Mrs. Robertson

RE: Disciplinary interview

Thank you for attending the disciplinary meeting yesterday, along with your ward manager. This letter is an official record of the outcome.

The panel appreciated your honesty in admitting your role and responsibility in the drug error. You agreed that it was a breach of the drug administration policy and could have resulted in serious harm to a patient.

The panel was assured by the support of your manager and that this incident was out of character.

The panel's decision is that a note will be made in your personal file about this incident and that, provided there is no repeat, the note will be removed on October 10th 2002.

We advise you to re-read the controlled drugs policy and ensure you comply with this procedure.

Yours sincerely

S. McLean T. Craig

S. McLean (Chair) and T. Craig (HR Manager)

ACKNOWLEDGEMENTS

I am grateful to all the people who guided and supported me over the years that I have taken to write this book. I owe special thanks to Prof. Mike Pringle, my 'critical friend' during the first draft stage.

My husband Ken, our children, my mother, sister and friend Caroline Adam never stopped believing that I could write and finish this work. I thank you for all the encouragement you gave me from the start.

Thank you to friends and colleagues who provided me with helpful feedback on earlier versions of the manuscript, especially Prof. David Haslam, Dr Gordon Linklater, Dr Colin Macduff, Fiona Hunter and Beth Struthers.

I am grateful for Daniel Allan's editing skills and his patience!

I have made use of numerous textbooks, articles and online resources over the years. I thank the library staff at the Wellcome Trust for their expertise as well as the staff at all the museums that I visited. I am happy to provide a full reference list if needed, but here are a few of the key texts:

Borden M. (1929) *The Forbidden Zone*, Hesperus Press, London

Lewis P. (1902) *Nursing: its theory and practice*, The Scientific Press, London

Lűckes E. (1914) *General Nursing*, 9th edition, Kegan Paul, Trench and Co., London

Mackenna R. (1916) *The adventure of death*, John Murray, London

MacPherson WG (1922) *Medical Services; Surgery of the war*, HMSO, London

Powell A. (2009) *Women in the war zone. Hospital service in the First World War*, The History Press, Stroud

Sawyer J. (ed.) (1921) *The Birmingham Territorial Units of the RAMC 1914 – 1919*, Allday Press, Birmingham

Watson JK (1912) *A handbook for Nurses*, The Scientific Press, London

Key internet sources

American Red Cross available at http://www.redcross.org/museum/history/ww1a.asp [accessed December 2010]

Matron-in-Chief BEF war Diary, France and Flanders available at http://www.scarletfinders.co.uk/110/html (national archives WO95/3988-91)

The medical history of WW1 – nursing documents available at http://www.vlib.us/medical/Nindex.htm [accessed October 2010]

The Royal Army Medical Corps and its work available at http://www.vlib.us/medical/ramc/ramc.htm [accessed December 2010]

Printed in Great Britain
by Amazon